AMAZ'N MURDER

Borgo Press Books by WILLIAM MALTESE

AMAZ'N MURDER

A COZY MYSTERY NOVEL

WILLIAM MALTESE

THE BORGO PRESS

MMXIII

AMAZ'N MURDER

FIRST BORGO PRESS EDITION

Published by Wildside Press LLC

www.wildsidebooks.com

DEDICATION

For My Dear Old Mum,
who would have loved this one.

CONTENTS

CHAPTER ONE

Pleasurably frightened, as a child, by the contents of her father's journals, Melanie Ditherson expected (hoped for?) a reality of bloodthirsty natives, or at least a slavering jaguar; she got neither.

"Sorry if I gave you a start." It was her Uncle Charles who looked romantically dashing in his bush outfit that included the brim-upturned hat he removed to wipe sweat from his forehead. His hair was stunningly silver; Melanie had always suspected he used some kind of rinse, but, unless he brought his own supply, his two weeks in the Amazon had produced no telltale roots of less magnificent color. "Haven't seen our guide, have you?"

"Gordon?" She made it you have to be kidding.

"Said he was off to use 'the facilities' and didn't bother to return. As he was headed this way...."

"Teddy is within hailing distance." Melanie waved her arm in a southwestern direction. "He said to call any time that Gordon might again decide to be a bother."

"Rather unpleasant business—that." Charles didn't refer to Gordon's more immediate disappearance, although that was unpleasant enough, but to what had happened the night before. "I hope you don't hold it against your dear uncle that he didn't vote in favor of our trotting back to civilization in retaliation for Gordon's unseemly behavior."

Melanie took a handkerchief from the front pocket of her pants and freed her face of as much perspiration as she could manage. "I'm the one who insisted we stay, remember?"

"Yes, but if I'd been a little more insistent...."

"We all made too much of it," Melanie rationalized. She left it at that, because she'd never assumed Gordon anymore immune to her harmless flirtations than any other man. Last night had merely proven her right.

"Having missionaries for parents doesn't make any child one." Charles' tone insinuated an access to more information than was at Melanie's disposal. "*Especially* it doesn't make Gordon one."

Melanie was curious for any specifics but she was detoured.

"Ah, I thought I heard voices." Carolyne Santire said, sweeping aside a large frond to join them. "Any luck, you two?"

"Plenty of *rubias*, myrtles, *leguminosse*, *epiphytic* orchids, *bromeliad*, and fern...." Melanie ran down the list.

"Don't I know it," Carolyne consoled. Unlike Charles' hair, hers, a henna-rinse red, was definitely coming in a different color—grey—at the scalp. She ran her fingers through the variegated results in an automatic exploration for whatever creepies or crawlies had hitched rides since her last search and seizure.

"Not only have I not found anything even vaguely resembling *Lygodium cornelius*, but I seem to have lost our guide in the process," admitted Charles.

"Surely, that young man learned from his mistake of last night and isn't up to any new mischief," Carolyne criticized Gordon-in-absentia.

"He didn't come *this* way." Melanie had no desire to get him into any more trouble.

"Left me on the other side of the gully," Charles lamented. "I could have broken my neck in my balancing act to get back across."

For not the first time, Carolyne knew Charles Ditherson was no way as decrepit as he was always letting on. After so many years of traversing gullies, chasms, sink holes, and an occasional abyss, he had a lot of expertise upon which to draw.

"I'm not a kid any more," he insisted.

Carolyne wasn't about to take any of his bullshit. "Were you as near to pasture as you insist, I doubt you'd have joined this little expedition."

"This is hardly the place to which an uncle willingly sends his niece without a chaperone?"

"Seems Teddy is bodyguard enough."

Charles snorted. "Teddy might protect her from Gordon Wentlock, but who, besides me, protects her from Teddy Rhingold? You?"

"Is anyone hungry but me?" Melanie changed the subject.

"You're hungry, even knowing as you do that Felix is in charge of the chow?" Carolyne's insinuation was that their cook-of-the-day wasn't likely to relieve any pangs of starvation: an anomaly when hours of traipsing the tangles left everyone famished at meal times.

"He's promised to follow package instructions, this time: 'put plastic bag in boiling water,'" Melanie reminded. It had been a promise forced from him after his last ill-fated Julia Child in the wild improvisation.

Not from Missouri, but California, Carolyne had to see to believe. "I guess it's chow time, nonetheless!" She wasn't enthused.

The three turned in unison and formed a line, Carolyne in the lead, Charles in the rear. Between each of them was space enough to avoid the constant whiplash from flora shifted forward and released.

Melanie relied upon Carolyne's sense of direction and focused her own concentration on pondering, once again, the absence of wildlife. Her father's journals were filled with tapir, jaguar, cavy, armadillo, sloth, peccary, anteater, and monkey. So far, Melanie had spotted none of the above, nor any anacondas which she'd once believed hung, like Christmas icicles, from every Amazon Basin tree. "I haven't even seen one snake," she commented aloud.

"Blame the tramp, tramp, tramp of many feet," said Carolyne. "Most of the indigenous animals have headed for deeper pockets."

Melanie found that answer insufficient. After all, this jungle was as wild and as greenery choked as any imagined. Surely, tramp, tramp, tramping human feet hadn't been nearly enough to stampede the whole indigenous wildlife population.

Carolyne was happy to elucidate. "Prospectors and geologists, like Roy Lendum, looking for gold, oil, emeralds, copper, iron, platinum, whatever." She was invisible except for the waves she made in the greenery that allowed Melanie to follow in her wake. "Hunters, museum people, zoologists, ornithologists, looking for animals and birds. Lepidopterists looking for butterflies. Tourists looking for the Great Adventure."

"I can't imagine even the most foolhardy tourist this far off the beaten path." Charles, too, had become just one more disembodied voice somewhere within the shifted shrubbery.

"Nonsense!" Carolyne was a teacher chiding a recalcitrant student who failed to see the obvious. "This isn't so far out of the way, so far removed from civilization, once you consider how few days of slash-and-burn remain between the Georni Ranch and here. How much of this forest, after all, is consumed daily by flames designed to 'reclaim the land' for crops and pasture?"

Charles should have known better than to disagree with Carolyne. She had a way, which he never liked, of making him feel he'd not done his homework; no matter that he could match her find for find, expedition for expedition, award for award, recognition for recognition, at least since she'd ended her professional association with his brother.

Carolyne droned on: "Come back next year if we don't luck out with our illusive *Lygodium cornelius*; I'll bet all you'll find, right here, where we now walk, is pasture with Kyle Georni's fat cattle grazing." Even Carolyne would have found such a prediction harder to believe if she hadn't seen, first-hand, plant-hunted jungles, just like this one, which once thrived, full and verdant, become open pastureland, almost overnight, stocked with Georni beef destined for world markets. All those short hours they'd jeeped from the ranch house to the edge of this jungle had once taken days of machete-cutting to maneuver on foot.

Charles slapped at a bug landed on one of his sweaty cheeks; he complained the mosquitoes hadn't been scared off by any tramp, tramp, tramp.

"You're getting soft!" Carolyne said but knew better.

Melanie expected to hear Teddy at any minute; he was assigned the section between hers and the campsite. To see him would be another matter; the choke of flora often made it impossible to see one's hand in front of one's face. She preferred stretches wherein giant trees, like supports for massive circus tents, suspended their high canopies of interlocked limbs and leaves, nothing below but groundcover clogged with decay and no sunlight. *This* was claustrophobic by comparison. Only her clothes kept the plants from flaying her alive; evidence was scratches on every part of her unprotected body.

"I need a rest," Charles complained; Melanie loved her uncle, but sometimes even she tired of his insistence that he wasn't up to the task. Excerpts from Cornelius Ditherson's journals, written during expeditions that his brother had accompanied, indicated just as many complaints from a Charles in his prime.

Carolyne stopped suddenly, which caused a pileup.

"Sorry," Melanie apologized for back-ending Carolyne, echoed by Charles who, by then, had stepped on his niece's left heel.

"Do you smell food?" Carolyne sniffed the air like a carnivore for rotting carrion.

"Vacuum-sealed food packets, my dear," Charles reminded. "Gone with the wind are the days of smelling the aroma of freshly killed game roasting over an open fire."

"Felix!" Carolyne called.

"Please, don't tell us you've lost the way," Charles punctuated. "I've counted upon you to eye spot reference points. Not professional of me, I admit, but my mind does tend to wander some with encroaching old age.

Carolyne's dilated nostrils, mere appendages of her intuition, "smelled" something wrong.

Melanie inhaled deeply, too, but took in only the usual combination of heat, humidity, fecundity, and decay.

"Likely, Felix has taken a few z's," Charles analyzed. "Far healthier for us than were he to subject us to whatever his latest concoction in the communal pot might be."

"I've a sixth sense for things not right," Carolyne bragged. "Or have you, Charles, forgotten how right I was in Chile?"

"I still believe I would have survived quite nicely without you having thrown me that rope, thank-you." It was a sore point with Charles that this wasn't the first time she'd brought it up to play one-upmanship. Charles wished for a jaguar so he might return the favor by yanking Carolyne out of harm's way, to brag about it until the grim reaper finally cut him down; then again, he doubted he had the strength to save even himself. This expedition had genuinely tired him out.

"See if I give you any assist next time," Carolyne threatened. "Then, we'll count the years it'll take you to extract yourself."

Melanie had previously been subjected to enough of her uncle and Carolyne's banter to ignore it now; no indication of Teddy's presence was her more immediate concern. "I'm surprised we haven't found Teddy."

"Teddy!" Carolyne called. Her only answer was the flight of those few birds left in the area. "Through here," she led the way into an even denser gauntlet which she said was "a short-cut." Melanie was battered by a renewed lashing of leaves and stalks; Charles complained bitterly of his own beatings behind her.

Carolyne's sudden, "Felix, what's happened!" was preview of upcoming events that warned Melanie of the worst even before she, too, followed into the campsite.

Felix Tenner, though conscious, was seated on the ground, hands-to-head, rocking to and fro.

"Overdosed on his own cooking, most likely," diagnosed Charles who was last out and the last to decide if it was something more serious.

Carolyne, down on one knee, quickly found, "A bump the size of a goose egg."

"Whacked from behind." Felix's voice, weak under the best of circumstances, was hardly audible. Luckily, everyone was close enough to hear.

Charles jumped to conclusions: "Considering the lead-in, our hormones run amuck guide is the most likely culprit, yes? Although, Teddy seems a more logical target, in his having rescued Melanie from Gordon last night."

"I'm not sure of that motive, but that's certainly a good place to begin," Carolyne agreed.

"Got me from behind," Felix complained.

"You already said as much," Charles reminded.

If looks could kill, Felix's expression would have sent Charles to The Big Arboretum in the Sky. Taking what Charles said as unadulterated criticism, Felix said. "I've yet to see someone with eyes in the back of his head; I'm no exception."

"Well, pardon me." The apology from Charles wasn't really an apology at all. "I suppose this means we must all fend for our own meals?"

That got him a Charles, this could be serious look from both Carolyne and his niece.

"I'm someone who thinks levity more conducive to rational thinking, especially in a crisis, than proceeding like chickens with their heads cut off," Charles excused.

"Charles, be useful and soak a rag for Felix's head," Carolyne suggested.

"What kind of rag?"

"Melanie, can you help your helpless uncle improvise?"

Headed for a towel in her knapsack, Melanie noticed how the main canvas flap on their radio encasement hung by only one ill-tied strap. That didn't interrupt her Florence Nightingale mission as much as did the radio part revealed by the breach. "Someone has battered our radio in!"

For the moment, Felix was forgotten, along with his aching head; Carolyne and Charles performed a mass exodus to Melanie.

"That young man's lusting after my niece has really gone too far," was how Charles judged the situation.

No way could Melanie think that. Gordon trying to steal a kiss was one thing, but taking his frustration to this extreme was out of the question; he simply wouldn't have.

Actually, the radio wasn't their only means of communication, even though the area had no reception whatsoever for cell phones. "Where's that 'satellite gizmo'?"

The piece of gear in question was a small contraption that Carolyne didn't really understand, except that it somehow, in an emergency, could be counted upon to bounce not only an SOS off some U.S. satellite but transmit longitude and latitude to would-be rescuers.

"Gone!" announced Charles after he'd joined the women in a futile search. "Gordon to blame!"

Melanie remained unsure, admitting only, "Yes, Gordon tried to kiss me. Yes, Teddy knocked the wind out of him. Yes, Gordon's forced apology sounded less than sincere at the time. On the other hand, his second apology, given me this morning, seemed sincerely genuine."

"Felix bonked himself on the back of the head, did he?" Charles offered in alternative. His niece obviously didn't recognize just how attractive she was, even in her slightly funky, two-week old jungle chic. Teddy, whom Charles still thought not the right fiancé for his niece, might have hit Gordon, but Gordon run amok was more a real example of a man driven to distraction by boiling passion. "Or, maybe Carolyne, or I, sneaked back and did this dastardly deed?"

"Charles, don't be ridiculous!" Carolyne insisted.

"Ms. Super Sleuth sees motives around here, other than physical attraction, does she?"

"Scientists—and may I remind that you and I are scientists— are supposed to look at things more objectively than the average man on the street," Carolyne decided.

"What average man on the street finds himself stranded in the Amazon with all lines of communication severed?"

"Don't jump to any conclusions, Charles, before we've heard

Gordon's side."

"You think Gordon went through all of this bother so he could sit down and explain it to us?"

"It's not just Gordon unaccounted for." Carolyne meant it as an objective let's wait until all of the alibis are in; Mèlanie took it differently.

"My God, where is Teddy?" Melanie managed to deliver with the same emotional emphasis of a scream.

Her answer was a distinct gunshot.

"From somewhere near the river," Charles isolated. He may have some diminished capacities, but his hearing was still good enough.

Two more shots confirmed.

"Could be a hunter," Melanie ventured. Immediately, she argued against it, "Hunting what, though? Hunting where? Far away?"

"Not far." Charles had a more experienced ear. "You don't need much jungle to muffle a sound." He drew his revolver and checked its load. He'd fought his share of enemies in hostile environments like this one, and he knew the procedure.

"This isn't happening," Melanie decided.

"Oh, but it is, my dear," Carolyne disagreed. She, like Charles, had been in predicaments where the only thing between her and safety had been a firearm and her ability to use it with precision. "The worst thing we can do is pretend it's otherwise."

Three to one, they voted to stay put; Melanie was odd-man (woman) out; even Felix, still doubled over with pain, cast his vote with the majority. Concerned for Teddy's welfare, Melanie was distraught by the decision. When Charles proceeded to make something to eat, his main concern apparently his belly, rather than Teddy's well-being, Melanie was made more upset.

Carolyne took it upon herself to explain how the combined voice of experience was preferable to the lone, illogical, but natural, contrary response of Melanie. Firstly, Charles was less callous than he seemed by his concern over whether to serve beef or lamb stew. "The last thing we want is to lower our energy levels," said Carolyne. "After a morning of expending calories, we have to restock or risk performing at less than optimum when the very best is exactly what's most demanded of us. We've food available, and it behooves us to take advantage of that good fortune. The absence of facts, regarding the real state of our situation, can't assure us indefinite access to provisions."

"Whoever was here, for some reason, didn't bother scrapping our food supply," Melanie reminded.

Carolyne was patient; after all, this sort of thing was new to Melanie, while Carolyne had successfully endured the mutiny of her bearers in the Gobi, as well as assassins in India who had intended an international incident by taking out the English/American botany team at Tumkur. "Maybe, whoever didn't, because we interrupted him before he finished," Carolyne suggested. "Maybe, he wasn't clever enough to see how stealing our food could be as debilitating as smashing our radio. Maybe, a lot of things. If he left us food, he can't be counted upon to be so obliging within the next hour, day, even week."

"Week?" Melanie shouldn't have been surprised. Without communications to the outside, they were at least that long of a forced march from the Georni Ranch.

"Now, as to our lopsided vote to stick here," said Carolyne, "rather than launch an immediate search for Felix's assailant, or Teddy, or for the source of the gunfire down by the river. It's a question of not having the faintest notion of the exact whereabouts of any of those. It's a big jungle, out there, my dear. Look how unsuccessful our concentrated efforts to locate even one *Lygodium cornelius*, a jungle plant, when any search for Teddy and Gordon would best be accomplished in just that same way: splitting the area into sections, one for each searcher. Except, as individuals, we're more vulnerable than as a group." She held up her hand to delay interruption. "We can't know the assailant will be any the less vindictive to you, or to me, than he was to Felix, and we shouldn't chance that will be the case. Teddy and Gordon, out there somewhere, know exactly where we are and the way to get to us."

"What if Teddy is injured?" Melanie asked, although she still refused to believe Gordon responsible. "What if Gordon is hurt? What if either of them fired those shots to get our attention?"

"Then, get our attention they did," Carolyne reminded. "However, their logical follow-up would be more gunfire, in an established rhythm, to indicate shots less likely aimed at an enemy and more likely a signal for help. What have three, erratic shots told us but that someone was off in the direction of the river with a gun? Is he there now? Is he injured, or is his intent to injure? We don't know, and it's preferable we do know. Our best bet is to wait until we have a better grasp of our situation. Until then, I suggest, you check your weapon to make sure it's operational."

"I could never shoot anyone," Melanie prophesied.

Carolyne's smile made redundant her, "You may be surprised by what you can do, my dear, if put to the test." She went to soak a towel for Felix; it was a chore originally assigned Charles, then Melanie, but forgotten by both. If you want something done....

They were joined as Melanie, surprised by how hungry she'd been, contemplated seconds from the stew pot. It was a good thing the new arrival wasn't the enemy, with full intent to do bodily harm, because, although he remained concealed, he was within easy striking distance of one and all when he requested, "Permission to join the party?" His voice was so near that Melanie dropped her mess kit in surprise. Still concealed, he filled in more pertinent details: "Roy Lendum, here. Remember me from this morning? I introduced myself, and you were kind enough to let me use your radio to relay a message via the Georni Ranch."

It was obvious by how Carolyne and Charles looked about that neither had located Roy yet. Melanie was only certain he was very close; she was right.

"I heard gunshots." Roy emerged from his crouch within a group of ferns not six feet from where Melanie had been seated before his announced presence had brought her to her feet. "I thought maybe you'd lucked out by bagging that rare bit of game. The idea of some fresh meat appealed to my meat-deprived taste buds."

"We suspect two-legged quarry." Charles replaced his pistol in its holster. "There's been a bit of mischief, as Felix and our radio can bear witness."

If he hadn't already, Roy noticed Felix's towel-draped head. Of the four, Felix had responded the last to Roy's unexpected arrival; he sat, eyes closed, and his head against a tree root that conveniently bowed up though the soil.

"I've seen no one," Roy admitted. His mental headcount was two short. He mentally went through the introductions of that morning. "Teddy and Gordon presently missing, right?"

"Both possible candidates for the gunfire," Charles conceded. "Although, we presently lean toward Gordon who...."

"*You*, personally, presently lean toward Gordon," Melanie corrected. "I'm not putting any responsibility on anyone until I have more to go on."

"We all need more input," Carolyne agreed.

Charles wasn't assuaged: "Gordon made a pass at Melanie just last night, and Teddy took exception. I used to wonder why, in all those adventure movies, there was always one attractive woman among all those virile men; it seemed to beg trouble, and this just proves my assumption right." He realized his faux pas and diplomatically made amends: "This expedition, of course, comes complete with two ravishing beauties."

"Charles, cut the crap!" Carolyne knew she wasn't a beauty, ravishing or otherwise; nor had she ever been. Certainly, she didn't look her best with her hair gone grey at its roots, clothes continually wet with the humidity and perspiration, bathing and toilet facilities next to nonexistent. Even Melanie, who had looked so good for so long, was beginning to go a little ripe around the edges; far less likely to spark unbridled lust in someone not hopelessly lost to the outside world for a very long time. Then, again, what did Carolyne know about men? Two husbands, and as many divorces later, still didn't exactly make her an authority.

"Pubescent boys will be boys," Charles concluded his summation.

"Not to where Gordon would endanger our lives and smash our radio," Melanie defensively insisted.

Roy was getting the specifics piecemeal.

"Took off with our satellite gizmo, too," Carolyne admitted.

"Wouldn't have run across a stray radio or space gismo, lately, have you Roy?" Charles knew it unlikely. Roy, a prospector and geologist, traveled light in order to cover a wide range of rough terrain. It was because he considered even his damaged radio excess baggage, jettisoned, that he'd appeared earlier that morning to borrow the use of theirs.

"I can offer a quick run-through of the immediate area," Roy volunteered, "if you'd like me to take a look."

"Would you?" Melanie was quick to accept.

Carolyne was reluctant. "We've decided it's best to stay put for the time being. Certainly, I wouldn't want you hit by a bullet that didn't even have your name on it."

The pros and cons were temporarily made moot by Teddy's call from a distance: "Hey, you guys, I'm coming in!"

Melanie would have rushed into the bush to meet him, but Roy, closest to her, put a cautionary hand on her shoulder.

Neither Roy, nor Carolyne, nor Charles took any chances; each had a pistol drawn. Even Felix drew his.

As was usually the case in the thick greenery, Teddy was heard long before he was seen. That he didn't go out of his way to be stealthy was emphasized by his virtual stumble into the small clearing.

"Teddy!" Melanie was the only one with welcoming arms, not an aimed gun. She hugged him close, her cheek so tightly against her fiancé's sweaty chest that she heard his runaway heartbeat and felt his rasping intakes of ragged breaths.

"Gordon is dead!" was what he said to them all by way of additional greeting.

CHAPTER TWO

"Gordon sneaked up on you, too, did he?" Charles' mind's eye had the scenario down pat. "Shot him before he knocked your brains out?"

Obviously, Teddy wasn't following the projection as well as the others. "Shot who?"

"Shot Gordon?" Melanie put to him. The idea made her queasy. She didn't want responsibility, and the tale, as conjured by Charles, painted her as some kind of femme fatale, right in the middle.

"You think I shot Gordon?" Teddy sounded incredulous.

"Didn't you?" Charles held fast to his theory of an attractive woman, two jealous swains, and the passion-spawning isolation of the Amazon Basin.

"We heard three shots." Carolyne blew a stray wisp of grey-rooted red hair out of her green eyes. "You did say Gordon was dead?" She didn't trust her memory.

"He's dead, all right, but I didn't kill him. My gunshots were attempts to save him; I was just too late."

"Take it from the top, why don't you?" Melanie figured any reality was better than her uncle's fanciful imagination.

"Jaguar got him," Teddy obliged.

"Jaguar?" It was Carolyne's turn at incredulity.

"Cat, big as a house."

Carolyne had trouble buying it. It contradicted her theory of wildlife, that size, forced into deeper jungle by encroaching civilization.

"It had to have taken him unaware; I didn't hear Gordon make a sound." Teddy gave Melanie a comforting hug. "It was the animal growls that got my attention."

Melanie shivered. Disappointed by a jungle so apparently sterile of fauna, she'd wished for one of the big cats, and here it was. It just went to prove that the bane of all wishing was the chance the wish might come true.

"Once I had the cat in sight, I saw it was mauling Gordon; I fired and scared it off. I may even have hit it. Whatever, it genuinely took off like a bat out of hell."

"Horrible!" Melanie didn't doubt.

"We've seen no previous sign of any big cats," Carolyne complained. "We've seen no sufficient amount of smaller animals to support a carnivore."

"Which might account for the animal attacking Gordon," Felix, eyes shut, added his two cents.

Teddy noticed Felix for what seemed the first time. "What happened to you?"

"The same fate as happened to our radio." Felix tried to open his eyes but decided against it. The pain was receding but had a long way to go.

"Someone sneaked up and laid poor Felix low," Carolyne clarified. "Same person apparently smashed our radio and ran off with our SOS device."

"Uncle Charles figures it was all part of Gordon's plan to get back at you."

"Get back at me?" Teddy answered his own question: "Because of our little to-do last night, you mean?"

"Seemed more than a little to-do to me," Charles argued.

"You think I'd blow Gordon away for his wanting to kiss Melanie? Lighten up, Charles!"

"I see it as a spontaneous reaction to Gordon coming at you with a club."

"What club? There was no club."

"I keep trying to tell him that the thing with Gordon was no big deal." Melanie couldn't believe her uncle kept trying to make it something more than it was.

"Oh, it was a big enough deal, all right," Teddy disagreed with Melanie. "It just wasn't so big that I'd kill the guy over it."

"You sound more magnanimous in retrospect." Charles held firmly to his way of seeing things.

"With time to think it over, I figure I might have tried a kiss from Melanie, too, in Gordon's shoes," admitted Teddy, an accusatory glance in Melanie's direction.

"Where's Gordon now?" Carolyne brought the conversation back to where she wanted it.

"That way," Teddy said, his arm movement encompassing a lot of the surrounding jungle. He narrowed it down: "Not far from the river. I was going to bury the poor bastard, but there are only a couple feet of topsoil."

"We better move fast," Carolyne took charge. "If a big cat is hungry enough to attack a man, your shots won't scare him far, especially if he's now wounded."

Melanie released her hold on Teddy. "I'll get my camera."

"God, Melanie!" Teddy was aghast.

Carolyne was less shocked. "It's best to have a record, Teddy. It'll be at least a week before we get out with the bad news, longer before anybody gets back here. A lot can happen to a body in that time, considering this environment."

"It's not something Melanie should even see," Teddy insisted.

Once again, Carolyne argued Melanie's case. "It's something none of us should see, but that doesn't mean we won't later be asked questions whose answers will be better accompanied with substantiation. Melanie knows photography better than the lot of us."

"It's okay, Teddy." Melanie was less certain than she sounded, but she went for her camera nevertheless.

Teddy continued to object: "It just, somehow, seems macabre to photograph the corpse."

"The police do it all of the time," Melanie reminded, camera in hand. "My college photography class had one of the cameramen who do that sort of thing come around to guest-lecture."

"From whom you gleaned enough insight to handle this?" Teddy didn't make it a statement.

Melanie was piqued. She wasn't a child but a grown woman good at her chosen hobby. Carolyne had had no trouble seeing that, so what was Teddy's problem? "I'm doing this as much for you as for anyone, you know?" Melanie said. His look said he didn't follow that, so she spelled it out. "You think Uncle Charles has given up on his version of the story, especially when he's had a few drinks? Without the very best photographic record of this, do you really want to tell the authorities that a jaguar killed the man you assaulted, and it did so at a spot that probably hasn't seen another jaguar in years?"

"Look, Melanie," Teddy was conciliatory; "while I'll concede that pictures *are* a great idea, I'd just prefer it if I took them. Or, how about Felix? He has a camera."

"Felix is staying right here with his headache," said Felix. "If whoever wants to finish me off, the way I feel, he's welcome to me."

"Shouldn't someone stay with you?" Carolyne suggested.

"If anyone had really wanted me dead, I'd likely be dead," Felix said and rubbed the bump on his head.

"Nevertheless...." Carolyne was prepared to argue the point.

"No baby-sitter required!" Felix insisted.

Meanwhile, Melanie had conflicting emotions: appreciation of her fiancé's concern, loathing of his assumption that he, Felix, or both, were better prepared to photograph death than was she, a woman. It was a streak of male chauvinism she'd recognized in him before; not appreciated.

"It's a matter of depth perception, clarity of focus, perspective," Melanie reminded. "There are certain learned techniques of photography that make me the obvious best choice. For instance, consider the scratch marks on the victim."

"What *about* the scratch marks?" Teddy asked.

"Has anyone else, here, realized that something like, say, a tube of lipstick, laid out beside them, can help immeasurably in later determining how long and wide the marks are, or, more importantly, how far apart they are, for comparisons, should the jaguar claim another victim?"

"I never realized you were such a forensics expert," Teddy said and didn't sound all that impressed with his discovery.

* * * * * * *

"How much farther?" Charles complained.

Teddy's answer: "Closer than Melanie or you should find yourselves wishing."

Melanie was no longer even vaguely flattered by Teddy's protective attitude. She found it condescending. When was the last time, not counting this one, that *he* had seen a jaguar-ravaged body? Had *he* been made dysfunctional by the experience?

Actually, he had looked in quite a state when he'd stumbled into camp; that memory made her less critical.

As predicted, the scene wasn't pretty. Melanie got ill before, during, and after photographing it; she wasn't alone if green faces and gagging reflexes were any indication. It was only her inherent need to do the job right that provided the impetus she needed to see her through it.

"How many pictures did you take?" Carolyne held Melanie's head while the young women dry-heaved for not the first time.

"A twelve-picture digital chip's worth." Melanie accepted another wet-wipe and wondered how Carolyne kept producing them from a seemingly endless supply. The taste in her mouth wasn't to be believed; Carolyne offered a breath mint.

"Wouldn't you agree that's enough?"

Melanie nodded.

When they rejoined the men, it wasn't Melanie's photographs any longer in question.

"Unbelievable!" Teddy didn't look happy. He slapped his hat against his right thigh; no dust resulted, but there was a spray of dampness and perspiration. "I tell you, I heard and saw the animal."

"No one denies the animal," Roy argued. "It's the time sequence suddenly in question."

This perked Melanie's ears, even before her uncle's follow-up, "It just pulls Felix's bonk on the head, and the radio's destruction, in out of left field."

"What does?" Carolyne asked.

"Roy here...." Teddy's hat-holding hand irritatingly swung in the prospector's direction. "...says we've a murder."

"Murder?" Melanie and Carolyne harmonized; Melanie, already weak, accepted Carolyne's offer of momentary physical support.

"Something about rocks in the head," Charles added cryptically. He corrected: "Rather, rock *on* the head."

"This rock in particular." Roy knelt on one knee and turned back the upper edge of the blanket they'd used to cover the body. Most of the dead man's face remained blessedly concealed.

"On which Gordon hit his head when the jaguar took him down?" Carolyne interpreted.

"Wrong sequence of events," Charles corrected but left Roy to provide specifics.

"No way would that rock be there for his head to hit, if left to Mother Nature."

"I don't understand," Melanie confessed.

Once again, Carolyne was quicker on the uptake. "It's river rock."

"So agrees our visiting geologist," Charles confirmed.

"Just over there is the river," Melanie pointed in that direction.

"And there the river has been for a very long time, geologically speaking," Roy explained. "But, dig down to bedrock, anywhere on this side of the river, and you'll not find another stone like this one, here. It's water-smooth and round."

"Rivers flood," Teddy reminded. "Stones in those rivers bang together and get smooth."

"Indeed," Roy agreed. "However, indicative geology says this river always floods eastward. It's a matter of a steep western gradient formed by an intrusion of igneous rock along an ancient fault line."

"All you grad students understand?" Charles was delighted by his comprehension. "We're right back to passion as a motivation for murder."

"You're back to saying I killed him, you silly old fool?" Teddy challenged.

"Self-defense is an acceptable motive for murder," Charles reminded. "Maybe, that rock was meant for your head before you wrestled it away from him."

"Assisted by a conveniently handy hungry jaguar? Take my word: had I wanted Gordon dead, I would have shot him and dumped his body where no on would ever find it."

"Stop, you two!" Carolyne insisted.

She turned back to Roy who seemed the only man present with his full wits about him. "Let me see if I've this geology stuff straight."

He obliged by reiterating in layman terms. "The river flows along a fault line with harder rock on this side than on the other. The softer, more easily eroded, soil has always seen the water flood in its direction. No matter the volume, the water wouldn't naturally have put that river rock, here, where it presently is. To have it here, someone would have had to go to the river and get it."

"There's always the possibility someone, for some other reason than murder, toted that rock here," Carolyne pointed out. "There was once a substantial Indian population in residence, correct?"

Melanie confirmed, in that her father's journals had mentioned as much. "Likewise, prospectors, geologists, anthropologists, zoologists, lepidopterists, botanists, and who knows who else tramp, tramp, tramping through."

"The world is full of weirder coincidences than a man attacked by a jaguar and gone down to hit his head on a rock brought in by natives to sharpen spear points." Carolyne decided that was a more comfortable alternative than murder.

Teddy turned on Charles. "If you don't buy that, you old fool, how about *you* as the killer?"

"I?" Apparently, Charles found that notion so ludicrous that it bore repeating. "I? Why would I want Gordon dead?"

"He attacked your niece. You weren't the one to protect her. That must have played havoc with your manliness."

"Absurd!" Charles looked around for additional support.

"You have an alibi for the time of the murder?" Teddy pressed; Melanie wished he'd quit goading her uncle, and vice versa.

"You tell me the exact time of the murder," Charles said, craftily, "and I'll tell you exactly where I was."

"It's doubtful any of us have alibis." Carolyne figured it was time to pull them together, their bickering not helping anything. "Gordon died between leaving Charles on the other side of the gully and...."

"With him at the last, weren't you, old man?" Teddy interrupted.

"Please!" Melanie gave a small tug on Teddy's muscled arm; he glowered but shut up.

"Just when did he leave you, Charles?" Carolyne stepped in.

"Eleven o'clock. I waited until almost noon to cross back over that rotting tree trunk he insisted was a viable bridge."

"He told you where he was headed, did he?" Teddy remained prosecutorial; Melanie suspected it was in return for Charles' romantic fantasies, but she couldn't enjoy her uncle pitifully on the defensive.

"He was going to the toilet if you must know."

"Mighty long potty break," Teddy decided to no one's appreciation but his own.

"He complained of dysentery. We've all had it."

Teddy enjoyed the spotlight shifted to Charles; Melanie continued to think her fiancé cruel to bombard her uncle who, despite all his ridiculous conjecture, had always given Teddy the out of self-defense. "I figure Charles followed Gordon, did the dastardly deed, and scurried back to camp before I found what his obliging accomplice, the jaguar, had left of the corpse."

"Even I could have gotten here and back without being seen," Melanie emphasized Carolyne's earlier comment that any one of them could have committed the deed—if the deed had been done.

Teddy didn't like her blood-thicker-than-water attitude. "Melanie had a motive, too, did you, my dear, having been mauled by Gordon even if in a different way than Gordon was mauled by the jaguar?"

Melanie's response was sarcastic to cover her hurt. "Thank-you so much for that!" She broke all physical contact with him and moved apart. "How quickly I've gone from poor little thing, hardly up to photographing a dead man, to cold-blooded killer responsible for making the man dead in the first place."

Teddy looked apologetic but didn't say as much. This did little to endear him to Melanie who stepped closer to Charles without completely closing the gap; Charles' accusations remained as ridiculous.

"Let's leave the cross-examination to those more qualified, shall we?" Carolyne couldn't swallow the love sick psychopath, the jealous fiancé in self-defense, the irate uncle, or the Melanie only got kissed, as real motives for murder. Maybe, she was too old to remember intense passion sparked by love, lust, infatuation, or whatever, but this Gordon-Melanie-Teddy-Charles quadrangle seemed too sophomoric as foreplay to murder. Pretty young women, even those with good-looking fiancés, had always flirted with other handsome young men; those same young women, as often as not, having second thoughts when things got too far out of hand. The world over, fiancés defended their bruised honors by fisticuffs, not murder. It was a rite of passage that only occasionally exploded into the seriousness of homicide. Besides, Gordon had simply not seemed all that smitten by Melanie, or all that resentful of his well-deserved comeuppance at the hands of Teddy, to go off the deep end and get himself killed in the process. As for her even imagining that Charles hit Gordon with a stone carried from the river, her mind's-eye picture of that would have made her laugh aloud if not for the sobering body laid out less than six feet from her.

"Do we bury the evidence?" Roy's question sounded more aptly put to cohorts in a crime than to the present group; belatedly, Carolyne realized he referred to the body. "If so, we'll have to take him across the river, in that any grave in this insufficient layer of topsoil invites vulnerability."

Carolyne didn't ask, "Vulnerability to what?" what with a hungry jaguar still on the prowl. Claws that had done what they had already done would have little trouble displacing a few feet of newly turned soil. Nor did she need it pointed out that any grave on the other side of the river was vulnerable, in its own right, albeit to subtler despoilers, like heat, moisture, and bacteria. Things were recycled mind-bogglingly fast in surroundings like these. Obviously, the killer, if there was one, had taken advantage by assuring expert analysis of his deed was more than a week away. Whatever forensics had to work with when they arrived, it wouldn't be nearly as good as if a radio transmission or satellite-transmitted SOS had brought them running sooner.

"Definitely, I don't think we should give the jaguar another chance at him," Charles decided. "Surely, between us, we can get him to a suitable site and buried deep enough."

"I say we inter him behind the waterfall." It was a suggestion made by Carolyne with some trepidation. She hadn't liked Gordon all that much, and antagonizing his possible killer wasn't something at the head of her to-do list. On the other hand, she never took kindly to people who played God, let alone to those who tried to put something over on her. If Roy hadn't pointed out the incongruity of that particular stone, would Carolyne have seen it on her own? Probably not.

She tried to minimize her present cleverness, in the eyes of any killer who might take umbrage to her efforts to thwart him. "The cave is closer and more convenient than ferrying the body across the river."

"Brilliant!" Melanie congratulated. "It's cooler, too, isn't it?

The body will be better preserved when the authorities finally do arrive on the scene."

Silently, Carolyne bemoaned Melanie having brought that to the attention of any killer. In consolation, it was unlikely any killer would have missed the obvious even if Melanie hadn't spelled out the obvious. Which was no derogatory reflection on Melanie's intelligence, except so far as Carolyne, never a beauty herself, had an inherent bias that made it difficult to equate prom queen with discoverer of a possible cure for cancer. She sometimes forgot the genes of Cornelius Ditherson were locked somewhere within that attractive package. Charles, not too shabby a scientist in his own right, had arisen from that very same impressive gene pool.

"Natural refrigeration, so to speak." It wasn't a question but Teddy pondering that possibility. "It might work."

"It'll certainly be worth the try," Roy agreed.

"There are those natural niches in the cave wall," Melanie reminded. "We can put Gordon in one of those and block it off with stones."

"Stones big enough to thwart any recovery attempts by Mr. Hungry Jaguar," Charles added his congratulations.

"Two at a time on the litter," Roy summated logistics, "the third walking shotgun and trading off duties with the other two." Felix, back at camp, wasn't counted. "The ladies can devote full-time to making sure the cat doesn't appear unexpectedly."

The speed and ease with which everyone fell into litter construction and assigned roles denoted universal acceptance. Although, Carolyne hardly expected the killer, if there was one, to draw attention to himself by arguing for a less acceptable—except for him—alternative course of action.

They were headed out when Melanie was distracted by a faint glitter of green. She stooped to retrieve the cause from the otherwise concealing mat of leafy decay. "Something else I suspect Mother Nature didn't put here?" she said and held up her discovery for more light.

"Is that an emerald?" Charles asked in amazement. Walking

shotgun, he'd seen Melanie kneel to claim the prize. Now, preferring a professional opinion: "Roy, my niece has a possible emerald, yes?"

None too ceremoniously, the litter, with Gordon on it, was lowered by Teddy and Roy, the latter's expertise immediately available.

"Damn if it isn't one of mine!" Roy surprised after his initial examination of the stone that wasn't overly large but definitely a beauty as far as its deeply translucent green was concerned.

"My niece found it while you were hitched to the litter," Charles indignantly begged to differ; he snapped the gem from Roy's hand.

Roy realized his announcement had sounded like a bully staking claim to some little weakling's prize marble. "I mean, it was once part of a cache I brought back from the headwaters of the Jurua."

"So, what's it doing here?" Teddy waited for Melanie to take the stone from her uncle and pass it on.

"Beats me. I sold it to John Leider awhile back."

"How can you be so sure it's the same stone?" Teddy was doubtful. "One emerald looks pretty much like another, yes?"

Roy had news for him. "Gems of this exceptional green don't grow on trees. They're damned hard to come by, and I remember every one I ever had the luck of finding." He retrieved a small spiral notebook from his shirt pocket, shuffled its pages, and pointed to a pencil drawing. "That's it; its inclusions form a distinctive 'J,' just slightly to the left of center. John's wife's name, Jane, starts with a J, too, and he was hot to have it. I jacked up the asking price, because of his obvious anxiousness to have it, and he still bought it."

"Inclusions?" Teddy held the emerald elevated between his thumb and forefinger; it converted all refracted light into green sparks.

"Its flaws." Roy wasn't a jeweler explaining stone qualities to a prospective buyer; he was a jeweler begrudgingly indulging questions from some know-nothing bum who'd accosted him on the street. "It's how you tell the real things from the fakes; it's the fakes, in the case of emeralds, that are always perfect."

"So, does this expand our list of suspects by putting Mr. Leider at the scene of the crime?" Suddenly, Charles was willing to welcome that additional scapegoat.

"There'd be a lot of people interested to hear it, if it does," Roy revealed. "Jane Leider included. John was due back in Manaus ages ago, but his wife insists he's never shown."

"Disappeared in order to off Gordon?" Teddy was magnanimously as anxious as Charles to shift the blame outside the immediate group.

"I can't imagine John misplacing an emerald, let alone this one," was the way Roy saw it. "Besides, I'd know if he'd reappeared around these parts."

"Maybe, my unexpected appearance on the murder scene didn't give him time to realize the emerald was gone," Teddy suggested.

"Meaning, we should keep our eyes peeled for a two-legged John Leider as well as a four-legged jaguar?" Charles ventured.

"Cheery thought!" Carolyne's tone came across anything-but.

"Congratulations, Melanie, it's a beautiful stone and will make a nice souvenir." Roy watched the gem pass back to its latest discoverer's hands.

"I get to keep it?" Possession pleased her, despite the tragic circumstances.

"At least until Mr. Leider comes to collect it," Teddy said ominously; it wasn't something Melanie wanted to hear; having heard it, she was sorry Teddy was so killjoy.

"Finders-keepers, I suspect," Roy was more optimistic. "Of course, the authorities will want to take a look."

"All chocked up as a very interesting interlude, but shouldn't we get Gordon taken care of before nightfall?" Charles suggested. "I suspect both our jaguar and Mr. Leider have better night vision than we do."

The ensuing burial proved anticlimactic, the trip down to

the river and behind the falls entirely without incident. One of several niches was sufficiently large so that Gordon fit without any undignified efforts to stuff him into a better fit. Convenient rocks, fallen from the cave ceiling over the centuries, made only a few additional stones necessary from the river.

The natural chill of the cave was enhanced by the sounds of the water that curtained the entrance without splashing anything but a leading lip of stone.

Roy asked Carolyne if she would read something appropriate from his weather-worn miniature *Old Testament*. She chose the "Twenty-third Psalm." That walk through the valley of the shadow of death was an old standard that always fit. She'd learned early that anyone who spent time in the wilderness should be prepared for the eventuality of dying there—herself or others.

Back at the campsite, they apprised Felix of the situation. He surprised Carolyne with his personal interpretations, and thankfully he did so in a private conversation. Had he publicly voiced his opinions, he would have found Carolyne completely unsure how to have handled them.

"If you ask me, put the blame squarely on you, or on Charles," said Felix.

Carolyne was flabbergasted by that insinuation. "On me? On Charles?" The echoing of his words was all she could manage.

"What has the death of Gordon accomplished, huh? It's nipped this little expedition right in the bud. It puts us on a beeline out of here, not only because we don't have a guide to take us farther, but because that guide's death, possibly by foul play, must be reported."

This, as far as Carolyne was concerned, didn't tie Charles or her to any murder.

"Neither you nor Charles wanted this trip to succeed."

It was a statement, not a question, and it left Carolyne wondering from where he and his lunatic accusations came. "I gave up a chance to teach at Oxford to assure the success of this trip!" She thought him mad!

"Assure its success, or assure its failure?" He allowed her no more than her what an absurd notion gasp. "The last thing you want is more accolades for Melanie's father. Cornelius Ditherson had way too many while he was alive, didn't he? Had way too many after he married Margaret instead of you, yes?" Her look of drop jawed surprise didn't fool him. "Did you think none of us saw what was going on when you pulled out, claiming an offer you couldn't resist from JanEx Pharmaceuticals?"

"It was simply a career move." She wasn't hot to discuss this, especially with Felix, especially here.

"Expected him to beg you to stay, didn't you, Carolyne?" It was a challenge. "Counted yourself chiefly responsible for all the successes of Ditherson/Santire, right? Didn't you locate *Habernia Carolyne-cornelius* in the Begum's garden; no matter Cornelius had put three years into cutting the legalities and red tape that put you two there at the right time? Didn't you find the illusive *Boletus Carolyne-cornelius*; no matter that Cornelius' friend of a friend of a friend got you access to that restricted Indian territory? You always figured Cornelius just a tag-along to be tolerated because he was such prime husband material."

"Don't be ridiculous!" How many, besides Felix, saw things that way?

"Surprised you, didn't he?" Momentarily his headache, still pounding beneath the wispy strands of his almost bald head, was forgotten. "Not only made do without you but proved himself more the plant-hunter than you ever were. Where were you when he found *Anemone cornelius* from which Crystin Companies developed their breakthrough arthritis pill, or when he discovered *Nymphaea cornelius* to give Crystin its active ingredient for Pelincidrinal-Z14? You were so far faded into the backdrop that it must have been hard, after all your years of imagining yourself the key ingredient of that relationship, to take in the reality."

Carolyne was too stunned by his vindictiveness to offer any immediate rebuttal.

"As for Charles, so long the ignored brother," Felix continued, "he could only gain his bit of the limelight once Cornelius was dead. How frustrating it must be for him to have some plant that Cornelius stumbled upon two decades ago suddenly come into prominence as a possible cure for cancer, just because Melanie experimented with the properties of a musty flora specimen pressed for years in the dusty basement of the University of Washington? You think Charles wants us to find enough *Lygodium cornelius* to confirm something in it destroys malignant cells in rats and may do the same for people?"

"He's here to do just that!"

"Except, we're scooting on out of here, our supposed objective not met."

"You think we won't be back to try again?"

"Back to what? Whatever the potential of our illusive *Lygodium cornelius*, it will likely be the victim of Kyle Georni's own personal slash and burn definition of progress. You think the authorities are going to renew our present permits, what with a possible murderer, let alone a man-eating jaguar, on the loose? This country is too indebted to U.S. banks, too hopeful that American aid is going to bail it out of its impossible financial predicaments, to ever risk the bad publicity that would attend the murder of prominent American scientists by man or beast. Melanie had trouble getting the permits in the first place."

Carolyne had quite enough and was finally recovered sufficiently to prove it. "People living in glass houses shouldn't throw stones!"

"Meaning?" He didn't seem threatened; she'd soon fix that.

"Whose name do you think was whispered to me as the 'other' man to whom Margaret was headed on that rainy night her car skidded off the road?" Carolyne had always wanted to believe Cornelius' wife was the slut Carolyne had always imagined her to be, but she had, at the time, resisted and laughed in Charles' face when he'd suggested Felix, this little nobody selected by Cornelius to fill the void left by Carolyne's departure, was ever Margaret's paramour.

"What an obscene, filthy-minded, ludicrous suggestion!"

Felix had taken way too long to formulate his response; even if he hadn't (look how long it had taken Carolyne to muster any response during his verbal attack on her), she refused to grant him even the shadow of a doubt; bad-mouthing was a two-way street. Felix wasn't finished: "Margaret was the finest woman I ever knew, and I resent your attempts to tar her reputation when she's not alive to defend herself."

After all the bilge his sewer mouth had just spewed, did he really expect her to stop now? "Just the response I'd expect from the man who bedded Margaret because he was so jealous of Cornelius with whom he couldn't compete in any way, shape, or form. The last thing you want is Cornelius to one-up you, once again, especially now, from the grave."

"You're eaten by jealousy toward a woman whose only sin in living was to love and marry the man you'd laid claim to for yourself."

"And you're a weak, no-chinned, no-account bastard who was too afraid to come out in the open about your sordid part in Margaret's death for fear Cornelius would sack you on the spot and no one else would ever take you on."

For just a second, she thought she sensed something about him ready to scream, "Yes, by God, yes!" right in her face. She was disappointed and a little frightened by his, "If I did kill Gordon, I suggest *you* watch *your* tail, from here on out!" said just before he got up and stormed off to the other side of the campsite, everyone else not hearing his threat but wondering what in the hell he and Carolyne were up to.

CHAPTER THREE

"Felix is a certifiable wretch!" Carolyne forked some of the Chicken Kiev that Charles had brought her; the food tasted as bland as it always did whenever Felix didn't make it even more completely unpalatable.

"I assume your reference goes above and beyond his questionable skills as a cook?" Charles sympathetic smile revealed white teeth all his own.

"Don't tell me you didn't witness our altercation while you played Betty Crocker for the second time in one day." She knew better.

"There was little chance of missing it, wouldn't you say?" Charles worked his shoulders against the smooth trunk of the tree he used for support. "Hearing it was something else again, although the facial expressions and hand gestures did Marcel Marceau proud. Jungle clearings are notorious for poor acoustics, especially when the actors insist upon keeping down their conversation to whispers and hisses."

"Would you like a quick recap?"

"Are you volunteering?"

She gave him a quick summation.

He surprised her with far less vehemence than her own. "I see where he might think that. Of me, I mean," he quickly amended to exclude Carolyne from any such correct thinking by Felix. "I was admittedly nondescript while in my brother's shadow."

Carolyne denied it, even if it was true: "Nonsense!"

"Felix's misconception is in assuming I minded all that

much—all of the time. Actually, Cornelius was never one of those brothers who got off on sibling rivalry. He was always quick to point out to me that a lot of his success was based on the luck of being at the right places at the right times. If people liked to think it was otherwise, they were entitled. It was important, though, that I know differently, because, given the right set of circumstances, bound to come my way, sooner or later, I'd come into my own. His words, not mine; something special about him, especially as a brother, no doubt about it. To the end, I was flattered whenever he asked me to accompany him on an expedition, and I believed him when he insisted each trip prepared me for my own great contributions, someday. If I got down the basics, I'd be as ready for success as it would one day be ready for me."

He shoveled a particularly unappetizing lump of gooey chicken and ate it. "Not that I was always free of jealousy, resentment, and all those other monsters that creep into relationships, in general, and into family relationships, in particular. At times, I could, and did, bitch up a storm about my secondary role. I could, and did, at various times, blame my lack of success on my brother, on flat feet, on bad knees, on influenza, on malaria, on my frequent bouts of dysentery. I don't suppose you ever noticed my tendency to bemoan my ills during the course of any given day."

"Can't say as I have," Carolyne lied through her teeth. She hadn't expected validation of Felix's slander and was put off by it.

Charles' laugh was one of his best qualities; he laughed now. It was a boom punctuated by an audible catch of breath, followed by an immediate repeat. Carolyne pictured the very first lexicographer as he listened carefully to Charles' laugh, then wrote: "Ha-ha!: an expression of surprise or joy."

The sounding never failed to make her smile, and this time was no exception. "So, maybe, I have heard you complain on occasion."

"It's a habit I was unable to shake even when I finally did

have a bit of luck. Remember my discovery of *Fitzroya char-lius*, or is my unfortunate throw-me-a-rope slide off the side of that mountain really your only memory of our shared experiences in the Chilean wilds?"

"You're not the only one ever beset by bugaboos, like professional jealousy," Carolyne was embarrassed to concede. "If I'd been two yards closer to that tree, it would be *Fitzroya Carolyneus*. I don't doubt you think that petty, a few finds already accredited to me at the time, but I was in a dry spell, as you might remember, having severed my ties with Cornelius. A new discovery of pseudo larch would have done quite nicely for my ego."

"As if you'd come to the end of the line! I recall several new plants added to your roster after that."

"Never anything as important as *Anemone cornelius* or *Nymphaea cornelius*."

What could Charles say to that? Cornelius held the record for discoveries used in major medical breakthroughs. There was a time when everyone expected his every find to provide some kind of miracle cure. Carolyne had started out her career like a house afire, but she had lost steam as Cornelius had gained his.

Carolyne laid her empty plate to one side and cast a furtive glance toward Felix ensconced in his don't approach me posture on the far side of the campsite; Teddy and Melanie were perfectly content with their own company; Roy had turned in, his bedroll now a cocoon-like silhouette against the fire built to keep any jaguar at bay.

"Maybe, just maybe," Carolyne admitted, "there is a thread of truth to the notion that I was a bit full of myself in my days with your brother." Had Charles known that there was nothing like offering his confession in proof of vulnerability, to coax a reciprocal confession from her? "Maybe, I did see myself as chosen by the gods and was slow to give Cornelius as much credit as was his due. Maybe, I did feel something for him, not just professional, that got bruised when he married the daughter of Crystin Companies' head honcho. But for that jerk over there...." She nodded toward Felix as if to indicate a feral rat run loose in the granary. "...to pick up on any of that and convert it, through his own convoluted logic, into a motive for murder, makes me see red."

"He's jealous of you; that's all."

"Jealous?" She could more easily accept his jealousy of Cornelius. Her accomplishments had never seemed quite good enough to inspire envy; the fading of her star, after leaving Cornelius, had made them seem even punier.

"Felix is a desk man, very good at it, too," Charles said. "Cornelius' estate would have been poorer, by far, without Felix's administrative skills. However, he's always seen himself as a man in the field. Maybe, he even assumed that's what he'd eventually be when Cornelius took him on; you certainly didn't languish long behind any office desk once you joined the team."

"Do you think Cornelius holding him back was what motivated Felix's affair with Margaret?" That's how Carolyne now saw it.

"You accepting that probability, suddenly? Seeing him seeing himself, at the time, better than Cornelius in bed, since he couldn't prove himself the better man in the field?"

"Something like that."

Charles shrugged.

"I'm now prepared to believe anything bad about the little weasel."

"Actually," Charles said, "I personally saw Felix rendez-vous with Margaret twice at a seedy hotel called *Seaman's Roost*. Why weren't they more discreet so as not to be spotted? Discretion, I guess, just wasn't among the characteristics of two people already prepared to risk so much. Anyway, the first time, I spotted her in the parking lot, getting out of her car. I would have pulled over, then and there, to say hello.... The idea of Margaret there for a liaison was so far out of my mind at the time that the obvious sleaziness of the venue didn't even register. Anyway, I was in the wrong lane of traffic for the turn and had to go around the block. When I got back, Felix was just pulling in. No longer any sign of Margaret, but her car was still there."

"You stuck around?"

"The potential for catastrophe took me out of there like a bat out of hell. A few miles down the road, I had myself convinced I'd seen nothing. There were probably a lot of women who looked like Margaret, driving cars that looked like hers. Same for Felix and his car. Those kinds of I have to be mistaken kind of mind games."

"You said there was a second time?"

"The very next week. Same time. Same place. Don't ask me why I was there; I truly believed I'd imagined it all. Still did when she drove in, just like before, and headed into the hotel. He arrived a few minutes later and followed her inside."

"Whatever did she see in him? He's not much to look at now and wasn't much better back then."

"Isn't it rumored that women love men for what's inside?"

"It's just a rumor, too, likely started by a very ugly man." So what that Tina Jackson had married Phillip Wayne whom Carolyne thought looked like a toad? And, it *had* to be pure accident that scare his own mother Darrel Wayne had landed a beauty like Candy Mills.

"I didn't stick around, nor did I ever go back."

"No temptation to get a camera?"

"And hurt Cornelius? Carolyne, my brother truly loved Margaret. Besides, I don't know how he would have handled having cancer and being a cuckold."

"Tell me about the night her car went off the road." Carolyne wanted that final connection.

"Tuesday night. Her and Felix's night. Eight o'clock. Their time. The *Seaman's Roost*, their hotel, only two blocks away."

"Would you believe the bastard was right here, only minutes ago, denying it all?"

"Probably took him by surprise that you called him out on it."

With that, Charles excused himself with, "Early to bed, early to rise...." He wasn't young any more, and trekking through any jungle, this one included, was no Sunday stroll through the park.

Carolyne, too, knew the advantages of sleep in the face of a scheduled early morning departure. However, she was still too keyed up by her confrontation with Felix; lying down would summon only more dark, sleep-denying thoughts.

She took advantage of Teddy's decision to turn in, too, and joined Melanie who, like Carolyne, wasn't ready for the day to end.

"That is a beautiful emerald." Carolyne sat down on the ground and took the gem Melanie handed over. "As Roy said: 'A nice little souvenir.'" She handed it back.

"Trouble is," Melanie said and pocketed the stone, "I came for more than a souvenir. The total repercussions of the day's events have just begun to sink in. I keep thinking of all those people in the world who die every day of cancer. I keep thinking of how many more may die because of a man killed, here, whether he was killed by man or by beast." She tried to muster a smile and did a pretty good job of it. "And, of course, I keep thinking how a major source of *Lygodium cornelius* could have been quite a feather in my cap, maybe someday making Melanie Ditherson a household name."

"That dream surely isn't dead."

Melanie was hopeful. "You think the authorities will allow us back, any time soon?" Her optimism was short-lived. "I'm not. They fought tooth and nail before they gave in this time. When they finally conceded the battle, I thought it was a sign good fortune would soon follow. What a mess it is, instead."

"How did you ever decide upon Charles, Felix, and me?" Carolyne wanted to talk to keep her mind off other things.

"I wanted the best, didn't I? More importantly, I wanted not only people who loved my father, and would see this as a marvelous final epithet for him, but the people my father loved and/or trusted."

"Wrong luck of the draw, as far as that certified wretch, Felix!"

Unlike Charles, Melanie didn't ask for specifics. Her laugh wasn't her Uncle Charles' laugh; it was her father's; it made Carolyne wish Cornelius wasn't dead of cancer, that old times could be lived again, that pain needn't always be so much of any relationship. "Father used to say, 'Love and like have, unfortunately, very little to do with a deserving recipient. It's to do with quite helpless emotions that take root, despite all efforts to control them, and grow against all odds.'"

"He must have figured I was doing my best at rooting him out of my life when I went over to JanEx." It wasn't exactly a question, because Carolyne knew the answer. At the time, she hurt a lot and meant to hurt him.

Melanie leaned closer and put a hand on the older woman's knee. "He never—ever—blamed you, you know? He told me he blamed himself, because he'd been too self-centered in thinking my mom was as good for everyone as she was good for him. He'd not even considered the prospects of things unable to go on as before. By the time he did realize it, it was too late. He admired your strength to see complications that he didn't see, as well as your determination to get on with your life. He always said he'd never have been where he was without you, without watching the way your instincts took charge in the field. Every time he made a new discovery, he'd tell me he couldn't have done it without those years of learning with you and from you. It made me quite jealous before I matured beyond most of that childish, stereotypical pettiness."

She moved her hand from Carolyne's knee to the woman's hand. She took those rough, square-tipped fingers and gave a squeeze. "My father was never very good with personal relationships. Oh, he loved and was loved. He was kind. He was considerate. He could be generous to a fault, and could forgive just about anyone for not being perfect. But, there was always a piece of him that was well-recognized; a piece devoted one-hundred percent to his vocation. His time in the field was his greatest passion. I truly believe he preferred plants to people."

Carolyne thought: He's not the only one.

"Dad didn't want me to go into medical research, did you know that?"

Carolyne, caught up in conflicting emotions, shook her head.

"'To be good in science, really good,' dad told me, 'you have to devote a portion of your life only to your work, and that makes the people closest to you think you're keeping something from them; it can lead to a great deal of unhappiness.'"

"Was Margaret unhappy?" God, yes! Please, God, yes!

Melanie repeated Carolyne's question, like a student in a spelling bee not only following instructions but taking the extra time to let her thoughts jell. "My mother came from a family of scientists, didn't she? She was a scientist, and she married a scientist. It was the only way of life she knew. I think she was happy only in that she didn't realize there was another definition of happiness that didn't entail some holding back, in even the most intimate moments."

It wasn't exactly what Carolyne wanted to hear. Deprived of complete satisfaction, she asked, "And you? Are you and Teddy happy?" Melanie *had* flirted with Gordon. Teddy *had* been the first to state Melanie's motive for murder. "You're a scientist; he's a scientist. Another match made in heaven?"

Melanie gave another of her laughs that attractively crinkled the corners of her eyes and made her seem more suited to cotillion gossip than to jungle machinations. "Definitely not a match made in heaven!" Her next laugh was at Carolyne's startled expression. "Oh, come on," she challenged, "are you seriously going to tell me you thought I'd say differently?"

Quite frankly, that was exactly what Carolyne had figured.

"I do *like* Teddy," Melanie admitted. "Did you like either or both of your husbands?"

"At what points in those relationships do you refer?" Carolyne parried.

"Exactly!" Melanie agreed. She smiled without vocalizing the laugh her twinkling brown eyes mimed for her. "I think he likes my celebrity. I think he likes liking Melanie Ditherson, daughter of Cornelius and Margaret, niece of Charles, granddaughter of the Cecilia and Geoffrey Crystin of Crystin Companies, *et al.*, *ad infinitum*. I can live with that, for the moment. Whether it will be good enough for the long haul—well, I'll just have to wait and see. I'll be interested in how he handles this setback, because he sincerely looked forward to the celebrity of our success here and from his projected part in the verification of my initial research. He's from a poor family, needed a full scholarship, had to maintain a high grade-point average, has this desperate compulsion to climb high socially and professionally; all of that kind of stuff. Why I latched onto him? Maybe, it's part of that old chestnut about the haves feeling guilty about all of the have-nots." She shrugged.

Carolyne was giddy from Melanie's candidness. Over and over, she forgot this pretty package's outside wrapping wasn't any real indicator of the real substance inside. How many times did she have to be hit over the head with that fact to remember it? "I really didn't mean to pry."

There was Melanie's smile again. "Of course, you meant to pry." Carolyne felt like a little girl, cookie in hand, denying a raid on the cookie jar, little consoled by Melanie's, "I don't mind. If I did, I'd tell you so, or don't you think I would?"

"I don't know what I think," Carolyne admitted. "Frankly, I find you something of a dichotomy."

"Really?" She wasn't displeased. "I'd always welcome your input, you know. On whatever. I admire the way you assessed your situation with my father, cut your losses, and moved on with your life without bitterness." Her next smile accompanied, "Outward bitterness, at least. I only hope I can handle any eventual separation from Teddy with equal aplomb."

Roy sat up suddenly, and it wasn't missed by either woman.

"Something, Roy?" Carolyne was apprehensive.

There was as minute of pregnant silence wherein everyone listened.

Roy said finally, "I thought I heard something."

Uncountable goose bumps suddenly pimpled Carolyne's flesh. She rubbed her arms vigorously to counteract her inner chill.

"It was probably nothing," Roy decided finally.

There was a universal sigh of, "Thank God!"

They'd divvied the night between them, Melanie to lead off the watch, Carolyne to follow. Carolyne was sure she couldn't sleep, in the interim, but she made the effort. She didn't want to face tomorrow dead on her feet.

The next she knew, she was aware of Melanie shaking her awake. She sat up so fast it left her slightly dizzy and decidedly disoriented.

"Sorry," Melanie apologized. "It's just your turn at watch. I hated to wake you, you were sleeping so soundly."

"Anything worth reporting?"

"A few sounds that Roy might have made heads or tails out of; not I. The jaguar eyes I spotted about an hour back turned out to be two moths committing hara-kiri in the campfire flames."

Carolyne got up and stretched; the prospect of more sleep was mighty inviting.

She threw a couple chunks of rotting wood on the fire. Sparks danced for a minute and highlighted her sleeping, or about to be asleep companions. She was tempted to rouse Felix, just out of curmudgeonness, but she controlled herself. She only had a few more days, and she'd be rid of the little monster. If the expedition got a new lease on life, she'd do her best to make sure the worm wasn't along for the ride; Charles would back her up, even if he wasn't as angry at Felix as Carolyne would have preferred him to be.

She squatted at the edge of the fire and welcomed the heat. The natural sauna of the day had deteriorated into a decided chill once the sun went down. Of course, the desert was even worse; after days of near sunstroke temperatures, Gobi nights had threatened her with frostbite. "Count your blessings, Carolyne," she mumbled and threw another stick on the fire.

Time stretched endlessly, eaten away slow second by slow second. Carolyne assumed an uncomfortable squat as a distraction against the continuing temptation of renewed sleep.

Sounds, like rodents scampering, began; they were like a breeze rustling dead leaves, without the breeze. Would Teddy's big as a house jaguar make as much noise? Carolyne's experience with big cats was limited. She'd spent time in their territories, but they'd always obliged by keeping out of sight and leaving her alone. Was her luck about to run out?

She tried less gruesome and disturbing thoughts, but conjuring the luxury of a lengthy tub bath, the delectability of a really good meal, and a complete make over in a beauty salon, were all too relaxing and made her more tired. Imagining her as the main course for a jaguar, or the victim of a madman, were more conducive to keeping her on her toes.

Roy stirred before schedule, but Carolyne was prepared to see her assigned time through. "I've at least a good half an hour more to go."

"I'm having trouble sleeping, anyway," Roy gave her leave.

She was gracious enough to believe him. "Nothing to report but the usual fantasies conjured by an overactive mind confronted by deep jungle darkness."

She checked her bedroll for whatever life-forms had proclaimed squatters rights in her absence, then scooted in. It was unbelievable how comfortable that bit of padding was.

All too soon, Melanie woke her again. This time it was indirectly. "I tell you, I know how I packed it!" Melanie was saying loudly to Felix.

Carolyne was pleased to see Felix didn't look happy, and she kicked herself out of her bed. "Something wrong?"

"I'm sorry if I woke you," Melanie apologized. "I wanted some toilet paper and found my bag rifled, Felix on duty."

"You don't know I was on duty when it happened," Felix defended. "When was the last time you checked?"

"Well, somebody scrounged through it," Melanie amended, "and I discovered that fact on your watch."

Carolyne wondered if she could be as certain of someone rifling her own disorganized possessions. "Anything missing?"

"My first thought was the pictures I took of Gordon's body,

but the digital chip is still there."

"I would have seen anyone," Felix insisted with renewed confidence.

"Unless you were sleeping on watch," Melanie challenged.

Felix's already florid face turned almost purple; little blue veins highlighted his cheeks. "I was not asleep!"

"My first thought would have been for my emerald," Carolyne confessed. Maybe prerogatives were different for someone who already had additional emeralds, plus a few diamonds, rubies, sapphires, and pearls, in the family vault back home.

Melanie rummaged through her bedroll and retrieved the gemstone.

"Problem?" Roy's adaptation to his surroundings had managed to get him to them before anyone even knew he was awake, let alone on the move.

"Melanie says someone has been going through her things." For the pure pleasure, Carolyne added, "She made that discovery on Felix's watch."

"There was nobody!" Felix responded on cue.

"Not even you?" Carolyne was grabbing at straws. Had Melanie narrowed it down to Felix, she would have said so. Nevertheless, it gave Carolyne pleasure to see the little maggot squirm.

"I was nowhere near her or her bag!"

"Scooted away before she came completely awake, did you?"

"Anything taken?" Roy kept out of the bickering. "Emerald? Photographs?" His order of prerogatives clearly matched those of Carolyne.

"Nothing that I can tell," Melanie admitted.

"Then, no harm done," Roy judged. "You might think seriously about sleeping *with* emerald and the digital chip."

Melanie was pleased he didn't suggest either would be safer if handed over to him. Teddy wouldn't have been as equal opportunity, or as diplomatic.

"Time to move out?" Charles had finally been aroused by their conversation; Teddy was the only one still out.

"Might as well," Roy conceded. "We should have enough light by breakfast."

He was right, although it was more a case of eyes adjusted to darkness than to actual sunlight released into the gloom.

Carolyne ate raisins and walnuts and washed them down with water. She hooked her canteen to her webbed belt and decamped with the others.

Charles and Teddy's disappearance occurred at midday. Noon was the hour Carolyne assigned it, although Charles could have gone as early as 11:30; that's when he was last heard from. As usual, travel had been accomplished not by visual contact, always difficult to maintain, but by an intuitive sense of stepping where the guy in front had stepped a few seconds before. Everyone was supposed to keep regular verbal contact with the person in front and behind, but exhaustion often made small talk a genuine effort.

"Charles!" Carolyne couldn't believe they'd lost him. His well-toned sixth sense should have kept him in line. If not, a few exchanged shouts, even now, should have returned him to the fold.

As for Teddy, who knew how long he'd been gone? There was the chance he'd merely followed after Charles, a case of the blind leading the blind, but positioned as he was at the end of the line, he might well have wandered off even before Charles cut loose.

It was frustrating they'd both been so quiet about it. None of the remaining four had heard anything that resembled a cry of disorientation.

"Teddy! Charles!" Roy fired two shots that received no reply.

Carolyne's acute dismay wasn't helped by her having been the weak link in the chain, from which both men had disengaged.

"We'll eat," Roy decided, "during which we'll shoot off a few more rounds. If Teddy and Charles haven't showed, or checked in, by then, we'll have to consider alternatives."

They had to consider alternatives.

The resulting vote gave Carolyne a sense of déjà vu: She was against a search party, because there were too many unknowns and too much jungle; Melanie was of the opinion, "We can't simply sit around and do nothing!" Roy volunteered to take a look-see; Felix sided with Carolyne, although it wasn't as any favor to her.

Two against two was normally a vote for the status quo, but Roy worked independently of the expedition's rules and regulations. He was used to making his own decisions, and he did so now. All the same, Carolyne blamed Melanie for Roy's rebellion, and, in a pique, imagined his macho response was more in reaction to the coquettish bats of Melanie's thick eyelashes than to common sense. "And when you don't come back, I'll see Melanie goes looking!" she called after him.

Lunch over, there was little to do but sit and wait. Sit and wait they did, then sat and waited some more.

Melanie was particularly concerned as it got later. She genuinely liked the handsomely rugged prospector; if she'd sent him into fatal danger, she would be no more pleased about it than Carolyne. She waited for the older woman to say, "I told you so!"

Carolyne would have said just that, too, except Roy hadn't exactly been led out of camp by a nose ring. He wasn't a novice at survival, and if he wanted to risk his neck to impress Melanie, that was his business.

"Let's get in a wood supply for tonight!" Carolyne ordered. Melanie was the expedition leader, but Carolyne, the more experienced and older, had launched a palace coup. "The last thing we need is a jaguar come to make the last of us its evening meal."

Wood-gathering kept their hands and minds occupied but only until they had every retrievable stick of burnable wood within safe foraging distance; it was a stockpile big enough to fuel a small city for the night.

The group's diminished number called for each to have more than one go at guard duty. "If it's something in any way suspicious, call out!" Carolyne was pure Sergeant-Major. "It's not likely a friendly will be walking around in the dark. Roy may be the possible exception. If so, we'll all want to be up for his report, anyway."

Darkness dropped with its usual absence of subtlety. Their isolated pocket of light seemed mighty small to those encapsulated within it. Theirs was a shared four down three to go mentality that begged for camaraderie, but Carolyne was still peeved at Melanie, and she couldn't abide Felix; Melanie was resentful of any blame Carolyne put on her for Roy's failure to reappear, and she still suspected Felix of having rifled her backpack; Felix was teed off at Melanie for her accusation of snooping, and his opinion of Carolyne hadn't changed since he'd accused her of Gordon's murder.

Things deteriorated farther when, halfway into the night, Melanie screamed everyone awake with, "There's something out there!" That something didn't respond to catcalls, cajoles, or threats. "I tell you, it was there!"

"Green, was it, with antennae?" Felix was tired and irritable. He was furious that he'd waited so long to get into the field, only to have the should be great experience end up like this. "Was the sound it made its request of you to take it to your leader?"

"Funny!" Melanie wasn't laughing. "Next time, I'll keep my mouth shut while it clops onto your fat head and hauls you off for din-din."

"Spare me the baby-talk!"

"Shut up, all of us," Carolyne insisted, "unless we have something constructive to say. All right? None of us will get back to civilization if we're continually pulling against each other."

"Well, isn't that the pot calling the kettle black?" was Felix's opinion.

"If you'd take the wax out of your ears, you'd recall that I included myself in that statement." She added to herself: "Felix, you are a pain in the ass."

The rest of the night passed without incident, everyone saved another rude awakening when Carolyne realized, on her own, that the ogre spotted in the bushes was nothing but a new set of shadows conjured by the last stick of wood added to the fire.

No one needed to be called at first light. Independently, each had decided the best plan was to get out as quickly as possible. If Roy hadn't found Teddy and Charles, they weren't likely to be found. If Roy hadn't saved himself, he wasn't likely to be saved. Experts were needed and wouldn't be forthcoming until apprised of the situation.

Carolyne was so convinced she wouldn't see Charles, Teddy, or Roy again, she took Roy's sudden reappearance as she would have any heart-stopping trauma.

"Sorry, I thought you heard me," Roy apologized.

Carolyne was still speechless when Felix and Melanie joined them.

"I found these." Roy extended his right hand.

"Arrows," Carolyne found her voice.

"Meaning what?" Felix made no move to touch them. All the South American arrows of his imagination came dipped in curare.

"It means nothing if they're artifacts jettisoned when the owner left the area." Carolyne wanted to make sure her voice was still with her.

"I've good news and bad news." All that got Roy was groans.

"I don't know about anyone else, but I could use the good news first," Carolyne decided.

Melanie and Felix provided Carolyne with a hearty, "Amen!"

"I didn't pull any of these out of any dead bodies."

"The bad news?" Carolyne really didn't want to hear it.

"No sign of Charles or Teddy, and these aren't artifacts."

Carolyne didn't need head-hunting Indians added to this already disastrous roster.

"Doesn't take an expert to tell they're not artifacts, either." He handed Carolyne two arrows and kept the third. He put the feathered end of his to his right thigh, gripped the shaft just below its sharp arrow point, and exerted enough downward pressure to bend the wood into a neat bow. "Green wood cut within the last few days."

"What Indians?" Melanie wanted to know. "Even the authorities agree there've been none around here for years."

"Natives have been known to be nomadic," was all Roy could come up with.

"Nomadic natives. Nomadic jaguars. Nomadic river rock. Nomadic what else?" Felix wanted to know.

"There's nothing here for natives to eat, by the way of large game." Carolyne was sorry the minute she said it.

Melanie wasn't going to let it pass, either. "The jaguar almost got someone to eat. Maybe, the natives were luckier."

"I think we should move out of here, and do it now." Felix read the writing on the wall, and he didn't like the story line. He certainly hadn't lived this long to become victuals for cannibals.

"Won't they beat drums, sing songs, make prayers; won't we hear them?" Carolyne had known Charles Ditherson for a good many years. She liked him. She was less certain he was dead, now that Roy had materialized, and she felt less justified in leaving.

Melanie's thoughts were more self-centered. "Hear Indians, and we're too close to them."

Felix didn't have to think twice, either. "Agreed!"

"It's a majority, Carolyne," Roy dashed her last feeble hopes. "We're not equipped to deal with some kind of native uprising, on top of everything else."

Such superb logic didn't make the logical more acceptable or easy to oblige. Carolyne had pulled out of New Guinea, forced to leave Mabel Funegan behind. No one ever found poor Mabel, and Carolyne didn't want more of that kind of guilt trip. However, then, as now, the decision seemed to have been taken out of her hands.

CHAPTER FOUR

"Drums!" Melanie's hysteria was contagious. Felix's face went white-washed. Carolyne's heart skipped a beat.

Roy, the only Rock of Gibraltar, insisted, "It's an SOS!"

That wasn't the general consensus, emphasized by Felix, "You have to be kidding!"

"I'm not. Just listen. Hear it? Boom, boom, boom. Boom... boom...boom. Boom, boom, boom. Equals SOS."

"I don't think so." Felix didn't buy it.

"Shut up and listen!" Carolyne was more open-minded. Her decision: "Damned if it isn't!"

"The natives are trying to suck us in." Felix's nerves were definitely on edge. "'Step into my parlor,' said the spider to the fly."

"Don't be absurd," Carolyne insisted.

"You think it's Teddy or Charles?" Melanie certainly preferred them alive.

"If so, they're telling every savage in the area where to go for good dining," Felix criticized.

"I want all of you to keep heading east," Roy instructed.

"While you're headed where?" Felix, who knew Roy had a better grasp of the territory than anyone else present, wanted him right where he was.

Roy ignored the question, and so did everyone else; the answer was obvious.

"He's right about what they're advertising." Carolyne's intention wasn't to hold Roy back but superfluously to make sure he was aware of the danger.

"I'll be careful." Then, quickly, he was gone.

"He's mad," was how Felix saw it.

"Sure you don't want to go along and give him a hand?" Carolyne was facetious, because she saw Felix as nothing other than a ball and chain. "He could probably use the help."

"You'd like me the ingredient in some cannibal's soup, wouldn't you?" His white-washed complexion progressed through its usual mottled reds to a brilliant scarlet. "You'd like my shrunken head as a souvenir on a chain hung around your neck."

He looked headed for a heart attack; the last thing Carolyne needed. "Don't be silly," she ridiculed.

They went east, which followed Roy's instructions and was the shortest route out. Carolyne had assumed the lead; Felix was in the rear but would have preferred a spot less exposed. Melanie, who had learned a lesson from the disappearance of Teddy and Charles, made sure everyone said something at least every five minutes.

The continuing SOS seemed a good sign. Likewise, so did their discovery of the trail they'd used on the way in.

"Finally!" Felix had lost track and had been doubtful of Carolyne's sense of direction.

The trail was good only in comparison to what they'd traveled as lead-in. Enough people had used it in the past to etch a visible dent in the vegetation, but nowhere did it show wear to bare ground. In fact, it no longer had a distinct beginning or end, rather like the roadway of some long-dead city that took up and left off without rhyme or reason to anyone but an archaeologist.

"Do you think the bridge is far?" Melanie wanted to put it between her and whatever she'd hopefully left behind.

"I do think I'm hearing the water the bridge crosses," Felix encouraged.

Carolyne didn't think he did, unless his hearing was far better than hers—which she doubted. "It's a good ways yet."

She knew exactly where she was.

When they reached the bridge, two hours later, the drumbeats ceased at that same moment in time. They were more aware of the former, however, because the bridge no longer spanned the void between the two facing rock walls; it hung like spider-webbing down the opposite side of the deep ravine. Without checking the rope remnants on their end, they knew the bridge had been purposely cut loose; all they needed to tell that was the stake, with its three human skulls by way of embellishments.

"Now what" Felix expected an immediate spear point to his gut.

"How are you at the broad jump?" Carolyne suggested.

Melanie took her seriously. "He'll never make it across."

"Of course, I'll never make it." Felix didn't appreciate being the brunt of Carolyne's humor. "However, maybe Carolyne will summon her broomstick for the ride across."

The absence of the drumbeats was parenthesized by the beat's sudden return. Its new shave and a hair cut six bits rhythm was more recognizable than the preceding SOS.

"Hopefully, someone is trying to relieve our anxiety," Carolyne decided upon hearing the thump de de thump thump; thump thump once again.

"Only minor consolation if it is." Felix walked to the edge of the abyss. Not to contemplate a leap for the other side, because twenty feet were at least seventeen feet too far, but to consider a down-and-up. Quickly, though, he decided none of them would succeed any attempts to get down and then scale the opposite wall, because even a mountain goat would be suicidal to give it a try. Besides, there was the additional obstacle offered by the roaring cascades of water at the bottom, in between.

The drumming stopped.

"Do we wait here, or what?" Felix faced the fact that Carolyne probably had more experience in these sorts of things.

"Maybe the chasm narrows off to one side?" Melanie was hopeful.

"Were that the case," Carolyne ventured, "I suspect the

bridge would have been built there, not here."

Felix didn't appreciate that hope dashed. "We can't go back," he insisted, as if that were Carolyne's next suggestion.

"Teddy, Roy, and Melanie, might work something out with ropes, when everyone is back." That was the only solution that came to Carolyne's mind. "I'm too old to attempt any adventurous circus acts, and you...." she speared Felix with her I dare you to deny it gaze. "...are certainly no more a human fly than I am."

Pleased she hadn't been excluded from Carolyne's all-star rescue team, Melanie tried, without success, to imagine the logistics of Teddy, Roy, and her making it to the other side and getting Carolyne, Charles, and Felix across with them—if, that is, everyone ever showed up.

What makes you think Teddy will be up to scaling chasm walls?" Felix didn't need Carolyne to tell him who was old and out of shape. "Correct me if I'm wrong, but wasn't that an SOS we heard?"

"Not the second time" Melanie chimed in optimistically.

"The second time, I assume, was Roy's doing." What had Felix ever done to deserve being stuck on this cliff edge with the Wicked Witch of the West and Pollyanna?

What did Carolyne ever do to deserve being stuck on this cliff ledge with a man who thought her capable of murder? Were she as cold-blooded as he thought, she'd knock the bastard over the chasm and let the rushing water flush him out to sea, like a turd to the sewer. "You want to explore...." She gestured right, then left. "...be my guest. I'll wait here."

"I'm taking bets it'll be our heads on that pole to greet Roy and whomever else—if they ever get this far," Felix wagered.

With more guts indicated than she was feeling, Carolyne walked to the pole and put a hand on the top skull. "These things are years old, not something lopped off their necks just yesterday." Her brave talk was to keep Melanie from following Felix into panic. "They have dirt encrusted in their eye sockets and in their cranium cracks, which says to me these old relics were dug up by way of improvisation for this performance and not specifically harvested for it."

"I'm supposed to be encouraged because the natives are only recently out for fresh game?" Felix was serious.

Carolyne was serious, too: "You're supposed to shut your lily-livered mouth and exhibit a bit of manly spine to give us women some much-appreciated moral support. If you can't manage that, keep your fears to yourself."

Melanie liked the old girl more and more. "Amen to that!"

Her pep talk over, Carolyne turned her back on Felix and the skulls; she found a bit of shade and sat down in it.

Melanie joined her. "Is Felix about to crack, or what?" Melanie asked

"Felix is not a happy camper." Carolyne was glad he sulked in a spot out of hearing. "He's stockpiled a lifetime of fantasy around how exciting life is in the field, and how boring life is behind a desk. His fantasies were a bit more digestible than the real thing, that's all."

"Do you think Roy, Charles, and Teddy are all right?"

"Until I find out differently, they're fine. Why should I get an ulcer before all the facts are in? If one or another isn't okay, I'll deal with that only when I have to."

"Shall we snack while we wait?" Melanie broke a trail bar neatly in half.

Carolyne produced one of her few remaining wet-wipes, opened its vacuum packet and shared it.

They savored chocolate and waited, but not, hopefully, for madmen, jaguars, cannibal head-hunters, or anyone in less than perfect health.

Charles was looked horrible when he rejoined them, aided by a trail-weary Roy and Teddy.

Roy had prefaced their arrival with more than one long and loud, "Hello!" This had been eagerly returned by Melanie and Carolyne in unison. Felix had only mustered, "Tell the whole world we're here, why don't you?"

Carolyne brought Charles a plateful of food and promised

him Felix hadn't anything to do with the preparation of it.

Charles wasn't willing to eat; his excuse: "Dysentery."

"You don't want to get dehydrated, Charles." Carolyne gave him her canteen and wouldn't take it back until he drank several swallows of its water.

"The dysentery," he explained, "makes a horrible experience even more so."

"I'm still not sure what happened," Carolyne reminded.

"Took Teddy out first, don't you know? Then, me."

"Who took you, Charles? Natives?"

"Teddy says, no. Says the guy spoke British. Wore a ring that cut Teddy's face. I never did see him. One minute, I was walking, the next...."

He rubbed the back of his head where a goose egg had been laid as big as Felix's in its prime. "I was blindfolded, gagged, tied to a tree. Teddy was blindfolded, gagged, and tied to a tree not six feet from me. Neither of us knew of the other until Teddy got free. By that time, I had stomach problems. I shudder to think how it might have ended with me dead and stewing in my own filth."

His stomach growled. He looked expectant, then grateful for an additional respite.

"You should eat something solid, even if it's just a spoonful." She reoffered the plate of glutinous stew. "If this won't stick to your ribs, nothing will."

He smiled; it was something he'd recently thought he'd never do again. He humored her by spooning up a small portion of the food. "Teddy was marvelous." He took another bite and hoped he wouldn't regret it. "Do you know anything about his father?"

"Teddy's father?"

"Mmmmm." It was confirmation, not a comment on what he was eating.

"I don't, as a matter of fact. Melanie likely does. Why?"

"I got the impression his father must have been exceptionally ill at the end: bedridden, soiled sheets, bed sores, that sort of thing."

Carolyne drew her knees into her chest and wrapped her legs with her arms. She wanted the conversation back on track. "You know about the arrows?"

"Yes."

"You saw the skulls on the stake?"

"I thought I was looking in the mirror." He risked another bite of stew.

"We thought your drumbeat was your captives celebrating a good meal."

"Teddy's idea: pounding on that hollow log. He'd reconnoitered and knew you'd headed off without us." He was quick to add: "Not that we blamed you."

"Roy did instigate a search." It was important he know.

"Must have been like looking for a needle—two needles—in a haystack. All that jungle; two men, tied to two trees. Hopeless. No chance for us if Teddy hadn't gotten free. Did you see his nasty rope burns in result?"

Carolyne nodded.

"Have Roy to thank, too. Came running when he heard our SOS. Damned fast, once he had something to work with." He'd had enough stew. "I haven't been as lucky since I fell off that mountain in Chile."

"I only wish I could have been there for you this time."

"I'd never have heard the end of it." His laugh was a ghost of the original, but it was good to hear.

Melanie joined them: "Good news!"

"Will my poor heart take the shock?" Charles ventured.

"Teddy said if you're not dead now, you won't soon be; Roy agrees."

"That is good news."

However, it wasn't "the" good news, and Melanie didn't keep them in suspense as regarded the latter. "Roy knows a way across."

"Seriously?" Nothing could have cheered Carolyne more.

"About a mile upstream."

"This means, we should have taken a look when you suggested

it," Carolyne said.

"It wouldn't have helped. Something to do with quirky river currents. Slip in on one side of the river, wash up on the other. Roy's prepared to take a rope over so we can ford."

"Who'd ever have believed getting out would prove more difficult than getting in?" Carolyne marveled.

"All rather exciting, though," was Melanie's ongoing opinion.

Carolyne and Charles exchanged glances and laughed in remembrance of their younger days wherein danger more easily rolled off their backs. These days, they less easily accommodated heady rushes of adrenaline.

Teddy came on over with the nasty scratch on his right cheek and the rope burns around his wrists. "Melanie told you the good news?"

"And weren't we delighted to hear it." Charles wanted a bathroom with all the conveniences.

"Now, if someone could assure me there aren't any nomadic Indians on the rampage." Carolyne wanted it all.

Teddy had no such assurances. "I didn't spot any, but the arrows are proof." He nodded toward the stake. "So is that."

"Charles said it wasn't Indians who had you." Carolyne liked to verify facts.

"Bastard had an accent, whoever he was, and called me 'Yank.' That sound like an Indian to you?" He traced the scratch across his cheek. "Had a ring on his finger, not through his nose."

"British?"

"Beats me! Roy knows of no Brits in the area. We might get something when we check for recent permits, but I came in under the impression we were it, as far as legal access. You have a different impression?"

Carolyne shook her head.

Their night wasn't a good one. Ill-conceived or not, the majority opinion was that this was the far boundary of territory controlled by a stark-raving mad killer, a jaguar, and wild natives; the expedition was still on the wrong side of that line. If they were to be victims, it was a kind of now or never moment, which made for restlessness. More than one wished they'd already succeeded in the river crossing, especially with the attending dangers of nightfall.

Made paranoid by her sleeplessness, Carolyne wasn't the only one who feared the person on guard was less diligent than he/she should be. Charles was up more than once with his dysentery. Melanie battled full to bursting kidneys until there was enough light to see. Teddy continually cocked and un-cocked his pistol; Felix told him to knock it off before he shot someone. Roy was the only one not heard from, except when assuming or surrendering his turn at watch.

It wasn't a very talkative group that crawled into more morning than it was used to; the ravine came complete with a rare expanse of blue sky that admitted just as rare indirect sunlight.

Carolyne ate raisins and walnuts and hoped the river was nearer the lip of the ravine, and less wide, a mile upstream. If she wasn't all that fond of rappelling, fording was something she'd tried to avoid since an unexpected surge of water had washed her off a guideline on the muddy headwaters of the Digoel in New Guinea; she still wasn't certain how she'd survived. Since then, she'd risked any flimsy bridge, swung like Sheena of the Jungle on any hanging vine, or jumped any reasonable distance in a single bound, rather than willingly commit to any body of water. Were this bridge, dangling temptingly across the way, attached to her side by even a mere thread, she'd be tempted to walk it in lieu of what Roy suggested.

Melanie approached the ravine. She nodded greeting to Carolyne, but that was the extent of it. She had her own psyching up to do. For her, this morning adventure was anticipated as much as feared. During the few minutes she'd slept last night, she'd dreamed herself neck-deep in the deluge, clinging precariously to a spider-web lifeline, roiling liquid all around her, as a war-painted savage delivered a machete chop to her only link with the shore.

"Ready?" Roy poured the dregs of coffee onto the fire.

Carolyne gave an affirmative wave. Her real feelings wouldn't help anyone. Melanie certainly didn't need to hear how the old pro of the trip feared becoming food for the fishes.

"Well, we're off," Melanie said as she joined up with Carolyne.

Carolyne thought: Yeah, off our heads for doing all this crazy stuff for a living.

"Would you guess hot, lukewarm, or cold?" Charles asked. Carolyne's what the hell are you talking about look made him elucidate. "The water, I mean. I've forded all kinds. A river in Iceland, within sight of the great Vatnajokull, almost boiled me alive; hot thermals had erupted through underwater vents; hot thermals always appear and disappear in Iceland, don't you know?"

"The closest glaciers, Charles, tip the Andes, a few thousand miles to our west." Carolyne was glad he looked and acted better, but she could do without the small talk. "As far as thermals—I've not seen any close, have you?"

"Chilly." Roy had eavesdropped. "It's the several underground streams that feed the river and cause the anomaly of current at that point that's going to get us across."

"I suppose a walk through the jungle will ready me for a cool swim," Carolyne was optimistic but doubtful.

Her optimism wasn't misplaced; Roy's "mile" had been as the crow flies. Via human foot, along a meander of terrain that refused easy passage, it was farther, took longer, and drenched everyone in perspiration.

"Do you think we'll lunch on the other side?" Charles was discouraged, although he should have known that distances, in jungle and desert, over hill and through dale, even along simple rural lanes, were relative.

Each time they were allowed a new view of the ravine through blockages of plants and stones, or across feeder gullies, the distance between cliff top and water narrowed. Less encouraging was the increasing width of the river surface that included no letup in the great splashing and foaming spray of rapids.

Roy's, "This is the spot!" seemed even less likely than Brigham Young's similar announcement to trail-weary Mormons who faced the dismal reality of the Great Salt Lake Basin by way of a building site.

"Where?" Melanie's question confirmed that Carolyne wasn't the only one at a loss.

"Six yards that way," Roy pointed. "Six feet down to the river. In, for a dunking." His finger followed the rumbling water back the way they'd come. "Out, where that ledge of stone juts into the water, over there."

Even squinting, Carolyne wasn't seeing it happen.

"You're joking." Felix, his mouth literally agape, was another disbeliever.

"Used to be the only way across in pre-bridge days."

"Right!" Felix had progressed into Doubting Thomas who wanted proof-positive of the stigmata.

"I read about it in Luke Wentlock's old journals," Roy assured. "Luke was here when the indigenous Indian populations were all in place."

Melanie was first with the connection. "Luke any relation to Gordon Wentlock, our very dead one-time guide?"

"His grandfather, a zealot Lutheran who showed up in 1841. Converts were as skimpy as hen's teeth in a country of predominantly Catholic immigrants; so, firebrand Luke decided the heathen Indians deserved saving for God and *from* the Pope. A regular fixture in these parts, he ferreted out all sorts of interesting tidbits of information."

"You knew him?" Carolyne didn't know why she found that newsworthy. Roy had prospected the area for years.

"I knew Gordon's father. Gordon's mother, of course, had died long before I appeared on the scene. Missionary work in these parts was a hard life for a woman. No derogatory reflection upon the fair sex, in general, mind you."

"All very interesting, but will it get us across the river?" Felix's eyes hadn't left the great churning water. He still hadn't pinpointed this "ledge of rock" to which Roy had referred.

"I've done this before," Roy assured. "Had to less than a month after I'd read it was here. Lightning struck the bridge platform that anchored supports on the other side; blew it to smithereens. It was cross here, or wait for a repair crew; a long wait, since Kyle Georni had told me there'd been no official repair crew since the Indians had moved out."

"I'm not going to like this." Carolyne had thought that all along and decided to make it vocal.

Roy briefed them where they stood, because the roar of the water made conversation impossible closer to the edge. "We'll make a raft for the backpacks, and then I'll cross with three ropes, each of which will be tied at this end. As soon as I affix my ends to the other side, the women come first. Last man over," which everyone, including Teddy, assumed would be Teddy, "will tie two of the ropes to the raft and come across on the third line. Together, we manhandle the raft across." Roy was confident. "The water will do all the work. Don't even worry if you get dunked or disoriented."

"I shouldn't worry while drowning?" Carolyne would beg to differ.

"You'll get to the opposite shore on any account. The deeper the water into which you sink, the swifter the diagonal current."

"Something to do with those underground streams that feed the river somewhere around here?" Carolyne hoped for a lengthy lecture on the interconnection of local geology and hydrology; it wouldn't make her crossing any easier, but it might give her time to think of some better way.

"The hydro-mechanics are interesting but complex. I'll be happy to go over them at another time," Roy parried.

Carolyne couldn't knock the solidity of the raft construction nor its buoyancy, both of which were tested. The raft so much wanted to float in a diagonal direction, toward the opposite bank, it was reluctant to return when they finally pulled it back and docked it.

Nor could Carolyne fault Roy's willingness to put his life where his mouth was. When the time arrived, he waded unhesitatingly into the water.

"Dear God!" Carolyne thought him a goner. Similar exclamations, even from Teddy who was supposed to watch for cannibals from the rear, told her she wasn't alone in her estimation.

Carolyne still thought she'd seen the last of him when everyone else insisted he was safe against the opposite shore.

"Marvelous!" Melanie clapped her hands.

Miraculous was Carolyne's view. What were the chances of five more miracles on one and the same day? She didn't need the odds to guess they weren't very good, no matter Roy's assurances to the contrary.

Roy affixed the ropes to a rock outcropping; the resulting tautness never escaped the water that continually overrode it.

Melanie said, "Good luck!"

Teddy said, "Ride the wild surf, momma!"

Charles said, "See you on the other side."

It wasn't until Felix's, "Amen to all of the aforementioned!" that Carolyne realized those were *her* farewells. She was actually expected to stroll out into that water as easily as a suicide Ann Bancroft had done in some remembered movie whose name Carolyne forgot. Well, Carolyne had con arguments, if anyone cared to listen.

Her deep breathing didn't help. What did help was her knowing that a balk, there and then, on her part might undermine Melanie and Felix's determination to follow. Worse, Felix might call her "CHICKEN!"—albeit true in the circumstances—and take her place in line with a parting catcall, "We're not all scaredy-pants!"

Well, she'd show Felix. She'd show them all. If she died, she'd lived an exciting life, to a ripe old age. Why not be remembered in stories told around camp fires? "Went into the drink like a trooper, did old Carolyne. Would have thought she was a fish the way she took to the water." That is, if anyone, lived to tell the tale.

Yes, Charles, the water is chilly. Around her feet. Around her ankles. Around her thighs. Downright cold as it knocked her off balance and swallowed her whole.

Her lungs hurt from her last lucky gasp of held air, and she lost all contact with the guide ropes. She collided with something hard that knocked the stale air right out of her. Reflexively, she inhaled water as a smiling Roy hoisted her, sputtering, out of the drink.

"Brava!" he congratulated.

She couldn't hear him over the roar, but she read his lips and was impressed he gave the word its proper gender; she'd heard many well-educated opera fans bellow "Bravo!" in supposed compliment to a female singer.

His strong, callused hands once again had her attention as he pointed toward the natural stairway up the embankment.

Carolyne nodded and risked moving on her weak legs that almost buckled twice before she gained high ground.

Watching Melanie follow didn't clarify Carolyne's dim memory of her heart-stopping journey across, anymore than having watched Roy had prepared her for the ordeal. "Once again, it just wasn't your time, Carolyne, old girl," she decided. "Some things are just not to be questioned, lest the Good Lord hear and think He made a mistake."

She was still woozy in a commandeered patch of sunlight when Melanie joined her.

"Whoever patents that ride for some amusement park has himself a gold mine!" Melanie finger-combed her hair to expose separate strands of it for drying. "Say a prayer tonight for scribe Luke Wentlock, Lutheran missionary, wherever he is!"

"I wonder if Gordon was the last of the Wentlock line." He hadn't reminded Carolyne of any son of a son of a firebrand religious man. Of course, she had no real basis for comparison.

"He never mentioned any brothers or sisters," remembered Melanie.

"Did he mention a wife?" If anyone would know, it was Melanie.

"A wife?" Melanie's tone was answer enough, but she supplemented, "I shouldn't think so."

Charles was in the water; they watched him. It seemed almost commonplace when he bobbed to the surface at the right place, at the right time.

"It's funny how you can spend time with some people and never know much about them." Carolyne wanted conversation.

"Mmmmm." Whether Melanie was in agreement or disagreement, it was hard to say. Her head was thrown back, her face toward the sun, her neck a graceful arc, her hair a damp cascade of wet, brown strands.

"Have you met Teddy's parents?" Carolyne asked.

"Oh, Teddy doesn't have parents." Melanie didn't open her eyes. She shook her head slowly to loosen more strands. "I mean, they're dead. Happened when he was a child. Why?"

"Just something he said to Charles when they were off on their little adventure, bonding."

Charles hadn't appeared atop the embankment. The trip, so close on the heels of his dysentery, left him utterly exhausted. Roy had reserved a spot for him at the lower level, off to one side.

"What exactly did Teddy say?" Melanie was interested.

"Some insinuation that his father was bedridden near the end," Carolyne said.

"I'll ask Teddy about it."

Carolyne was flabbergasted. "Oh, I wouldn't want him to think I was prying." So, what if she were? "Charles was just curious. Blame my asking you on him. I told him you might know."

"Count on me to be diplomatic," Melanie assured. "Besides, I'm curious. All Teddy's sad tales have included very few specifics of *mater* and *pater*. I think his mother was a house-wife; his father made shoes, or, maybe, repaired them." She shook her hair vigorously.

Felix was in the water; his danger seemed so minimized that neither woman was much concerned.

Melanie turned from the sun to Carolyne. "Do you find it strange that Teddy keeps his family history from me? Our being engaged and all."

What could Carolyne say to that?

Melanie continued. "I'm no longer as good a catch as I would have been had I located a supply of *Lygodium cornelius* and discovered a cure for cancer, but I'm more than good enough to offer him job security and social connections. It's not likely Crystin Companies will go under any time soon, or that a Ditherson will be struck from the Seattle social register."

"I find modern relationships a little hard to follow." Relationships in Carolyne's prime hadn't been any easier. Would things have been different if she'd slept with Cornelius when she'd had the chance? Could she have worked bedroom magic to seal him to her so that Margaret went unnoticed? The thought of her as a femme fatale made her almost laugh.

"Teddy couldn't have killed Gordon," Melanie had decided from the start.

Carolyne didn't follow the logic. "Even if he thought Gordon and your relationship was developing into something serious?"

"I've flirted with other men before. There have been fights before, usually in very public places as part of Teddy's she's mine and the world better know it mentality. Yet, he and I remain together. Do *you* think there was something serious going on between Gordon and me?"

Carolyne certainly had thought it at least possible.

"It was a game, like all the other men I flirted with were games," Melanie assured. "Murder was never a part of it. It would risk Teddy losing me, screwing up his hard-won career, letting him face prospects of god only knows how many years in some dirty South American jail full of AIDS-infected perverts."

Charles and Felix appeared at the top of the embankment. Felix gave Charles a helping had, but both men were wheezing.

"Charles, are you okay?" As far as Carolyne was concerned, Felix's friendly enough send-off to her, on the other side, didn't erase past wrongs.

"Feel like a drowned rat!" Although he preferred a spot next to Carolyne and Melanie, Charles was too pooped to protest when Felix led him off to one side.

It was Teddy's turn in the water, and Melanie brought the conversation back to him. "He really wanted this expedition to succeed. I was prepared, and still am, to commit millions of Crystin Companies' dollars to develop and exploit possibilities hinted at by my preliminary research. Teddy knows he's scheduled to be part of that project. He'd have cut off his nose to spite his face had he killed Gordon and sent us all scurrying home prematurely."

Felix's shadow usurped sunlight already claimed by the two women. "Are either of you as worried as I am about all our supplies suddenly on the opposite side of the river?"

"A point well-taken," Carolyne begrudged him; the most opportune time for an enemy strike was when his opponent overconfidently considered the foe outwitted. Their supplies would be permanently out of reach if someone suddenly, now, cut their tenuous links to them She got to her feet; Melanie joined her. "We'd better lend a hand in hauling the raft across."

"Carolyne, give me a hand up, will you?" Charles called.

She could have told him not to bother, but he wouldn't like the insinuation, no matter how much and loud his moaning and groaning, that he wasn't strong enough to make a measurable contribution. Besides, whatever little he could manage might make the difference.

Felix went ahead. Melanie followed with Charles and Carolyne.

CHAPTER FIVE

Their combined efforts launched the raft and pulled it onto the course they'd all rode before it. It started to disintegrate mid-channel. Cries of dismay rose above the roar of the water, and everyone pulled harder. The additional strain on the collapsing construction caused a faster breakup. The first of the backpacks tumbled into the river.

Carolyne watched her pack shift precariously and drop off. She was furious, not only that this was happening, but that she had, against all intelligent reasoning, been lulled into assuming it wouldn't.

She was surprised when Roy dipped into the nearby water, just missing the dangerous collision of several free-floating raft logs with the ledge of rock upon which they stood, and successfully rescued one of the backpacks. He swung his dripping prize behind him where Teddy waited to beach it.

Five of their six bags were similarly retrieved as a result of the river current and Roy's fast action. Four of the five were intact; the fifth had dumped most of its contents as Roy tugged it from the water.

They stayed put long enough to know the last bag wasn't going to be recovered. They carried what they had up the embankment.

"Cut through!" It was Melanie's comment on her bag which was the worst for wear. "Check these flaps; all sliced open, slick as a whistle. A knife, not river rocks, did this."

"Does look that way," Roy confirmed.

"Were the raft ropes cut through as well?" Felix had progressed to the next logical step.

"We all checked before we started across," Teddy insisted. "Everything was tied and secure."

Roy didn't find that contradictory: "Someone could have come in low from the jungle, kept the raft between us and him or her, and done the deed while we concentrated on getting all of us across safely."

"Why didn't this someone just cut the guide ropes, after we were all across, and keep the load for himself?" Teddy wanted to know. "No way could any of us have gotten back to stop him."

Carolyne had an answer: "That wouldn't have made it look like an accident."

"This cutting of my bag's flaps makes it look like an accident?" Melanie denied and flicked one of the cut flaps in question.

"Did you believe, when the raft went under, that we'd salvage all we did?" Carolyne supplied the missing pieces. "How could the saboteur have known we'd fish incriminating evidence out of the drink?"

"Who the hell is doing all of this, anyway?" Teddy wasn't alone in wanting the answer.

"Whoever it was killed Gordon," Melanie had it figured, "and tampered specifically with my bag to make sure any possible photographic evidence possibly to link someone to the corpse wouldn't make it through to this side of the river."

"The digital chip was in your backpack?" Roy's disappointment sounded through, as well as his unspoken accusation that she should have kept it on her person to lessen the risk of its disappearance.

"What about the emerald?" Carolyne figured Melanie as foolish as not to have hand carried that, either.

"I have it here." Melanie pinched off one corner of her jacket pocket to indicate the gem inside.

"Too bad those jacket pockets weren't big enough for the

digital chip, too." They *were* big enough, which was Roy's point.

"I wasn't thinking, sorry," Melanie apologized. If he thought she'd hoped for something like this, he was mistaken.

"What do you want to bet he's already made off with Gordon's body, by way of absconding even with that physical evidence?" Roy asked. So much for Carolyne's efforts to preserve the corpse.

"Figure it's John Leider?" Teddy threw out for discussion. "Something to do with the emerald?"

Roy had no answers so gave none. "He's known for his quick temper, especially where his poke is involved."

They left off additional conjecture to take stock.

Forced to travel lighter, they could travel faster. If they ate only enough calories to get them through any given day, they could reach the Georni Ranch with what they had, hungry but without acute malnutrition. That wasn't saying they wouldn't be dog-tired.

In fact, by the time the end was nearly in sight, Carolyne couldn't remember when she'd been so tired. What's more, she'd gotten that way with no additional traumas than the day-to-day effort it took to put one foot in front of the other: apparently, they'd left behind the man-eating jaguar, the skull-collecting natives, and the mad killer. Anyway, catching the killer no longer seemed as important as enjoying dreams of deep, feather-down beds, surrounded by acres and acres of delicious food. If she tried really hard, she could smell the wood burning in some giant, outdoor pit, over which a whole steer turned slowly in the flames.

Carolyne's imagination wasn't nearly as vivid as she thought. Melanie smelled it, too. "Smoke!"

"There!" Felix pointed.

Carolyne, too, focused on enough bad news to override all the absence of same over the last few days.

It looked like smoke, smelled like smoke, too soon tasted like smoke. If it had looked, smelled, and tasted as much like a duck, it would have been a duck. A distinct crackling, like a few thousand breaking twigs, said it wasn't alone. In emphasis, a brilliant tongue of orange-yellow flame incinerated a not so distant treetop in two seconds flat.

Carolyne joined right in the ensuing every man and woman for himself and herself panic, and it wasn't something of which she was proud. Even a brief what do we do powwow might have gleaned enough input to decide the best alternative upon which they could have all acted in unison. As it was, her main concern, aside from escape, was avoiding collisions with other panicked expedition members running full tilt in the bushes around her.

Roy proved the most concerned for his fellow man. He appeared from seeming nowhere and grabbed Carolyne's arm. He jerked her in an entirely different direction than she was headed with, "Here, this way!" as the bushes into which she'd been headed were consumed with a fiery "Whoosh!"

As tired as Carolyne was, and as old as she was, how could she be moving as fast as she was? If she extended both of her arms, she could probably fly out of there. Except, Roy now had her hand and cracked-the-whip, just like a particularly mean-spirited boy Carolyne had once endured on a childhood play-ground. It took considerable effort for Carolyne to remember that Roy was trying to help her and not throw her into cardiac arrest.

She didn't see the pool until they were literally over it. Their drop into it was reminiscent of the one taken by Butch Cassidy and the Sundance Kid in a movie of the same name; anyway, it seemed that way. Actually, it was only six feet from the lip of the embankment to the surface of the water, three more feet until Carolyne's feet sunk into an additional foot of ooze at the bottom.

The force of her landing, though, buckled her knees and folded her five-feet-nine-inches approximately in half. Her head flipped forward on a neck that could pass for silly putty. She had escaped one drowning, in the river, only to fall prey to another, at least until Roy—as before—pulled her head above the water.

"Are you okay, Carolyne?"

Compared to being dead? Compared to being trampled by stampeding buffalo? Compared to long, relaxing nights knitting in a rocking chair on the front porch of some old folk's home?

Her, "I'm fine," came out as if she'd said it in a goldfish bowl. The brackish water, still draining from her eyes, ears, nose, and mouth, tasted as if she'd said what she'd said in a toilet bowl.

"Get ready to go back under!"

It was like the movies, except wasn't there supposed to be some kind of hollow reed through which to breathe? Did Roy know that wouldn't necessarily work, because fire needed the very same air to burn that they needed to breathe? Or, hopefully, Carolyne had gotten those scientific facts wrong.

Luckily, neither theory was put to the test. Although several bushes burst into flame along the ledge above, there was no overshooting canopy of fire to ignite the vegetation below, or on the other side, nor any drool of fire as far as the water. The crackle and roar went elsewhere, leaving them in smoke-filled silence.

"This old lady thanks you from the bottom of her traumatized heart." She hoped it safe to wade ashore; her legs were about to give way, and she preferred a collapse onto solid ground.

"Here, lean on me."

Her reservoir of energy was depleted, zilch, zero, the big goose egg. Only Roy's reserves got them to the shoreline through the sucking mud.

Carolyne collapsed in a quick slide down Roy's left side and leg. The man's thigh and calf were hard as tree trunk.

"I hope you don't mind if I'm not immediately up to moving?" *he* said; she laughed appreciatively at his diplomatic good humor. He squatted beside her, his black hair singed, his tanned face sooty. A nasty scratch on his cheek matched the one some bastard's ring had dug earlier across Teddy's cheekbone; Carolyne wished she looked as good as he did. "How about some favorable news?" he suggested.

"Aside from the fact that we're alive?"

"Aside from that."

"Why not?" She certainly didn't want to contemplate the fate of the others. Poor Charles: kidnapping, dysentery, near-drowning, forced march, now this.

"Tonight you'll sleep in a real bed."

"Do you suspect a connection between the Georni Ranch and our near barbecue?"

"The location is right."

"Kyle might have picked a less spectacular way of saying hello."

"Except, he hasn't done any burning since his father died."

"Must be about time, huh?"

"Told me he didn't plan to slash and burn much more."

"Maybe he doesn't figure a few hundred acres are much."

"He gave me the opposite impression."

"When was this?"

"When Jean-Michael Teruel came around and complained how the crazy American lady was trying for permits yet again."

"Jean-Michael Teruel: the government representative?"

"The same."

"Talked over Melanie's request for permits with Kyle Georni?"

"As a courtesy. Unofficially, the land is/was Georni land."

"Annexed via a few generations of bribes and greased palms in high places, I've heard it rumored."

"Had Kyle not wanted you in, you would have stayed out."

"You were actually there?"

"Even I enjoy the occasional amenities of civilization, and Kyle is a gracious host. Besides, my permits were up for renewal, and I had a bit of buttering up to do."

"The Georni family takes a percentage of your prospecting profits?"

"That's the way it works. That's the way it's always worked. That's the way it'll continue to work until I've the clout to go over Kyle Georni's head and deal directly with the politicians in Brasilia. Don't consider that a major complaint, because Kyle takes a smaller percentage than his father did. Not because his bargaining position isn't as strong; he's simply fairer. We're talking less greed as regards land, as well as money. That's why this fire surprises me. He actually mentioned ecology in his discussion with Jean-Michael."

"Words come cheap," was how Carolyne saw it.

"You do have a suspicious mind."

"You don't?"

"I like Kyle. What can I say? I liked his father far less."

"His father is dead. Dead men don't say, 'Go out and kill a man so I can end, for a very long time, irritants like this American expedition.'"

"Has no real ring of duplicity; sorry 'bout that," Roy decided. "Kyle needn't have even mentioned ecology; no one of importance around here cares. No one around here, at least at the moment, can stop him burning all of the jungle between here and the Pacific. Why tell a nobody, like me, that he has as much pastureland as he needs? As far as your little group, Jean-Michael didn't expect Kyle to consent; the bigwigs in Brasilia didn't expect him to consent. His allowing you in caused more tongues to wag than had he kept you out."

"So, maybe it isn't a perfect hypothesis, but I'm working on it. That's what we scientists do."

Roy had his second wind, but Carolyne needed a few more minutes. She could have been magnanimous and sent him to reconnoiter, but she didn't want to stay behind and wonder what he found. Besides, she felt safer with him around. He'd been there for her at the river, and he'd been there for her at the fire. That counted in her book.

"You read about this pond as a fire-stop in Luke Wentlock's journals?" she asked to make conversation.

"This pond is actually one I previously stumbled upon, quite on my own. I'm talking stumbled in the literal sense. Right from up there." He pointed to their launch pad. "It wasn't one of my more cognizant of my surroundings moments."

"Tell me some more about Gordon Wentlock's people."

"My first day in the area, I was told by three different people:

'You want to know anything about this neck of the woods, ask Jeremy Wentlock. His father, Luke, was everywhere, saw it all, wrote it all down.'"

"And Jeremy said, 'Here, read my father's journals; they'll save me from talking myself hoarse.'"

"Not exactly."

"But, it eventually did come to that?"

"Yes, but Jeremy wasn't an easy man to get to know. I don't think Gordon ever got to know him."

"My second husband, Randolph P. Santire, Senior, had a son when I married him. I never met anyone, except Randolph, Junior, who didn't like Randolph, Senior. I even liked Randolph, Senior, after our divorce, which is more than I can say for my first husband. The moral: Being a father to a son, or a son to a father, is no easy business. Probably the only things worse is being a stepmother or stepson."

"Randolph, Junior, and you didn't get along?"

"I'm not the mothering type"

"No?"

She would have preferred an argument, but she gave him points for no direct agreement.

"My story to be continued." She was up to moving out and confessed it.

He helped her to her feet and watched her first tentative steps. "No one says we can't hang around here a little while longer."

"I'll be fine if you keep my mind off my aches and pains with more talk about Luke Wentlock's journals."

"They were genuinely interesting, even just as a local history. If I'd known Gordon was just going to give them a toss, I...." He shrugged. Here's where you fill in the homily about spilt milk."

"Consider it done."

They paused on the fire line; some bushes and trees were only half burned.

"Let's hope there was no *Lygodium cornelius* growing here," Carolyne said in a small prayer, "or any other plant that might have cured cancer, or AIDS, or Parkinson's, or.... Here's where *you* fill in the appropriate blank."

"Does look a bit dismal."

"It *is* dismal. I hope the few cattle this cleared land can sustain are appreciative of the cost paid by humanity for fattening their bellies for slaughter."

"This *Lygodium-whatever*; that's what you came for?"

"Your Mr. Wentlock didn't mention it in his journal, did he? Not that it necessarily would do us any good. Melanie's father, who ran across the only known sample, way back when, was quite detailed in his records, and quite specific as to locale. My guess is that it just couldn't survive any longer in its ecological niche. A jungle is one large laboratory in which experiments constantly succeed and fail."

"Kyle's father kept you from looking for a good many years?"

"Actually, to be fair, ignorance played even more of a role in keeping us out; ignorance of anything to see but an insignificant plant that couldn't look like much when growing in the wild when it looked so unimpressive when dried out and pressed in a binder. You see, finding a new plant isn't the half of it. Years go into research to find what each plant, if anything, has to offer, whether a cure for some disease, ingredient for some cosmetic, or just a particularly colorful bloom for someone's garden. You can't usually tell just by looking, either, and such alternatives for each plant are seemingly infinite. There are archives filled with still untested specimens from days when new plants were nowhere as hard to come by as they are today. A new plant you or I find today, or one Cornelius Ditherson picked up in his time, has to wait its turn. There aren't enough researchers; of those there are, some only like to work with aesthetically attractive plants, others only with mosses, others only with grasses. Some believe they don't even have to experiment with erotic flora but only need go no farther than their own backyards to make a major breakthrough; it was the common periwinkle, after all, that provided a source of antineplastic."

Walking wasn't easy, because the fire hadn't wiped the ground clean. Most of what was killed was denuded but standing. Some trees, vital wood locked behind protective epidermis of water-rich barks, weren't dead at all but would soon be taken out by the men and bulldozers to follow.

"Melanie discovered *Lygodium*'s potential, right?" Roy ventured.

"In a very dark and very gloomy corner of a very dark and very gloomy sub-basement of the University of Washington. On a day she would have preferred to be skiing, except she'd broken her leg on a slippery sidewalk before she got near that winter's ski slopes. She'd been through the specimens before, but this time she remembered some cancer research recently begun at Crystin Companies on plants similar to *Lygodium cornelius*. She decided to run a few preliminary experiments on the plant Cornelius had picked up here. Upon such chances of fate are based such repercussions as my being here, now, wondering where Melanie is, not to mention where Charles, Teddy, and even obnoxious-at-times Felix is."

"You'd be surprised how many pockets of safety exist in these fires," Roy encouraged. "A rain forest is pretty wet by definition."

Normally, that might have been overly optimistic, but this time it had taken only one such pocket to save the other expedition members who, via four different routes, had ended up in one and the same water-soaked gully.

Carolyne hadn't been so surprised by a survival rate since they'd all successfully made it across the river. Actually, she thought Felix looked better with all the hair on his head singed off, eyebrows and eyelashes included. Melanie's hair needed some work with scissors to balance out spots where some hair was now missing. There was a new burn on Teddy's left forearm to accompany the rope burns still not healed on each wrist.

The joyous reunion was cut short only because none of the participants wanted another night out-of-doors. Beds and bedrooms beckoned, as did baths and bathrooms, dining and dining-rooms.

"It was ghastly!" Immediately, Melanie knew Carolyne

thought she'd referenced the fire; there was no denying *it* had been ghastly. "The death of Teddy's father," Melanie better defined to what she referred.

Carolyne wondered how that bit of trivia resulted from the last few minutes.

"We were huddled together, sure we were about to be roasted alive," Melanie said, "and I said, 'Here I am, about to die with you in some godforsaken jungle, and I don't even know anything about your father.'"

Carolyne suspected a relationship in real trouble if such circumstances had elicited a conversation of that caliber.

"'What about my father?' Teddy asked. I said, 'Like how did he die, exactly?' Was I diplomatic, or what?"

What it was...was strange. "No kiss. No hug. Only, 'How did your father die?'" Carolyne was incredulous.

Melanie sensed veiled disapproval. "You had to be there."

That didn't mean Carolyne wasn't interested. Maybe, she'd been so unlucky at love because she didn't know what to discuss and when to discuss it. "You were saying?"

"Teddy was young when it happened. Too young to drive, but that didn't stop him; nor did his father not owning a car: Teddy 'borrowed' a neighbor's."

Carolyne didn't follow but waited, none too patiently, for the connection.

"His father had some kind of an attack. Down on the floor, rolling around. Teddy drove him to a hospital. Hospital wouldn't take him; no health insurance. He drove him to a private clinic; repeat, except some doctor—or a least someone who looked like one—said: 'Your old man will be fine, son. Take him home, give him a couple of aspirins, and don't call me in the morning!' Something like that. Neighbor never did know his car had been used as a taxi."

It was a story too fantastic not to be believed.

"Melanie!" Carolyne suddenly thought the younger woman a little unsteady on her feet.

"Just a bit dizzy," Melanie admitted. "I guess a girl can't

make it through what I've been through and maintain her total cool." She held out her hands; they were shaking.

"Why don't I suggest a break? They'll not begrudge this old lady a respite, do you think?"

"Actually, I'd prefer we reach the ranch ASAP. Do you mind?"

Mind? They couldn't get there fast enough, as far as Carolyne was concerned.

"Okay, back to Teddy's father." Carolyne pushed a burnt twig out of the way but got a sooty whiplash from another.

"He died at home, three days later, and Teddy didn't know what to do," Melanie said. "He figured: no health insurance, no funeral. He sat and waited for some miracle. Finally, Public Health was alerted that the Wentlock house had a peculiar odor."

Conversation was interrupted when the group drifted together to maneuver a particularly smoky area. They were greeted on the other side of the opaque screen by two men with hand-held cameras and another man, decidedly irate, less than five-feet-two in height who screamed, "Cut! Cut! Cut! Who in the hell are you people?" He had a pseudo-English accent, and whoever had kidnapped Charles and Teddy had "sounded" British. Not a ring on any finger, though. Would he, bound to think Teddy and Charles destined to die while tied and gagged to that jungle tree, have bothered to strip himself of incriminating jewelry? No finger seemed to have any lingering telltale indentation or tan line to indicate any ring had recently been removed.

"Who the hell are *you* is the real question," Roy lobbed right back.

"Does Kyle Georni know you're trespassing on his property?" the short man challenged.

Roy grabbed him by an open collar and threatened to make him airborne.

Apparently, so manhandled, the little man had second thoughts about his ability to control the scene. "I'm Richard Callahan, movie director. Directing a Galin Balstrom video at the moment."

"Who is Galin Balstrom?" Roy wanted to know.

"I sure as hell have never heard of him, either," Teddy was equally unimpressed.

"Are you and Balstrom the ones responsible for this?" Carolyne waved her arm in a way that encompassed the smoke and destruction; it didn't seem a coincidence that there were cameramen with cameras still running.

"Impressive, yes?"

Her slap knocked him off his feet.

They commandeered his transport for the ride to the Georni Ranch house, and Carolyne made no apologies when she learned the filming in progress would be pro-ecology, all proceeds donated to the Greener World Society.

"You sometimes have to burn to build." Richard rubbed his sore jaw. The whole side of his face, like some cave wall, held the petroglyph-like imprint of Carolyne's open palm.

"With thousands of acres burned daily, you have to set your own fire?" Carolyne was dubious. "We could have been roasted alive."

"I didn't know you were anywhere close." It was a good argument; there was no way anyone could have known they were headed back. What wasn't as good was his: "We couldn't risk filming where those in charge figure our message bad-mouths their livelihoods."

"You're just like those reporters who recreate crimes in order to pass them off as the real thing!" Carolyne labeled.

Richard was aghast. "I'm an artist! I did *Honeymoon at Loon Lake*." That got no reaction. "I did Galin's Cola commercial."

Carolyne remained unimpressed. "I don't drink soda," she lied. At that very moment, she would have gladly traded Richard Callahan, his cameramen, and their cameras, for one frosty bottle.

Richard left off trying. Kyle Georni would take care of these interlopers. The last thing Richard had expected, cheerfully out that afternoon to orchestrate and film the burning of the Amazon, had been the near incineration of six people who looked and acted as if they'd escaped from some loony-bin.

Kyle, though, wasn't interested in extolling Richard's film credentials, nor Richard's clout in New York and Hollywood film circles. He paid no attention to Richard, or to the cameramen, except to dismiss them: "Galin is in his room, asking for you." Kyle's accent was pure Portuguese.

"You look a sight!" was Kyle's description for every member of the ill-fated expedition? "What are you doing back so early? Find that plant for which you were looking?"

"Melanie launched right in. "Firstly, someone came around and...."

Carolyne interrupted: "I think you should call your friend Jean-Michael, or, at least, someone with some police authorization; we can tell it all once and not bore you."

"You're back because of trouble, then?" Kyle divined.

"Major trouble," Carolyne defined.

Charles had something on his mind. "Do you think I might use a bathroom?" His dysentery over, he wanted to wash away all residue.

Kyle gave instructions to get them all settled. "I'll send word as soon as Jean-Michael gets here. We'll all meet in the den."

Once in her assigned room, Carolyne wished Jean-Michael would take his sweet time. The bed looked so inviting, she was tempted to plop right down in it and fall asleep. Only the stains she'd leave on the snowy bedspread, not to mention on the ironed sheets, decided her in favor of the bath water, drawn for her by Mary, the maid.

Wasn't it heavenly, her big toe dipped through the tingling bubbles for that first exalted contact of weary flesh with hot water? Her whole foot followed the submerged toes; and, then, in slipped her ankle, her calf, until the water rose almost to her knee, the soap to mid-thigh. Slowly, she joined her first leg with the second, took hold of the sides of the tub, and shivered with unadulterated pleasure as she slid along the sloping porcelain to bury herself to her breasts in sweet-smelling foam. She felt reborn.

After long, luscious minutes, she emerged from water that

was so muddy it had killed the suds.

"My God!" It was Medusa staring back at her from the mirror she'd carefully avoided until now. Frantically, she turned for help to the heavy-set Indian woman who she expected had turned to stone but who turned out to be not only alive but with access to a large pair of shears.

Carolyne wanted her hair back to its henna red. She would have settled for her natural salt-and-pepper. What she got, once Mary had done her work, was a short, spiky, two-tone coiffure that would have done a punk rocker proud. Was Galin Balstrom looking for a back-up singer? Was Richard Callahan hiring extras for his next heavy-metal video?

She thanked Mary for doing all that could be done with the material available, and had almost reached the bed, that drew her like a magnet drew an iron filing, when she was summoned to the den. Jean-Michael Teruel had arrived, and so had the local police chief, Rodrigo Barco; that meant nine for the room since Galin Balstrom, Richard Callahan, and the cameramen hadn't been invited.

The den was an impressive, masculine room, filled on every side with stuffed examples of the wildlife that had once roamed the area. Here were the dead peccaries, tapirs, armadillos, and civets that Melanie's father had seen alive but Melanie never had; there were more of the taxidermy animals in storage.

Carolyne—she suspected it was a matter of seniority—was designated her group's general spokesperson, although it was understood everyone would get his or her say. She proceeded in her most objective manner.

She'd gotten to where Roy had pointed out the geological significance of the river rock upon which Gordon's head, one way or another, had collided; the door banged open to frame a very pregnant, very distraught young woman.

"Gordon is dead?" The clutching of the woman's fists to her breast was thespianism at its most dramatic. Her Portuguese accent got even thicker, with "Please!"

"Dead!" Kyle confirmed.

The woman dropped to the floor in an immediate swoon. There was no one close enough to catch her, although Charles made a valiant attempt.

Everyone but Kyle rushed to offer assistance. He finally got up, walked over, and looked down on the busy efforts to revive her. "Gentlemen, ladies. May I present my sister, Alexandra Mata Jornella Georni: Gordon Wentlock's pregnant whore."

CHAPTER SIX

"Are we talking an evening of surprises, or what?" Carolyne decided she shouldn't have made it a question but a statement.

Melanie had just surprised her fellow expedition members by turning over to Police Chief Rodrigo Barco the digital chip—assumed lost when crossing the river—that contained the pictures she'd taken of Gordon Wentlock's body.

"You said the pictures were gone," Teddy accused.

"I lied," Melanie readily admitted. She wasn't about to apologize for a deception which had worked. "If someone was out to be rid of the pictures, I wanted that someone...." She gave Felix a we know to whom I refer look. "...to think he'd succeeded. Once he thought the photos deep-sixed, he'd hopefully not need to make any more effort to get to them."

Rodrigo Barco offered his congratulations on Melanie's cleverness, in having substituted unused for exposed chip, as far as her backpack, and he promised to have the pictures printed out, via his sources, immediately.

Even Carolyne had to admit that Melanie's ruse had been damned clever. She would have preferred Melanie trusting her with the truth; but, she was prepared to accept this all's well that ends well scenario.

Teddy was less pleased. "You couldn't even trust *me*?"

"Of course, I could trust you," Melanie smoothed, "but why bother with explanations, even to you, that I knew I would have to repeat here?"

From there, the meeting continued. Later, drinks were

served, then the evening meal. Melanie asked the whereabouts of the video star and crew and was told they'd opted, whether by choice, or by assignation wasn't specific, to eat in their rooms; no one asked about Alexandra Mata Jornella Georni, although it was about her that most everyone really wanted to know.

After dinner, there was cognac and cigars for the men, sherry for the ladies, and more talk for everyone. Although, the latter steered clear of the more gruesome events.

When everyone finally called it a night, it was with Jean-Michael and Rodrigo's assurances that they would keep in touch. A helicopter would be sent at first light to recover Gordon Wentlock's body, if it were still in storage. Also, a closer look would have to be given the emerald that Melanie had picked up at the murder site, since it was possibly evidence in the disappearance of John Leider.

Carolyne entered her room with full intention of making a beeline for her bed. It just so happened, though, that Alexandra Georni sat directly on the target area.

Carolyne was confused: "I'm sorry, do I have the wrong room?"

"No! No!" Alexandra hurriedly crossed the distance to shut the door. She moved with exceptional grace for such a pregnant woman; her swoon had been as equally graceful. "I must know about Gordon; Kyle won't tell me."

To the contrary, Kyle had already told her what Carolyne considered the most important detail. "He's dead."

"Oh!" was accompanied by a flood of real tears.

"I didn't realize Kyle had a sister. Were you here when we came through before?"

Alexandra wiped her eyes. "Actually, I wasn't." She chose a chair and gracefully eased into it. "I was staying with a friend, where I thought I was safe. She wasn't a friend, though, and I wasn't safe. Are you sure Gordon wasn't faking his death?"

Carolyne knew a dead man when she saw one. "I'm afraid, my dear, there's no chance of that."

Alexandra tucked a stray, glossy black strand of hair back

into the knot tied slightly off center at the nape of her slim neck. Her big brown eyes looked bigger through the magnifying lenses of more tears. She looked very vulnerable.

Carolyne wasn't about to tell her that Gordon had made a pass at Melanie and gotten himself beaten up because of it. Only if the cad had still been alive would Carolyne have seen it kind to warn Alexandra away.

"I was sure he loved me."

"I'm sure you thought so." Carolyne remained unconvinced and must have let her sarcasm show through.

"He told me we were going away together as soon as he got back."

Why not before he left? was what Carolyne wondered.

"He wanted me to see Rome and Paris with him; just the two of us."

"When you said 'away', you meant far *away*." Carolyne multiplied what they would have paid Gordon, based upon how much his other customers had paid him for guide services rendered. She didn't calculate that was nearly enough for three to set up housekeeping at the *Hassler* or *George Cinq*. More likely, he would have headed off alone, financed by whatever—stay away from my sister and her baby—funds he would have managed to squeeze from Alexandra's brother.

"Now, he's dead." Alexandra still didn't sound as if she believed it. "I'm alone with a brother who now hates me and is disturbed by any thoughts of my baby. I must get away."

"Men can be very forgiving." Carolyne hoped that was the case with Kyle.

"Forgiving?" Alexandra's eyes flashed. "Who is my brother to forgive me? Who asked him to interfere?"

Carolyne had no answer, except that she had no desire to get involved in a family feud, especially when she agreed with Kyle that Gordon had been a jerk. What's more, Kyle would have a say as to whether the expedition would or wouldn't be allowed back in.

"Kyle had him killed; I know he did." Alexandra's conviction was that of a woman deprived of her beloved by an evil brother. "Kyle's arm reaches a long way. From here to there, for him, is nothing."

Carolyne already had Kyle on her list of suspects with motives. She saw him as a rancher with designs on jungle for additional pasture—no matter his assurances to Roy that he was ecology-minded. What ecology advocate would burn down several acres so some goofy rock star could prance among the ashes and sing about saving trees?

"Won't your brother be looking for you?"

"He's already found me." However, Alexandra got the message. "You're right, he shouldn't find me here. He could get violent if he thought you sympathetic."

As soon as Alexandra left, Carolyne collapsed on the bed and fell asleep without thinking, even without undressing. This didn't guarantee a good night sleep. She woke up, more than once, and thought she was in the jungle with jaguars, natives, killers, high cliffs, deep waters. Her bed was too soft, after minimal mattresses of dead leaves over hard ground. Her clothes were uncomfortably binding, but she was too tired to remove them. Her room was too sound-proofed by thick walls and thick doors; the architect and builder had not only wanted all house occupants insulated against harsh equatorial heat, but guests, especially, undistributed by early-morning activities that inevitably accompanied the workaday world of any func-tioning ranch.

When she got up, she was surprised by the time. Her eyes and head were achy, her nose and throat were dry, and her mouth tasted like cotton balls. Her condition wasn't helped by the bathroom mirror, cruel as usual, that revealed a hairdo arranged by restless tossing and turning; she couldn't straighten the flattened, nor comb down the spikes. She let a hot shower do her corrective styling.

She returned to freshly laundered, ironed clothes laid out on her made bed. She selected a pants and blouse, and then risked another check of the looking glass. No beauty awards!

She ruffled still-damp hair and added a touch of lipstick and rouge to highlight her tanned complexion. "Take it, or leave it, humanity!"

She'd stayed at the ranch before and knew the routine. Breakfast was a catch as catch can buffet on the terrace and in an adjoining room; it lasted from early morning until the transition to the midday meal served at noon.

There was still plenty of food when Carolyne found Melanie at a patio table with an attractive blond boy.

"Get a plate, Carolyne, and join us," Melanie invited.

Upon closer examination, the boy was a young man, somewhere in his early twenties. He had lines at the corner of his black eyes, and more at the edges of his pouty lips; he wouldn't likely age well. At the moment, though, he possessed a somewhat "used" attractiveness that Carolyne found appealing.

"You don't look like a rock star," Carolyne commented after introductions; it must have had something to do with his hiking boots, shorts, and khaki shirt.

"Wait until I put on leather drag, spike my hair, and hang my neck with gold chains." Galin's voice was a gravelly rasp that even Carolyne considered sexy.

"You've not heard any of his songs, then?" Melanie sounded like a long-time fan, but she'd not displayed any foreknowledge upon confrontation with Richard Callahan on that burnt stretch of land.

"He starred in a television cola commercial." Carolyne knew that much.

Galin saw through that, though, his resulting smile as attractive as the rest of him; his teeth were white against bronzed skin of the kind few blonds managed in the tropics. "You've talked to Richard." It wasn't a question.

"So true." Carolyne tasted scrambled eggs that were just the way she liked them. "Speaking of Richard, has he been anywhere but around here, during any of the last few days? A couple of our party had an unpleasant confrontation, not long ago, with an as yet unidentified 'Brit'."

"He's not actually English, you know?" Galin said and smiled. "That accent of which he's so proud is purely affectation."

"I know," Carolyne admitted to never having been fooled. "Nevertheless...."

"Sorry, but I've seen him everyday," Galin disappointed.

Carolyne shrugged off the setback. "So where is everyone?"

"Richard and the camera crew are off to photograph the desolation, one day after," Galin said. "I think Richard actually wanted up and out before you came after him with another backhand." He couldn't repress his attractively large grin.

Melanie ran farther down the roster: "Kyle and Roy ate early for a powwow with Inspector Barco; Alexandra remains unheard from and unseen; Teddy is at the pool; Felix took a Jeep into town; Uncle Charles, would you believe, actually hitched a last-minute ride on the helicopter that left early this morning to collect Gordon's body—if the body is still to be found. My uncle never ceases to amaze me!"

Carolyne was no less astounded by Charles' recuperative powers.

"Carolyne, did you know that Galin knew Gordon?" Melanie asked and stabbed a piece of melon.

"They do say it's a small world." Did Carolyne sound as curious as she was?

Melanie was a "fisherman" who knew she'd set her hook. "They met when Gordon helped select sites for the videos from Galin's *Amaz'n Galin* album. You know: the album that went platinum before it officially hit the stores."

Carolyne only briefly wondered how a record managed to do that, but she wasn't really interested enough in the rock-and-roll business to ask. The Galin-Gordon connection was something else again. "*Amaz'n Galin?*" She didn't want him to think she looked down on what he did for a living; she merely found the new music so damned loud and—probably luckily—undecipherable, most of the time.

"A play on 'Amazin', i.e. 'Amazing,' and 'Amazon'." Melanie

had a lot down pat. "It was a concept album."

"A run-thorough theme," Galin elucidated. "'Love is a Jungle,' 'Man-eating Woman,' 'Eaten Alive,' 'Hot nights, Cold Lady,' etcetera. Richard was contacted to rush-shoot a couple of the videos for play on YouTube."

"I don't recall his mentioning any of that." Carolyne combined more ham and eggs; she punctuated with a bite of butter-soaked toast. "There was only something about 'a honeymoon'."

"*Honeymoon at Loon Lake*. Shirley Lynn's debut *movie*."

"Tell Carolyne why Richard didn't boast the *Amaz'n Galin* videos," Melanie coaxed.

"Mmmmmm," Carolyne encouraged in lieu of showing a mouthful of chewed food.

"Richard pulled out halfway through the shoot: breach of contract," Galin said. "I brought in Dillon Crane at the last minute, at additional expense. At the time, I swore it would be a cold day in the Amazon before I'd ever work with Richard again. Trouble is, he's damned good at what he does, and Dillon just followed through on Richard's original schematic to make the videos visually spectacular. They extended the album-life by providing three number one on the charts, over and above the original two that took off without visual promotion; so, I forgave him...obviously."

"Which finds you two here on this ecology video?" Carolyne was still angered by Richard's pyromania. "Shouldn't you be out pantomiming a song or two in the burn?"

"I'm too valuable to get too near any flames." He managed not to come across conceited. "Most of the interfacing will be done in a stateside studio with technical equipment that will have it looking as if I'm singing, 'Armageddon Now!' dead-center the holocaust. Most of my shots were taken the first day, before the burn. I'll do more amongst the ashes, later this afternoon."

Melanie figured other aspects were of more interest. "Go over, again, the reason why Richard pulled out of the *Amaz'n Galin* shoot."

"You mean, tell you about Susan?".

Carolyne's left eyebrow arched in encouragement. "Susan?"

"Susan Delaney." Galin wasn't immune to the excitement of Gordon's murder. "Richard's main squeeze at the time. A genuinely statuesque beauty who once thought she could sing but latched onto Richard, or vice versa, when it was apparent she didn't have the vocal cords to succeed."

"Seems Alexandra wasn't the only woman to succumb to Gordon's charms." Melanie could almost see and hear the little gears rolling inside Carolyne's head. "Susan fell like a ton of bricks for the big white hunter."

Carolyne associated 'big white hunter' with Africa, but she could stretch the point.

"Richard didn't take it well," Galin continued his contribution. "Really went bonkers. Insisted he'd been about to marry the girl; although, by then, he had graduated from calling her 'girl'."

Melanie was less reticent: "He was calling her 'a two-timing bitch'!"

"Day-long crying jags." Galin shook his head. He found the memory disgusting. Susan hadn't been all that special. Then again, Galin, unlike Richard, wasn't five-feet-one and didn't look like a toadstool. Still, even the shortest and ugliest in the business, especially the short and ugly with Richard's kind of clout, could expect better. The broad must have been a real whiz in bed. "He couldn't work. Everything came to a stop. Finally, he just pulled up stakes and headed home. Gordon and Susan went off somewhere to play house while I had to wait around in Belem for Dillon to clear his schedule and fly down to give me a hand. When Dillon arrived, Gordon came back sans Miss Delaney."

"Richard now here at the moment Gordon drops dead," Melanie stated the obvious.

Galin supplied more details: "Says he was ninety nine one hundredths percent cured the moment Susan came running back with some sad tale about how Gordon had dropped her like a hot potato, not more than a minute after he'd run off with her. Not that Richard took her back. Hell, no! Afterwards, he wanted to exorcise the rest of his demons, and he figured here would do it. He had this concept for a save the jungle song and video that was just right for me; tree burning gets big publicity in the States these days. What's to produce oxygen when all the jungles are gone? That kind of scare tactic. He even proposed Gordon to scout locations, but Gordon was off with you."

"Richard lucked out when Kyle volunteered to put some acres to the torch?"

"Did you really smack Richard for setting his fire?" Galin's ever widening smile revealed the faintest dimple in his right cheek. "I asked him how he ended up with that handprint on his face, but he refused me the specifics."

"Kyle allowed the burn as a favor to an old family friend who owes Richard for getting his son out of a cocaine mess in Los Angeles." Melanie had mined.

Carolyne remained unconvinced that a favor was any excuse for destruction.

If the women were already enthralled, Galin had more to keep their interest. "Actually, Richard and I met John Leider, too."

Melanie kept him going: "When? Where? How?"

"Just before Richard pulled up stakes and Gordon ran off with Susan. Gordon knew this spot on the Amazon just perfect for what we needed for an *Amaz'n Galin* locale, but Leider was there before us and wasn't happy to see us. He put bullet holes in our boat, one of which missed but gave Richard's hair a new part; ask him to show you the scar. Leider wouldn't believe we were there to film, not even when we showed him cameras and my leather costume. I swear he had us figured for claim jumpers; Gordon's presence seemed to have him all the more convinced. In the end, Gordon took us to another spot but complained that Leider had usurped the better location. Shortly, thereafter, things fell apart."

"You do know that Leider is now missing?" Carolyne figured

his exchange of information with Melanie had been a two-way street.

"News of Melanie's emerald wasn't kept under wraps for long." Galin had heard from Richard who'd heard from one of the cameramen who'd heard from the servants. "Some kind of birthday gift for his wife?"

"So says Roy who sold it to him," Carolyne confided.

"It's kind of hard to put Leider's disappearance on Richard's doorstep just because of that once upon a time scalp wound; Richard hasn't been in Brazil since the *Amaz'n Galin* videos; passport control, here, and in the U.S., makes that easy enough to check."

Nevertheless, Carolyne definitely suspected some kind of tie-in of Gordon's death with the missing John Leider, unless the man had had an offer on the "J" emerald that he simply couldn't refuse.

"Yo!" Roy heralded as he came around the end of the house with Rodrigo Barco in tow.

"Any word?" Melanie scooted her chair to make room; Carolyne and Galin followed suit.

"The helicopter pilot just radioed in," Roy filled in. "No sign of the murder weapon where we left it. No body, either; made to look as if some animal had dug the corpse out for dining."

"No way a jaguar!" Carolyne was convinced by this point.

"They did find jaguar pugs," Roy said, "but, I suspect, you're right. The animal probably nothing more than a convenient disposal unit for whoever did dig out the body."

Suddenly, Carolyne had no appetite for the food remaining.

"There's a last bit of bad news, I'm afraid," Roy informed. "Inspector, do you want to do the honors?"

Rodrigo fished his document case for the manila envelope he deposited into an empty space on the table.

Carolyne recognized his invitation and took possession. The contents were underexposed photographs, but of what?

Melanie, more than one photography class under her belt, was quicker on the uptake. "None of my shots came out?"

"I'm afraid not," Roy confirmed.

"I don't believe this!" Melanie decided. Granted, she had been upset when she took the pictures of Gordon's body, but all the operations of her camera were second nature to her by now. How was it possible, after all her efforts, that nothing was produced? "Felix!" she voted total responsibility. "The night I discovered my backpack rifled, he'd already gotten the filled digital chip and substituted an unused one from his own supply. So, when I exchanged unused chip for what I thought was the real stuff, I was doing nothing but replacing his unused chip with one of my own."

"Why would Felix make such a switch?" Roy asked, seemingly anxious for someone to provide Rodrigo and him a clue.

It was Carolyne, of course, who had the answer: "Because he...." She cut herself short, fearful of what effects bad-mouthing Melanie's mother would have on her relationship with Melanie.

Rodrigo had been long enough on the job to recognize an opportunity when he saw one, and he suggested Carolyne say what she had to say in private.

Melanie looked left out; Galin and Roy looked none too pleased, either.

Reluctantly, Carolyne joined Rodrigo on the far side of the patio.

Carolyne explained to Rodrigo her theory as to how Felix may have killed Gordon so, with its guide dead, the expedition would fail in its mission and, thereby, keep Cornelius Ditherson from any additional, albeit posthumous, credit for discovering a plant soon to be used in a cure for cancer. As the murderer, Felix wouldn't have wanted any photos surfacing to indicate Gordon dead of anything except by jaguar; Felix, in the past, having assuaged his envy by having had an affair with Cornelius' wife, Melanie's mother. Carolyne assured that Charles could confirm all she said. She, also, mentioned how, considering her good relationship with Melanie, she had been reluctant to bring up the Margaret-Felix affair in Melanie's presence. "There are those who think I was jealous of Melanie's mother, because Margaret stole Cornelius from me. However, I never had any real chance with Cornelius." It was something she'd decided long ago but, until now, hadn't been up to admitting.

Rodrigo promised discretion.

Carolyne didn't rejoin Roy, Galin, and Melanie, although Rodrigo did. Carolyne wanted time to figure some logical excuse for having excluded them from her discussion with Rodrigo. If the others thought she withheld information from them, they'd be less apt to volunteer to her their ideas, and Carolyne did so enjoy the continuing intricacies of this who done it.

She borrowed a Jeep from the ranch motor pool and drove into town. It gave her a chance to think; it gave her a chance to run down a bottle of henna. She needed all the mental, as well as all the cosmetic, help she could get.

Besides, Manaus was fascinating in its second boom, filled with turn of the century remnants from the lucrative rubber trade that contrasted with the modern high-rises from the present commercial successes of a town declared a free port in the nineteen-sixties.

Here were some of the best fishing facilities in the whole Amazon region: for tucanari, surubim, piraiba, pirarara, and 180-pound durado.

Eight hundred plus miles upstream from the Amazon mouth at Belem, Manaus was a centrally located jump-off for anyone interested in traveling the more inaccessible areas of the Basin. There were still pockets of jungle where animals, like jaguars, roamed on a regular basis, not just as occasional visitors in search of a tasty human being.

Large ranches, like the Georni spread, made notable contributions toward pushing back the forest, but Carolyne drove through groves of cocoa, rubber, and guarana that were footholds prepared to expand at the first opportunity.

She pulled into the *Hotel Amazonas*. The *Tropical Hotel Manaus* was larger but another eighteen kilometers up the beach at Ponta Negra; it wasn't gorgeous landscaping, natural zoo, casino, shops, or floating river bar that Carolyne wanted, though.

It took three hours to be squeezed into a full docket of looks-conscious tourists and get the complete treatment offered by the hotel beauty salon, but it was worth it. She looked better, felt better, and had her new supply of touch-up henna. During her turn under the dryer, she'd decided to come clean to Melanie, Roy, and Felix, but only if Melanie pressed the issue.

She assumed she might run into Felix who'd driven into town before her. The city was large, but the *Hotel Amazonas* was a popular watering hole for locals and tourists alike.

However, it was Richard Callahan she spotted as she pretended to examine a display case of indigenous Indian handicrafts and weapons (the arrows looked disturbingly familiar); actually, she preened in the glass, once again complimenting the metamorphosis accomplished via the ministrations of the skillful beautician.

In a hurry, Richard didn't see her as he was lost amid taller people and exited through a side door.

Carolyne gave chase, because intuition said he was up to no good. What other explanation for his not being where he'd told Galin he would be? If he'd merely wrapped up shooting for the day, he still deserved another piece of her mind; anyone who burned down the jungle in the name of ecology was someone who needed to be set straight at every turn.

Following wasn't as easy as Carolyne had been led to believe by movies, books, and TV. Or, her problem was a quarry that didn't jut up in a crowd but, rather, sank into it. Richard's shortness easily disappeared him behind people, cars, bicycles, even—seemingly—trash cans.

It was his wake she followed. People glanced after him, and Carolyne knew they reacted to the sight of the hurried little man. She caught an occasional glimpse of his trousers, or his shirt, through a forest of legs. Cars screeched to sudden stops as Richard crossed in front of them.

Her efforts made her perspire; the last thing she wanted after paying for her "cure". Why chase Richard down a dirty Manaus street when she could wait until evening and confront him over cool cocktails on a cool patio?—"By the way, Callahan, what were you doing today in town when you were supposed to be busy shooting burn scenes for your video?"

She stopped, but only because he stopped. He was half a block away, his back to a building. He checked his watch and turned in her direction. Rather than wave him down, she played inept private detective, in some B-grade move, and turned to feign interest in a store window that turned out to be a solid brick wall.

Embarrassed, she turned back, and his—I'm not happy to see you—expression said he'd spotted her for sure. She took two steps in his direction, determined to begin again where she'd left off when she'd knocked him flat, but his attention really wasn't on her. It was focused, instead, and always had been, on a younger woman who approached him from not quite Carolyne's direction to stop, arms akimbo, and tower over him, like some stereotypical Amazon of mythology.

At the same moment, Carolyne felt an imperceptible tug on her purse, reminiscent of Rome when a young hoodlum on a motorcycle had come abreast, reached out and taken hold of her purse in preview of the real wrench that would have disconnected her arm from her shoulder if her purse strap hadn't conveniently broken.

Reflexively, she braced, and her free arm swung her free hand to clamp her purse. She'd have this little bugger pulled off his cycle and laid in the street before she'd budge.

This kid, though, wasn't on a motorcycle. He just stood there. His hand was no longer on her purse, although it had been on it to get her full attention. First thing, Carolyne made sure all the purse zippers were still zipped, all the snaps still snapped. Second thing, she wondered why the youngster wasn't six blocks away by now.

He spoke her name: the last thing she expected. He tried again and enunciated more slowly and clearly.

"Who wants to know?" It was the seemingly harmless ones

who caught you unaware and did the worst damage. She pulled her purse closer and waited for him to make his next move.

He produced a folded piece of paper.

"What's that?" She was suspicious.

Her name was apparently the extent of his vocal English vocabulary.

She took the paper, and he left her with a swiftness that surprised and impressed her.

She had the page half unfolded when she remembered, "Richard!" Her exclamation drew startled glances from two men, neither of whom stopped; probably neither named Richard.

Richard and the woman were gone. Carolyne blamed the now absent boy for the diversion; the paper would be blank when she opened it.

Wrong!

It was a woman's neatly written script that invited "Mrs. Santire" to "join Mrs. John Leider for tea." Carolyne checked her watch. If the tea in question wasn't all that far away, it could be what the doctor ordered. It held far more interesting prospects than accosting Richard and his Amazon on a busy Manaus street.

She went back to the hotel, and, as if she were a paying guest, she requisitioned a map of the city from the clerk behind the front desk. Then, she had him pinpoint the Leider address on the map and red-line the most direct route there from the hotel.

She arrived within the hour, not sure she was in the right place. She didn't exactly know what she'd expected by way of a residence for Mrs. John Leider, wife of missing prospector, John Leider, but it wasn't this Italian-Renaissance villa in direct throwback to times when Manaus had seen fabulous fortunes made and spent overnight in mad quests for rubber put in so much demand by Mr. Goodyear's discovery of vulcanization.

The villa was no comparison to the greatest surviving relic of that area, the ostentatious *Teatro do Amazonas*, which Carolyne had passed to get there, but, at least, as viewed through its gates, it was in an even better state of repair. Carolyne's preference for the villa over the Georni ranch house which, likewise, had seen very little expense spared in its construction was probably a case of aesthetics triumphant over functionality.

Despite her success in the beauty parlor, Carolyne wasn't dressed for high tea. She'd expected hot water poured from a rustic, tin kettle into chipped porcelain cups. Nevertheless, she rang the bell on the gate.

"Yes?" The reply came from a weather-proofed squawk box.

"Mrs. Santire for Mrs. Leider."

The expected reply: "Who for whom?" The actual response: "Yes, please,"

The gate swung open with a click, and Carolyne, very much the poor relation come to call, steered the Jeep up a driveway of crushed pink quartz and parked in front of a large, double, teak door that opened its left side as if on cue.

Jane Leider was as much a surprise as her home, and not just because she didn't send a servant but came personally down the three half-circle steps that echoed the arch of the porch. She extended a hand upon which rode the biggest emerald Carolyne had ever seen. "Thank you for coming on such short notice, and I hope you'll forgive my unorthodox method of invitation. Someone at the hotel knew of my interest. Unfortunately, my note arrived after you'd left, and it was necessary to pass it to one of the youngsters better able to maneuver city streets in pursuit."

"I'm delighted he caught me." She was, too. "You have such a lovely home." Wasn't that the understatement of this year and last? "One of the 1890 constructions, isn't it?"

"1894." She wore a cream-colored pantsuit of some soft material that clung to all the right places and camouflaged all the bad; good care and plenty of money made her look thirty. "Are you a student of our local architecture?"

"Only insofar as I've always found it fascinating," Carolyne admitted.

"Fascinating enough for the 'grand tour' of the house, or would you find that not only tedious but presumptuous?" she came across genuinely concerned that she didn't want to inconvenience.

"I'd be flattered to have the grand tour." The first thing Carolyne had done when initially checked into the Georni Ranch had been an in-depth view of those premises—literally from top to bottom.

Now, the women strolled gardens whose indigenous plants were Mediterranean in arrangement, confinement, and cut. Sculptures were Greco-Roman, white-marble representations of fauns, nymphs, goddesses and gods, centaurs, and satyrs. A bronze-dolphin fountain spewed water that spread wide and long into a cool, reflecting pool.

"My grandfather built this house." Jane's voice was low, cultured, in no way out of place amid the surroundings. "Our family emigrated from Venice; thus, the Italian influence."

Marble had been brought from Italy, tiles from Portugal, porcelain from England, furniture from France, wrought iron from Germany. Ceilings and walls were decorated with mirrors that reflected murals of harp-playing angels cavorting with half-naked Amazon Indians.

Carolyne was transferred back to 1894 when no expense had been spared by rubber barons who brought artisans and artists in by the boatload; who bought an evening of entertainment from Sarah Bernhardt, Caruso, and Pavlova, for exorbitant fees; who thought nothing of shipping all personal laundry to Paris for just the right press or fold.

The tea service was Spode Fine Bone China, the tea: green Gunpowder sorts, the silverware: Regency. While the ladies ate crustless cucumber sandwiches, time ticked on a nineteenth-century, French, lapis lazuli clock bracketed by matching François Rude candelabra.

Jane kept up a polite banter that drew out small talk of Carolyne's life as well as her own. Carolyne regretted the upcoming moment of truth, because she enjoyed herself and had so very little to offer as regarded Melanie's "J" emerald that had to be Jane's chief concern.

"We were lucky and got out of rubber before the disastrous bust; I forget who tipped my grandfather, but we owe whomever this house, life-style, and acquisition of the cheap land suddenly so valuable today."

Carolyne refused another sandwich. It was time to pay the piper; she knew she didn't have the price. Without being asked, she told Jane all the facts as she had them.

"One final room to show you," Jane said when Carolyne had completed. She got to her feet and led the way.

It was accessed through a large bookcase that swung open in the library.

"My husband checked in on a regular basis." Jane motioned toward the short-wave. She pulled a binder from a shelf and opened it.

Carolyne divined a larger version of the type of log that Roy had once produced of his gem discoveries and sales. Like him, Jane provided a drawn diagram of the "J" emerald that Roy had sold to John Leider. Likewise, she had a color photograph of it that included a caliper to provide scale. "Would you say this is the stone in question?"

It certainly seems so. I'm sure that Melanie would let you have a closer look."

"You might assure her that I have no plans to make any legal claim. Not that I'd have a leg to stand on, except, of course, for my conviction that John would never have sold that particular stone."

"Nor lost it."

"Nor lost it," Jane agreed.

"Which says what?"

"I can't be sure. I do know that when my husband disappeared, he had not only this emerald in his possession but at least these other five as well." She flipped back the preceding pages and paused at each for Carolyne to see the diagram, the color photo, and the accompanying handwritten notes. "The diagrams are based upon coded information broadcast to me from my husband at various times while he was in the field."

"Coded?" Roy had once borrowed the expedition's radio in order to broadcast seemingly numeral nonsense."

"Airwaves are easily accessed. Not everyone with big ears is honest, as any prospector with his own secrets and codes will tell you."

"And the photographs of the gemstones?'"

"These six were on a digital chip passed to me by Roy Lendum, given him by John at the time my husband purchased the 'J' emerald in question. Roy was incoming civilization, at the time, in order to renew permits and what-not."

"The proceeds from the sale of so many emeralds could have taken your husband a long ways from the Amazon."

"As part of some he left his wife theory?" Jane suggested but didn't sound upset. "Except, more money than you're talking from those emeralds was available in banks right here in Manaus; John's money, still untouched. Why make it more complicated than it need have been to pack up and walked out on me? Did he think I'd make a scene? Did he think I'd attempt legal action? You can easily find that John wielded more than enough clout to counteract mine. I trusted him implicitly. He had full access to all of my business affairs. I assure you, he left everything in impeccable order; no running out because he'd embezzled company funds."

Would Jane benefit if Carolyne failed to bring up one logical possibility? "Your husband had reason to want Gordon Wentlock dead?"

"They weren't friends. There was bad blood. But murder him? Lose the emerald your friend, then, found? Be so careless as to leave Gordon's body to be discovered by one of you? Leave our lucrative business behind? Leave this house?"

"Leave you?"

Jane smiled. "No relationship is perfect, ours no exception. But taking everything into account, yes, I think we might add that to the long list."

On her drive back to the ranch, Carolyne slowed at the approach to a steep downgrade that bottomed out with a sharp left turn that skirted, rather than penetrated, a thick growth of banana trees. The first time over this stretch of roadway, she'd overshot the dip in the roadway at only moderate speed; that had been enough to launch her and her vehicle as substantially as Roy and she had been launched over the lip of that jungle pool which had saved them from the fire. Being airborne had been scary enough, but the jarring landing, on shock absorbers that had seen better days, had telescoped her spine and clattered her teeth with a force she'd thought, at the time, had cracked them.

Now, she edged the car smoothly into the drop; indication she'd learned from her past mistake.

Someone else hadn't been so lucky: at the bottom, where the turn veered sharply, there was a tunnel plowed into the underbrush, the rear of a Jeep visible beneath a banana tree knocked off vertical; two bunches of bananas looked like chandeliers hung in a room off-kilter.

No convenient place to pull over, she took the makeshift pathway provided by the damaged Jeep.

She expected the worst.

The audible groan indicated a survivor but didn't assess the damage to the crumpled body curled in a nest of crushed vegetation.

The victim rolled before Carolyne knelt to warn that movement might be dangerous until injures could be determined.

"Dear God!" She saw a bleeding and battered Richard Callahan.

She wasn't sure he recognized her. There was something about his eyes that was definitely unfocused. His speech was slurred but still pseudo-Brit. He, maybe/maybe not, said, "Brakes. Gone." Then, he passed out.

CHAPTER SEVEN

Carolyne tried to be calm and coolly consider her alternatives.

Richard solved her dilemma with short-lived unconsciousness. "You'd better drive me to the ranch infirmary." He attempted to stand but couldn't quite manage.

"Maybe I should go get help?" The zone was dead, as was almost everywhere thereabouts, by way of cell phone.

His condition made him irritable. "Maybe you should just give me the hand I've suggested."

If she could get him into her Jeep under some of his own power, it would be easier. On the other hand, "I'm not sure you should be up and around before a doctor sees you."

As usual, he found her impossible! "I'm only moving as far as your Jeep."

If they could make that happen. She made the effort. It wasn't easy, because he wasn't as capable as he thought and as she hoped. More than once, she had to support them both which nearly dropped them. His final deposit in the Jeep's backseat wasn't as graceful or as gentle as she'd planned. Nor was it any too soon, because, once again, he was dead to the world.

She estimated she hit every bump on her way out. The road was a washboard. She glanced back several times to see Richard slide farther down in the seat. She stopped to reposition him, not pleased his head kept bleeding. Head wounds could be nasty things, but he'd seemed lucid enough for those few moments he'd been awake.

The distance seemed endless; there was little consolation in Georni land stretched as far as the eye could see.

When she reached the main complex, she had visions of Richard quite dead. Of all her alternatives, this one had become the wrong one. She should have never listened to him, or moved him, because the easiest way wasn't always the best way.

Roy saw her and waved. He read something in her failure to stop and ran after her to the infirmary. "What is it?"

"Richard's car crashed on that steep section of roadway between here and Manaus."

"Better get him inside."

Having gotten him this far, she was more cautious. "Maybe, we'd better have Dr. Seln check before we move him."

"Maybe," Roy agreed. He was already en route to the door. Shortly, he produced Dr. Ferdinand Seln who gave permission to move Richard inside. Roy managed the transfer with no need of assistance—for which Carolyne was grateful.

Dr. Seln assigned chairs outside the curtained examination area.

Roy didn't stay. "I'd better tell Kyle."

Shortly, Kyle appeared, sans Roy, before the doctor was ready with any verdict. "Ferd?"

"Take a seat with Mrs. Santire, Kyle. I'll be with you both as soon as I'm ready." The doctor's accent was some hybridization that Carolyne couldn't place.

Kyle turned to Carolyne. "Roy said it happened on the Tlesselan Grade. No one can persuade old Tlesselan to shift his bananas."

Carolyne didn't know Tlesselan, but his stubbornness was a menace. Not that he was totally to blame. "Richard said something about his brakes gone out."

"Wrong place for that to happen." Kyle's observation was superfluous. He phoned Inspector Barco, came back, and sat down.

A short, dull hum indicated an x-ray. After that distraction, Carolyne realized Kyle eyed her strangely. "I put my head on wrong this morning?" She sounded testy and was glad he laughed.

"You look fantastic," he complimented; she thought he was sarcastic—she didn't feel fantastic. "Your hair, right?"

She remembered the beauty parlor. "Some major repair."

Dr. Seln appeared, only briefly. "My preliminary doesn't indicate anything serious, but I want to do a more thorough go-over of the x-ray."

"We'll be optimistic." Kyle settled back, ready to wait.

Carolyne had no intentions of deserting her post, either, until final diagnosis. She didn't like Richard but didn't wish him harm. She wanted proof positive that her assistance hadn't been detrimental.

Dr. Seln returned to the world behind the curtain.

"While in town, I had tea at the Leider villa," Carolyne told Kyle. She wanted input and figured he was the man to provide it.

"Had you to the Villa Borgia, did she?"

"Is that what she really calls it?"

"An 'in' joke," he apologized. "Reference, I guess, to the Italian influence."

"Weren't the Borgias Spanish?" It was her attempt to impress.

Kyle was no less astute: "Spanish in origin; Italian by temperament."

"Rather unsavory reputations, if I remember my history. Patricide, wantonness, vice, high crimes."

"Perhaps my analogy *was* a little wide of the mark. Then again...."

He had her curious. "I found Lucretia...." Her reward for her further reference to the infamous Borgia clan was his smile. "I mean, Jane," she needlessly corrected, "exceedingly charming."

"I'm sure she was." Jane had a way about her that he'd come to resent more and more over the years. "She can be quite charming when she puts her mind to it. It's the result of all those years in private finishing schools."

"She was interested in Melanie's recovery of the 'J' emerald."

"Wants the gem back, does she?"

"Actually, she seemed more concerned about the where-abouts of her husband."

"Could be, but she always seemed so much happier whenever he was away."

Carolyne gave him silence in which to continue. Some people were acutely uncomfortable in silence and would fill it with the most marvelous tidbits if given the opportunity by a skillful listener. Of course, there were those not at all cowed by it; Kyle was one. If Carolyne wanted anything more on Jane Leider, she'd have to work for it. "Mr. and Mrs. Leider weren't the ideal couple?"

Kyle contemplated not taking the subject farther. He never had spent all of his venom, regarding Jane and her family; whether or not Carolyne was the right sounding board, she was at least available. Better yet, she wouldn't be around for long to remind him of any slips of the tongue, here and now. "I'd hate to have any of this come out as sour grapes."

If he thought that would have her diplomatically cut him off at the pass, he was mistaken. "Actually, Mrs. Leider seemed almost too attractive, too gracious, too good to be true."

"Would you like a drink of something?" Kyle detoured.

A jigger of rubbing alcohol, you mean?" She didn't mind the tangent, as long as it was only temporary.

He smiled, which put his dark good looks to their best advantage. He liked anyone who held their own in a conversation, and he appreciated Carolyne's wry sense of humor, noticed as far back as their first meeting. "Ferd, I'm raiding your liquor cabinet!"

A reply came from somewhere behind the pulled curtain: "You know where I keep the key. You might ask Mrs. Santire if she'd like something, too, while you're at it."

"The good doctor still sees me as a self-centered brat apt to forget simple good manners." It wasn't really criticism.

"You and the doctor go back a long ways, do you?" She calculated the doctor's age, based on his shock of pure white hair and his myriad worry lines.

"I was a difficult delivery, and he's never forgiven me the extra work I caused him." He brought her two fingers of liqueur in a clear glass. "Curacao," he identified.

"How'd you know I was fond of oranges?" She gratefully sipped while he again settled into the chair beside her.

"This used to be Fernelli land," he said. "Not just the Georni Ranch but all of the other ranches, large and small, around here."

"Fernelli land?"

"Jane Fernelli Leider," he provided clarification. "Thomas Fernelli was the real powerhouse and made the family fortune in rubber. Also, he got out of rubber before it went bust. After which, he bought up cheap land and supplanted rubber as king in these parts."

"We're talking Jane's grandfather?"

"As opposed to Arthur Fernelli, her father, who, as a walking catastrophe, gave poor Thomas many a cause to turn over in his grave."

They clinked glasses and drained off the resulting liqueur; Kyle went for refills which Carolyne didn't refuse. There was nothing like alcohol to smooth tattered nerves and foster bonhomie.

"Thomas Fernelli founded the dynasty and enlarged its net worth; Arthur Fernelli let Thomas' legacy slip away, slowly at first, then in a great, huge hemorrhaging. John Leider to the rescue! Of course, there were a few of us as willing to play White Knights, too: myself, Roy, Janner Tyrol, Simms Mason; but, John beat us out, because he had founded lucrative Leider Platinum by then and came from a family fashionably old guard. Before the rubber bust, the Leiders were really even a few steps above the Fernelli on the social ladder: a definite advantage over those of us late on the scene and seen only as scavengers eager to gulp down whatever Fernelli holdings Arthur let slip. One thing about John, he might have had none of the polish the Leiders had before him, but he did have luck as a prospector and the skills to exploit his findings into a stockpile of profits. You'd have to look far and wide to find anyone in the whole Amazon

Basin who did as well off its natural resources."

"A little rough around the edges, was he?" That had always been Carolyne's assumption before getting a counter-glimpse... of Jane and the Leider villa.

Kyle answered indirectly. "Before you can exploit platinum, gold, silver, or emerald finds, you have to do a lot of dirty digging to get to them; John was good at getting down in the dirt. Years in the wilds, with only animals for companions, didn't match Harvard or Oxford as imparters of social grace."

Carolyne found it difficult to imagine such a man master of all she'd surveyed at the Leider villa.

Kyle saw where Carolyne's thoughts wandered. He emphasized the picture he'd painted. "He was the bull in that China shop. Not that he didn't enjoy the role, because he wanted all the trappings. He liked the Leider name back in prominence. He liked the Fernelli beholden to him. Hadn't Thomas Fernelli lorded it over everyone, John's grandfather included, when the bottom dropped out of rubber? The Leider properties had been some of the first Thomas had swallowed up at rock-bottom prices. So many complicated egos, superegos, ids, libidos, and angst; enough Freudian stews to keep a team of psychoanalysts smacking their lips for years: all pretty much unrecognized and ill-understood by one poor simpleton who merely thought, 'Isn't Jane Fernelli beautiful, and wouldn't it be grand to have her as my wife?'"

"You: that one poor simpleton?" She wanted to hear it again to be sure 'poor and simpleton' came off as ludicrous from her lips as it had from his; it did.

"Oh, I wasn't always this suave, cosmopolitan, sophisticate you see before you." He scratched one armpit, like a monkey.

Her laughter said more than words how Jane had come out on the short end of any bargain that had lost her Kyle. Carolyne didn't forgive him for allowing Richard Callahan's burning of jungle acreage for a video, but no one was perfect.

"To Arthur Fernelli, my dad was newly arrived and newly rich and took advantage of Arthur's rampant cocaine, gambling, and womanizing habits, and his catastrophic business sense, to set up housekeeping on sacrificed Fernelli land; no matter the land had passed into Fernelli hands at the expense of gentry fallen on hard times."

"Jane, I suppose, had nothing to say about anything?"

"She loves that house. She loves her jewels. She loves the haute couture of Paris. She loves the discos of New York. She loves being rich. She couldn't survive poor, and even she had to know her father drained family coffers at a dangerous rate. I doubt she put up much of a fuss at the solution. I'm sure it was coincidence her father dropped dead two weeks after the wedding, no chance for him to reap the benefits of John's hard-won money. There's nothing clandestine about John's disappearance, if you ask me; the jungle is a very dangerous place to be, as Gordon Wentlock might bear witness. It's merely coincidence that John conveniently happened to disappear at a moment in time when Jane no longer needs him to bolster faltering finances."

"You think she killed her husband, or had it done?"

"It's so very easy for a man scorned to think only the very worst of the woman who scorned him."

Carolyne was empathetic. All these years later, she still smarted at how Cornelius had opted for Margaret, that bit of rejection occurring without the additional indignity of Cornelius needing to balance bank accounts.

"Ironically, I can thank Jane for how well-off I am today." The liqueur was warm in his stomach and provided an enjoyable flush behind the tan of his cheeks. "At the time of her engagement, I was as crushed as much as any of her other rejected swains, but my father was livid—for all the wrong reasons, many of which I've criticized in Arthur Fernelli. Dear dad had been hyped on the possibilities of our social upgrading. When I failed him in my failure to storm the palace and make off with the princess, he worked harder to make the Georni name something to be reckoned with. I certainly own more land than Jane, although those little plots of mineral-rich soil John left her are more valuable. If I have contacts in high places, whom I count as personal friends, that doesn't mean Jane can't buy the same favors."

"A debt owed or one repaid: you allowing Richard to burn those acres of your land?" She had a one-track mind when an estimated one plant species bit the dust with every acre of rain forest burned. Kyle had no doubt she'd already advantaged the rumor grapevine; Carolyne confirmed. "Something to do with a problem similar to the one riding on Arthur Fernelli's back." There was something, even at her age, about an attractive, intelligent male, that made her want to shine—and simultaneously get his goat. "Cocaine?"

"Suffice it to say that the young man in question, a very silly son of an old family friend, is nonetheless the favorite of his father, the father so feeble as to the point he would most assuredly not have survived the apple of his eye having fallen on desperate times. I suspect the young man will eventually do something of equal foolishness, from which not even Richard Callahan's connections will be able to extract him, but the old man should be dead, of more natural causes, by then, and I couldn't be bothered."

"It's true, then, that this burn was the exception to your rule?"

"I no more want suffocation in an atmosphere of carbon dioxide than the next guy."

Carolyne could expound the pros all day. "Not to mention the destruction of unique animals, insects, and plants, any of which could provide major scientific and medical breakthroughs."

"Yes, not to mention those."

"The land already cleared is sufficient for your needs?" She was dubious, because land claimed from the jungle wasn't as fertile as the original lush growth would seem to insinuate. Continued fertility depended upon constant recycling of minerals from the ground, to vegetation, to ground again; that cycle broken by any introduction of livestock into the equation.

"I've more than enough money to last me a lifetime. A few less dollars and cattle, down the road, won't change that."

Outside, a car crunched gravel that wasn't as pink as that of the Leider villa, but was definitely just as noisy.

"Company!" announced Kyle and knew, since the auto proceeded directly to the infirmary, that the newly-arrived was probably Rodrigo Barco. He was right.

Rodrigo greeted them with the news that the brake fluid of Richard's wrecked car had purposely been drained. He asked after Richard's health as the three proceeded into the infirmary.

An invisible Dr. Seln answered: "Not bad, as far as I can tell. No broken bones, a superficial head cut that bled a lot but isn't deep. Of course, it's hard to tell about bumps on the head, and he did receive a nasty one of those, probably when his car hit whatever the immovable object."

Rodrigo had questions, but Richard was still unconscious.

Galin's appearance was unexpected only in that Carolyne had expected it earlier. She'd forgotten he was scheduled for an afternoon shoot. He'd only just returned, steamed at Richard's no-show, to hear of Richard's accident from Roy. "Is Richard all right?"

Dr. Seln: "He's momentarily in a coma, but that's not uncommon in these cases. I won't underestimate the potential for concern, but the prognosis is good. If he's not come around by morning, I may amend."

"Someone drained his car's brake fluid." Carolyne hadn't missed Rodrigo Barco's announcement, and she knew what it meant.

So did Galin: "Who'd want Richard dead?"

"Is Susan Delaney about five-eleven, auburn hair?" Carolyne's subconscious had worked overtime. She had a good record of going to bed with a problem and awaking to solutions provided by sleep; this time she'd skipped the sleep.

"So are a lot of women, even in Brazil." Galin's rendition of the Richard-Susan altercation might have led Carolyne to such a conclusion, but, as far as he knew, Susan was a few thousand miles away.

Except, Carolyne was privy to information Galin didn't have: "Richard met such a woman this afternoon, not all that long before his 'accident', and he didn't seem all that happy to see her."

If the police inspector had even less facts than Galin, Rodrigo was soon filled in.

Rodrigo called his headquarters and gave someone Susan's name and her description. He hung up and asked to speak with Carolyne in private.

"You two are sharing a lot of secrets these days." Galin remembered Carolyne and Rodrigo's tête-à-tête of that morning.

Rodrigo's smile was noncommittal. He indicated by pantomime that Carolyne should join him on the porch. He led her down the stairs and invited her to join him on a stroll.

Carolyne was as curious as Galin; though, if Kyle had seemed unsurprised, it was because he was already aware of the subject about to be discussed.

To Carolyne, Rodrigo admitted to having had a talk with Felix, after one of Rodrigo's men had spotted Felix doing some heavy drinking at the floating bar of the *Tropical Hotel*. Rodrigo, there, having confronted Felix with Carolyne's reference to Felix and Margaret Crystin Ditherson having had an affair, during Cornelius Ditherson's lifetime; Charles had by then confirmed all that Carolyne had told Rodrigo earlier. Rodrigo punctuated with a cough.

Carolyne guessed, right then and there, what had happened. "He denied it?"

Rodrigo admitted that Felix had done just that.

Carolyne had more trouble with Felix's denial of the facts than she expected. "You believed him?"

Rodrigo assured that he was making every effort to check out the facts of Felix's denial. At least for the moment, Rodrigo had concluded that Felix did have a logical reason for all of his meetings with Margaret Ditherson: valid above and beyond taking Margaret to bed.

"What reasons?"

But, as a matter of courtesy, Rodrigo had promised Felix to keep them confidential. However, Rodrigo did suggest that

Carolyne might, sometime, want to bring up the subject with Felix, if just to put her own mind at ease; although Rodrigo wouldn't suggest she do it any time soon. Felix was decidedly distraught that Carolyne had passed on her suspicions of adultery, with additional suspicions from Charles.

"May I remind you," countered Carolyne, "that Charles saw them twice at that seedy hotel?"

Rodrigo admitted that Carolyne's deductions, based upon the facts she had, were logical. And not until Rodrigo had thoroughly checked out Felix's story would Rodrigo absolutely be assured that Felix's explanations were the real ones. However, at the moment, Rodrigo was prepared to give Felix the benefit of the doubt.

"Without allowing me the facts to do the same?" Carolyne was disconcerted.

Rodrigo's upturned hands gestured his helplessness. He had, after all, to respect Felix's privacy, just as he had promised Carolyne, during the meeting with Carolyne, that morning, to keep Melanie in the dark.

"I see." Except, Carolyne didn't see.

Not that Rodrigo thought her wrong to have relayed the rumor; quite to the contrary.

Rodrigo steered them on an angle that intercepted the main house. He bid her farewell at the front porch and headed back to the infirmary.

Charles, Melanie, Teddy laid in ambush, and Carolyne was roped into telling her story of how she'd rescued Richard. In finale, she pleaded tiredness in a way that invited Charles to accompany her as far as her room.

When she farther isolated the two of them behind a closed door, Charles asked, "What's up?"

She told him.

"You're not serious! Felix came up with something Rodrigo actually bought?"

"That was my definite impression."

"And he didn't give you a clue as to what?"

"'Ask Felix, but not any time soon' was, I believe, how he put it."

"Felix has probably been working on some logical cover story ever since you confronted him with his adultery. The man is no fool."

Carolyne checked her watch. "Agreeing with that, I think my day would be improved by my having a short nap."

Charles took the hint. "Yes, of course." He did add, before parting, "You do look smashing."

"You do say the nicest things." She pecked him on the cheek in a way allowed between friends who went back as far and as long as they did.

When he was gone, it hit her how tired she was. Nonetheless, the nap she craved wasn't summoned by her lying down. She settled for a leisurely wander along the upstairs outside balcony that was momentarily hers alone to enjoy.

There was a breeze, cool, as if it had managed the miles from eastern seaboard, or western glaciers, without a loss of chill. Carolyne faced it and the rustling leaves of a tree whose sole occupant, a macaw with scarlet plumage, sampled an assortment of green-to-overripe figs. The view through gnarled branches was of ranch buildings and parenthesizing pasture-land. The only indication the ranch once sat in a claustrophobic choke of vegetation was an attractive island, here and there, of virgin trees: someone's effort to control erosion by retention of occasional root matting. Carolyne considered such holdovers as genetic banks from which Mother Nature could someday draw for regeneration if and when some catastrophe erased interfering humans.

The balcony extended around the entire exterior of the second floor: an antebellum-like walkway hung on the same square pillars that supported the roof.

There was a lived-in quality to it all that Carolyne now realized she'd missed in the formal gardens, antique furnishings, and rose-quartz driveway of the Leider villa whose fairy-tale setting was look but don't touch.

She was brought up short by movement in what had been Gordon's room on their trip out. Now, Gordon dead, it was assigned to someone else.

Its curtains were pulled across its windows and French doors, but some piece of furniture interfered, or some flaw of the curtain mechanism made the cloth cocoon incomplete. A peephole offered itself through which Carolyne had spotted the movement.

Without forethought, she moved closer and expected a maid. However, it was Roy behind a desk.

Carolyne was embarrassed, her position easily that of a Peeping Tom. When Roy looked up, Carolyne's wave was an automatic fancy spotting you there; she hoped she came off innocent.

To her surprise, he paid her no mind but returned to what he'd been doing. Obviously unseen, she felt wrapped in a Tarnhelm of permanent invisibility as she determined her view of him was secondhand, a mirror reflection of his section of the room.

There was nothing unusual about Roy's examination of his notebook, but Carolyne felt uneasy about seeing and not being seen. She sidestepped to the French doors and knocked on a pane.

Roy had trouble with the curtains and the latch; they both finally opened. "Carolyne, how's Richard?"

"The long-range prognosis is good, although he's still unconscious."

"Dr. Seln will have him up and around in no time."

The jungle was safer with the pyromaniac bedridden, but she didn't say so.

She was surprised when Roy invited her in; sometimes, she forgot the days were long gone when such an invitation might be misconstrued as something other than harmless.

He asked her something more about Richard; she calculated the angles of desk to mirror to window and asked him to repeat his question.

"He's not said how it happened?" Roy complied.

"Rodrigo said the brake fluid was drained from Richard's car."

"Drained: as in attempted-murder drained?"

"Seems an old girlfriend may be in town from whom he parted on less than pleasant terms."

"Thank God this one comes with a possibly logical explanation." He motioned her into an easy chair. "Can I get you a Scotch? I'm afraid it's the only thing I have on hand."

Her two glasses of liqueur with Kyle had certainly produced some enlightening conversation. "Maybe a very small one."

"Great!"

The bottle and tumblers were handy on a nearby dresser.

The segment of window through which she'd spotted him had a tendency to be glared over on the inside; her presence on the outside had been additionally disguised by distortions of the mirror's surface on which he would have had to see her.

He brought her glass. She sipped very good Scotch; he sat across from her.

"I had tea with Jane Leider." A now familiar refrain.

"The widow is out of mourning and into entertaining, is she?" It didn't come out complimentary; he hadn't meant it to.

"Kyle told me that you and he used to court Jane when her name was Fernelli."

"Boasting, was he?" He sipped.

"Regretting might put it better."

"Yes, maybe so," Roy agreed.

"And you?"

He shrugged, settled back in his chair, and took another swallow.

Carolyne decided on another tack. "I'm sorry; I didn't mean to pry. It's just that, with Jane a suspect." She left it at that, hoped for a response, and got it.

"You think Jane killed her husband, or Gordon? As for the latter, it would likely have been vice versa; it was she, after all, who wouldn't give Gordon a tumble, even when he, like with every other woman within miles, tried."

That was a bit of news. To mask her surprise, Carolyne swallowed too much Scotch and almost choked. By the time she recovered, flush from her efforts, Roy had wised up.

"You meant the death of her husband."

"If John Leider is dead."

"There is that, of course." Where was the conversation headed, and was it any danger to him? "How is old Jane holding up? Did you know she and I are the same age? Of course, I haven't had the benefit of a lifetime of creams, yearly injections of blender-reduced sheep glands, not to mention cosmetic surgery."

"You haven't suffered from the deprivations." It was flattery but not fabrication. He looked good and must have known it. Surely, he preferred his rugged good looks to Jane's milk-toast perfection.

"Is this where I say, 'Flattery will get you anything'?"

"I'll settle for conversation."

"Through which you expect insights into the disappearance of John Leider?"

"And now, admittedly, maybe, even into the murder of Gordon?"

"Curiosity killed the cat?" he ventured. "To which you respond, 'Satisfaction brought him back'?"

"I'm not all that convinced of reincarnation."

He got up, got the bottle and brought it back. He filled his glass and offered Carolyne the same. "I'm not very talkative when I drink alone," he coaxed when she hesitated.

She estimated the present alcohol content of her blood and weighed the benefits of playing detective against the horrors of a hangover at her age.

"So, what did Kyle tell you about our courtships of Jane Fernelli, so I won't cover the same ground?"

"You're mistaken if you imagine he was indiscreet," she said. He'd filled her glass; then, again, no one said she had to drink it. "You were mentioned only briefly, in the same sentence as Jenner Tyrol and Timms Mason."

"Simms," Roy corrected. "Simms Mason."

"Yes," Carolyne conceded. "My memory isn't as good as it once was. Not improved by...." She lifted her liquor.

He looked dubious but had nothing better to do. "Simms was a buyer of gemstones for Sterns. Now, he's in some jail in Sao Paulo, having bought at lower prices than he reported."

Carolyne filed that away and waited for more.

"Jenner was the youngster amongst us. A wife, like Jane, would have eaten him for breakfast, but he thought he had a chance with her. Maybe he did. His grandfather had lost a bundle in rubber, but there was an uncle, Lord Somebody, in England, who was luckier in finances, if not in love, whose wife died in childbirth. Jenner was scheduled to inherit and did—just last year. At the time, though, Jane and her father.... I presume Kyle mentioned Arthur?"

Carolyne nodded. She matched him swallow for swallow but let most of her liquor stay in her glass.

"The Fernelli reasoning, as I suspect, went, 'Why wait for Jenner to inherit, when we can work things out, here and now, by going with one of our other alternatives?'"

"You, Kyle, Simms, John Leider, or Gordon?"

His smile appreciated her return to a familiar theme. "Gordon wasn't in the running. Not then. Not ever."

"Because he was Lutheran?" Carolyne finished with that good possibility.

Roy nibbled: "Because he was poor. Church-mouse poor." There was no harm in fully following the bait: "I daresay the Fernellis might have overlooked his religion had there been any need to do so; the god of all capitalists is Mammon."

Carolyne didn't believe that camel through the eye of the needle generalization.

Roy, though, knew what he knew. "There was no money to be made by any Lutheran missionary, and what Gordon made as a guide was diddly-squat as far as what Arthur and Jane had their hearts set on. Arthur blew more cash in one night of 'friendly' poker than Gordon could expect to see in his lifetime."

"The Geornis were wealthy *and* Catholic."

"John Leider was wealthier, just as Catholic, and from a more socially acceptable background. The Leiders were in Manaus when the Fernellis were still looking for a tramp steamer out of Italy."

"And you?" Carolyne braved another swallow of Scotch. She always forgot how good it tasted. Its smokiness contrasted nicely with the equally enjoyable sweetness of the Curacao gone before it.

"Protestant, not nearly as wealthy as Kyle Georni, and from a family of U.S. mine owners who would have passed social muster far better before a few key coal veins petered out. In short, I didn't have a chance, knew I didn't but couldn't resist playing with the big boys."

"I got the impression that Kyle figures himself a winner in having lost."

"One, he's alive. Two, the odds are good you'll see him at supper. Neither can be said about John. Looking at things that way, I, too, consider myself a winner in having been a loser."

"Kyle never even mentioned Gordon having ever made a pass at Jane."

"Possibly he didn't know. I didn't until John appeared on my doorstep one evening and insisted I tell 'my friend' that Mrs. Leider was disturbed by his 'unwanted attentions'. I never did learn, in any detail, to what unwanted attentions John inferred. Gordon wasn't any more forthcoming."

"You and Gordon were good friends, then?" They hadn't seemed all that buddy-buddy the short while Carolyne had seen them together at the camp.

"'My friend' should be in quotation marks, although John assumed more than Gordon's interest in geology kept him hanging around me; when in fact, Gordon just saw more money in prospecting than in being a guide, just as he'd seen more money in being a guide than in being a missionary."

"You always give pointers to your potential competition?"

Old dame didn't miss an opening, but Roy had been mellowed

by the Scotch—a few lead-in drinks already under his belt even before Carolyne had arrived. "I've always been generous with anyone who wants to give prospecting a try. I remember how it was when I first got here, and John Leider acted as if I came expressly to steal all the area's goodies meant for him—Jane Fernelli, later, included among them. He made so many people angry with his attitude that singling out his wife as his potential killer, even now, is probably not seeing the forest for the trees."

Carolyne tried her some people naturally fill a silence method of interrogation; this time it worked.

"John's likability wasn't increased by his uncanny ability to search out and find the biggest and the best mineral caches," Roy said. "Those who dig for years, and get nothing but dirty, experience attacks of the green-eyed monster when someone goes down every time and comes up a winner. Even I, with enough formal background in geology to know John's finds were based on solid scientific foundation and hard work, felt short-changed on occasion, and I've made a better living than ninety-nine percent of those, like Gordon, who think a modicum of science and a landslide of luck are all that are needed."

He paused for breath and punctuated with Scotch. Did Carolyne see any of this as anything but prerequisite red herring? "Did Jane or Kyle mention Prince Mahoud Najheez?" he asked, and didn't Carolyne's eyes light up at that bit of exoticism?

"No."

"Of The Roundili Emirate?"

"No."

"With its bottomless bank vaults of petrodollars and its ruler's passion for emeralds?"

"No, Roy." She didn't want her information spoon-fed; she wanted it smorgasbord.

"He wants emeralds. He wants big ones. He's so prepared to get anything really good that the potential for profit sent John back into the field this last time."

"Apparently, John had at least five emeralds on him when he disappeared, over and above the one Melanie found. Anyway, so says Jane."

"If that's what Jane says, cross her off your list of suspects in the killing of her husband, unless she killed Gordon, too. She's way too greedy to have killed John and not gotten the emeralds. If she got them, by killing John and/or Gordon, she'd have sold them, no one the wiser." He could see the wheels spinning in the old babe's henna-rinsed head.

"She wouldn't have killed either herself." To Carolyne, Jane pushing through the jungle was ludicrous. "She would have hired someone."

Was Carolyne serious, or did she expect Roy to play Devil's Advocate? He said, "Why admit to you that she doesn't have the gemstones if that puts you into someday asking, 'How could you sell something to Prince Najheez that supposedly disappeared with your husband?'"

Carolyne wasn't likely to be privy to any sale of emeralds to Prince Najheez, by Jane or by anyone else. Nonetheless, the world had, more than once, proved itself proverbially "small", so why would Jane needlessly make such an obvious *faux pas*?

"While you think about that, ask if a geologist's wife wouldn't know better than to hit Gordon over the head with that particular rock."

Carolyne was ahead of him. "She couldn't know you'd be there to enlighten us. Therefore, she couldn't have anticipated and said to someone she hired, 'Be sure not to hit Gordon with a stone from the river, because that would look suspicious.'"

"I like things as clear-cut as this attempted murder of Richard Callahan by this ex-girlfriend of his."

"See that as clean-cut, do you?"

"You don't?" Did he have to ask?

Did Carolyne want to get into this? Should she presume the more input the better? Or, did a plethora of facts and opinions do anything but further muddy murky water? "The woman at one time left Richard Callahan to be Gordon Wentlock's lover," Carolyne said. "After Gordon dumped her, she headed back to Richard who no longer wanted anything to do with her. If

Richard had Gordon killed and wanted to make it look as if Susan tried to take them both out, same trip through, he could have drained his own brake fluid; hell hath no fury...and all of that."

"Mercy me! The complicated web we weave!" He shook his head and ran his fingers through his black hair. "So, why would she oblige Richard by showing up here?"

"I never said I had answers." She finished her Scotch and was afraid he'd refill it; as interesting as farther conversation might be, she knew her limits and came to her feet. "Thanks for the talk and the drinks."

He was getting a headache, and he needed a shower and a nap; so, what was she up to now in her going to a segment of curtain and giving it two hearty tugs? She turned back to Roy, who looked as if she were crazy, and said, "It wasn't hanging properly."

"Oh?" He sounded doubtful.

"A woman is better at telling. It's fine now." She was damned near babbling.

He gave her the benefit of the doubt. "Thanks."

"I'm off." Staying longer would accomplish nothing; her thought process was booze-induced deteriorating.

Her steps were uncertain. She had trouble finding the French doors; there seemed no access through the curtains she'd just realigned.

Gallantly, Roy helped and was no help at all. "Where in the hell is it?" He meant the means to her exit.

When "it" appeared right where it should be, right where Carolyne and Roy imagined they'd each looked for it at least ten times, it was a big surprise.

"I was beginning to think you'd yanked those curtains one too many times." He'd not lost his sense of humor when he'd found his headache. He held the breached curtain to one side while Carolyne stepped through into blinding brightness and a breeze suddenly sucked dry of all coolness and moisture.

"I'm definitely drunk." She thought she made that admission

exclusively to herself.

Nonetheless, Roy responded through the now-dropped curtain, "Welcome to the club!"

With difficulty, Carolyne divined the shortest route back to her room and took it. Her fingertips dragged along windows and walls for balance.

Suddenly, a woman with very red eyes stared at her from less than an inch away. The woman was she, at the sink, three aspirins death-gripped in her right hand, and she had no idea of how she'd got there. The bathroom was filled with steam from water about to overflow the tub.

In the minute it took to decide whether she should stop the water, or take the pills, there was a waterfall of soap bubbles onto the floor.

When god-only-knew-how, she managed to turn off the water, she, then, tried to recall whatever the law of physics that promised: Enter the tub, and there will be even more water and soap cascaded onto the floor. Until she figured it out, she returned to the sink and swallowed the aspirins.

The next mystery: Why was the water level lower in the tub when she returned to it? And what was that obscene sucking sound?

"Overflow hole!" She wasn't as far gone as she'd thought and watched the small opening, once completely covered, in not having been designed for the deluge she'd fed it, now manage to function better with the water turned off. Carolyne's only complaint: "You really must learn to drink without slurping."

She adjusted the temperature with a combination of concentration and fumbling dexterity that raised the plug and added cold water from the tap.

Finally, she was in. And wasn't it heavenly? No doubt about it: her efforts had been worth it.

"Now, just don't fall asleep, Carolyne," she instructed, her eyes shut. "If you do, you'll probably drown. And wouldn't everyone have a field day trying to figure out the way and how of that?"

CHAPTER EIGHT

The bath relaxed her. Her nap, on her bed, afterwards, surprised her it not leaving her with a headache or any other expected attributes of a hangover. It was like her younger days
when she could drink everyone under the table and still get up
at the crack of dawn to hunt plants in steamy jungles, on misty
mountaintops, at foggy seashores, or on arid plains. However,
another bout of drinking, any time soon, would tempt fate, and
was, thus, to be avoided at all cost.

For once, she was satisfied with what she saw in the mirror.
She wouldn't look much better unless someone chanced upon
the Fountain of Youth and gave her a swallow.

She twisted a henna-dyed lock of hair but gave up when it
refused realignment.

Although the younger, Roy looked far the worst for wear
when they met at the top of the stairs. His squint produced
wrinkles at the corners of his eyes and indicated a headache
not yet controlled by the handful of aspirin he'd fed it. He'd
nearly decided to forget the evening meal and, now, wished he
had. Carolyne's bubbly, liquor-unaffected "Hello!" mocked his
misery.

The outburst of racket downstairs was so sufficiently muffled
by the poor acoustics of the curved stairwell that neither Roy
nor Carolyne got the full blast of it until they were around the
bend and had a clear view of a bloodied Charles on the parquet
floor, Melanie kneeling beside him; her handkerchief dabbed
his split lip. Felix struggled noisily to be free of Teddy who held

him in a hammerlock.

When Felix spotted Carolyne, his expression was downright nasty. "You dirty-minded, foul-mouthed bitch!" No doubt to whom that was directed, and it nailed her to the spot. No way would she get nearer to someone so obviously out to get her. "Spread any more malicious lies about Margaret and me to the cops, or to anyone else, and I'll have your black heart for dinner!"

He wrenched forcefully, combined it with a torque of his torso, and ripped free of Teddy's grasp.

Carolyne was ready to backtrack. Long ago, she'd learned to calculate odds and retreat, no matter how ungracefully, if they were stacked against her.

Felix, though, headed for the door. His last-minute about-face focused his—I'll hate you forever—glare directly on her. "I've warned you; pay heed!"

Then, he was gone, the screen door slammed behind him.

"Someone has been drinking!" Teddy still smelled Felix's rancid breath.

Carolyne thought he meant her; Roy thought he meant him. Carolyne realized her mistake first. "Rodrigo said Felix started drinking in town this morning."

"And kept right on, by the looks of it," Teddy judged. "Whatever was that all about, anyway?"

Outside, a Jeep engine revved.

"I hope this doesn't mean another auto accident on the Tlesselan Grade." Roy's head was better in the aftermath.

"He definitely shouldn't be driving." Carolyne thought her concern magnanimous, under the circumstances.

Tires burned rubber and splattered gravel; Felix had an inflated opinion of his driving capabilities.

No one risked getting run over in any kind of attempt to stop him as Jeep sounds retreated into the distance.

Teddy helped a groaning Charles to his feet.

Charles held Melanie's handkerchief to his sore lip. "The man is stark-raving mad!"

"Does anyone have a clue?" Teddy had been thoroughly engrossed in attempts to break up the fisticuffs and had missed parts of the verbal exchange.

Melanie had seen and heard a lot more. Her inquiring glance, first at Charles, then at Carolyne, demanded an explanation.

"If I could see Charles and Melanie alone for a couple of minutes." Carolyne made it more command than request; she had no intention of spreading the story of Felix and Margaret's adultery any farther than necessary.

"By all means, have a conference." Roy was delighted by whatever new reduction of chatter; the noise hurt his head.

"More secrets?" Teddy was less gracious in being left out—once again.

"Melanie can fill you in, later, Teddy," Carolyne wasn't sure that would happen, but she wanted this over and done.

The selected group sequestered in the library, behind closed doors.

Melanie waited. She didn't have to point out the reference Felix had made regarding her mother.

Carolyne took a deep breath and began the tawdry tale of Felix, Margaret, *Seaman's Roost*, and Charles as unwilling witness. She followed with how Felix might have killed Gordon to sabotage the expedition's chances to give Cornelius even more, albeit posthumously, glory. "To cover his ass, Felix could have stolen the photographs of Gordon's body and substituted the blank digital chip."

"Damn!" Melanie couldn't believe how anything could be so askew, yet appear so logical. It was a jigsaw whose pieces could be arranged two different ways, and, each time, come up with a recognizable picture. She wrung her hands, paced the floor, and repeated, "Damn!"

Carolyne launched into her reasons for confiding, that morning, the same to Rodrigo Barco. She admitted how Rodrigo thought Felix had some kind of alternative story with equal merit.

"I'm sorry, Melanie, but I did see your mother and Felix."

Charles' nose quit bleeding. "I made every effort to spare you from hearing about it."

"Oh, Uncle Charles! How wrong you and Carolyne have been about mother and Felix!" If Felix had decided none of this was anyone's business, Melanie disagreed with him in thinking, at this point, that Carolyne and Charles couldn't be trusted with the truth. In fact, keeping it from them had resulted in this mix-up. Although, Felix probably didn't even know she knew the truth, in that her parents certainly never gave any indication they knew she'd periodically eavesdropped on their private conversations.

"If you tell me to rely upon Felix to fill me in, when you know something, I'll scream," Carolyne threatened.

"That probably would be best," Melanie hated to admit. "Relying upon Felix, I mean."

"Did Felix's beating up on your Uncle Charles appear to you as if he's ready to discuss any of this?" Charles didn't think so.

Carolyne didn't think so, either. "Why don't we proceed to next best?"

In case Melanie missed the point, Charles spelled it out for her: "Melanie, tell us."

In for a penny, in for a pound: "My father knew about Felix and mother meeting every Tuesday at that hotel," Melanie told them.

"Seaman's Roost?" Charles wanted to make sure they talked about the same thing.

"Yes," Melanie confirmed.

"I can't believe he knew and didn't do anything about it." Carolyne may not have known Cornelius all that well, in the end, but she knew him well enough to know some things.

"There was nothing romantic about the meetings," Melanie proceeded.

"What do you imagine they were doing there?" Carolyne insisted Melanie be realistic, painful as that was.

Charles responded to Melanie's pause, "Well?"

"The hotel manager was Burt Evans, Denise Tenner's lover."

Carolyne didn't see how that explained anything. Who were Burt and Denise anyway?

"Denise Tenner was Felix's sister," Melanie supplemented.

"I didn't know Felix had a sister." Charles didn't see where any of this went, either.

"Did you know he had a mother and father?"

Carolyne recognized sarcasm when she heard it. "Melanie, please!"

"Burt and Denise both had AIDS."

"AIDS?" Charles remained frustrated. "Whatever does AIDS have to do with this?"

"RZ11-2."

This was another case of spoon-feeding, and Carolyne was having none of it. "Do, please, give us connections, so we can stop pulling teeth."

"RZ11-2 was an experimental drug at Crystin Companies that showed initial success against AIDS in monkeys; everyone thought it might prove the major breakthrough in providing the cure."

Carolyne racked her brain but had left Crystin Companies for JanEx by that time.

"It wasn't ready for human testing, but Felix knew about it and was desperate over his sister's deteriorating condition. He begged mother to make RZ11-2 available to Burt and Denise. She talked it over with father, and they verified everything Felix told them about the failure of all the then available drugs to do men or women much good. Mom had access to RZ11-2, and she managed to smuggle out weekly dosages. After mom died, dad continued until it proved, three years before Crystin Companies' official confirmation that the drug had proved no significant dent in combating the virus in humans."

"Dear God!" Charles felt like an old fool.

Carolyne was furious. "Why didn't Felix just say so?"

To Melanie, the possibilities were obvious. "He couldn't know how either of you would react to the illegality of what was done."

Carolyne didn't buy it. "I refuse to believe I come across, even to Felix, as that inconsiderate or uncaring."

"He still sees you as the spurned woman, and Uncle Charles as the overlooked brother. If what had been done had ever gotten out, or if it ever got out even now, there could be legal repercussions—for the company, for my parents' good names, for Felix as an accomplice. An investigation won't take good intentions, or humanitarian motivation, as valid reasons for violating FDA rules and regulations."

How much of this had Felix had to tell Rodrigo Barco to offset what Carolyne had passed on? No wonder Felix was furious with her and Charles.

"If not to cover his murder of Gordon, why would he steal the photos and replace them with blanks?" Carolyne was interested in Melanie's rationalization of Melanie's accusations of that.

"I didn't say he didn't kill Gordon and steal the photos; he probably did if his twisted logic blames my parents for the failure of RZ11-2 in the death of his sister. I'm just saying your theory of motivation doesn't include his sleeping with my mother."

Kyle rapped on the door. "Shall I hold supper?"

Carolyne let him inside. "I imagine you're apprised of this evening's little drama." His silence coaxed more. "Also, I assume Rodrigo Barco keeps you enough up to date so you know why the scenario occurred."

"Rodrigo and I go back a long way." His answer was appropriately vague.

"I've filled in Carolyne and Charles on my idea as to Felix's outburst," Melanie said. If that wasn't specific enough, "I overheard my parents discuss my mother's weekly meetings with Felix."

"Rodrigo suggested to Felix that he might be more candid with some of you, but...." Kyle shrugged.

"Somewhat of a mess." How else could Carolyne see it?

"Rodrigo has a cousin with AIDS. It's made him particularly sensitive, and he can be counted upon to have been exceptionally discreet in whatever his inquiries to validate Felix's story,"

Kyle assured.

"I hope so." Carolyne saw a domino effect that could involve the U.S. Federal Food and Drug Administration.

"I've sent someone to make sure Felix's inebriation doesn't get him into more mischief," Kyle said. "By the way, Richard has regained consciousness."

"Marvelous!" Melanie expressed the all-around consensus on both points.

"Any news of Susan Delaney?" Carolyne went three for three.

"If she's in the city, Rodrigo or Jean-Michael will find her."

Carolyne wasn't hungry, but her appetite improved when supper provided a convenient diversion. If Teddy, Roy, Galin, and the two cameramen, Hal and Jacob, were excluded from a piece of the puzzle, they didn't press for inclusion. If there was no sign of Alexandra, no one asked about her, either—nor was her whereabouts volunteered.

"Really delicious!" Initially, Carolyne had found *feijoada*, Brazil's national dish of bubbling black beans, pork, and sausage, a bit intimidating.

"Have you tasted the delicious *vatapá*?" Melanie poked her spoon at a dollop of the shrimp stew that was flavored with coconut and palm oil.

Galin was so much taken by the *batidas*, potent drinks of homemade whiskey and fruit juice, that Carolyne was amazed how unaffected he seemed by his overindulgence when he joined her at breakfast the next morning. Ah, youth!

She ate bacon and eggs and wondered, late out of bed again, where everyone was.

"Rodrigo Barco has requested our presence." Galin's voice was even more raspy than usual. "It seems his men picked up this statuesque American woman, named Susan Delaney; our second and third opinions wanted."

Carolyne pushed her fork to one side.

"Said, 'Finish your breakfasts, first, though.'" Galin stole the last of her bacon. "Are we finished?"

Carolyne couldn't stand people who, uninvited, scavenged other people's food; Galin, though, somehow remained charming. Even the way he chewed was winning. Carolyne was more determined to see one of his videos. If he was naughty-boy appealing to her, he must send prepubescent teens into cardiac arrest. She drank the last of her freshly squeezed orange juice.

"Shall we proceed, immediately, to our civic duties, or detour long enough to let Richard thank you humbly for saving his ass?" Galin asked.

"You think he's up to humble?" He hadn't acted humble at the time.

"He might not tell you, but he told me, this very morning, that he's convinced he'd be far worse today if you hadn't stopped with a helping hand. Are you of a mind to take advantage? Any aspirations for a career in rock and roll?"

She wasn't convinced Richard had a gracious bone in his body.

That went to show that a book couldn't always be judged by its cover, or by a superficial skimming of its pages. "I'll send flowers once you're off somewhere where you can't pick your own bouquet during three minutes of leaning over any balustrade," he said, propped up in bed, his head in a bandage as skillfully wrapped as any Elton John turban. "You scheduled for any future plant forages into Antarctica?"

She had a retort that referenced his thank god inability to torch an ice field, but she refused to come across less gracious than he did. "I'm just glad you're okay."

"I promised Carolyne free tickets and backstage passes to my next concert." Galin stole the last of the bacon off Richard's infirmary tray with the same aplomb he'd exercised in robbing Carolyne of hers.

Carolyne would decide, after hearing an example of Galin's singing, whether his offer was reward or punishment.

"Shall I tell you that Carolyne and I are, this very minute, off to see Susan Delaney?" Galin said.

"They know about Susan?" Richard sounded surprised.

"Don't they tell you invalids anything? Carolyne spotted you two on Manaus streets yesterday."

"I was in the *Amazonas* when you were on your way out." Carolyne didn't add how she'd immediately given chase, then and there.

"So, thanks to Carolyne, we would have caught the she-vixen even if Susan had succeeded in successfully accomplishing her mischief in draining your brake fluid." Galin heaped praise. "And, I would have learned, eventually, why you, once again, missed a shoot."

"I had every intention to be back in time for the shoot," Richard assured.

"Hal, Jacob, and I improvised, but I doubt it'll meet your standards. So, hurry and get well, because burn-spots turn green pretty fast in this fecund environment, and it would be ungracious to set fire to more jungle when your savior is so dead set against it."

Richard was prepared to squeeze more acres out of Kyle, if it came down to that. However, he said, "The doctor says I should be up in no time."

"Until then, we must be off to turn the key on Susan's jail lock." Galin pantomimed the incarcerating turnkey and provided a voice-over, "Clink!"

"You said she's the one who drained my brake fluid?" Richard held them awhile longer.

"You team up with the most interesting people," Galin said. "All the women I know wouldn't likely know a drip pan from a bed pan."

"Confidentially, I'm surprised Susan knows the difference," Richard marveled.

"She only needed money to hire someone who knew the difference," Carolyne reminded. "Like Jane who wouldn't have had to set foot outside her villa to have had her husband and/or Gordon snuffed."

"Ah, the deductive reasoning of the scientific mind!" Galin congratulated. "Carolyne is right. A few dollars here, a few dollars there, and good-bye, Dicky and/or Gordon!"

"Isn't, 'I won't call my director Dick,' somewhere in our contract?"

"I think Carolyne and I must shove off now, Richard. Do your best to get well in our absence." He took Carolyne's arm and headed for the door.

"Mrs. Santire!" Richard brought them to a stop.

"So formal, Richard?" Galin chastised. "Surely, 'Carolyne' is more apropos for the woman who saved your life."

Richard ignored him. "I don't forget a favor, Mrs. Santire. I owe you."

For whatever the reason, Carolyne didn't find his promise enticing. "You owe me nothing, Mr. Callahan. I would have done the same for anybody."

"Richard, though, isn't just 'anybody', are you Richard?" Galin's smile was charming; his tone was not. "He's very, very special. Just ask him."

Carolyne waited until they were outside and almost to the Jeep which Galin had requisitioned from the motor pool. "Do you like Richard Callahan, Galin?"

"God, no, Carolyne! What's to like about a short, ugly, egotistical prima donna? I do happen to think he's one of the best video directors in the business. Garret Tilbee and Dillon Crane might be a shade better, but who's to know?"

They were driving off when Melanie and Teddy spotted them, and Melanie waved.

"Is that a happy couple, or what?" Galin's query dripped sarcasm. "Engaged, while at the same time her eyelashes bat like butterflies in heat, and her look is more come on than that of any I've had from a hot-pants groupie."

The subject wasn't one with which Carolyne was comfortable. "If I understood mating rituals, I'd be in anthropology, not bio-sci."

"You're not going to tell me to be careful? Charles did. Roy did."

"Why should I be redundant, then? Although, you should probably be careful."

"She flirted with Gordon Wentlock, didn't she? Suddenly, old Gordon hit the dirt."

"I've yet to hear anyone prove even a tenuous connection. Not that it hasn't been tried, either."

"Fascinating: one man drops dead in the middle of nowhere, and everyone for miles around has a motive for murder."

Carolyne gave him that much. "Yes, fascinating, indeed."

"Richard: Gordon stole his girl. Susan: Gordon used her and threw her aside. Kyle: Gordon got his sister pregnant. Alexandra: Gordon left the incriminating bun in her oven. Roy: Gordon competed for his woman and for his minerals. Jane: Gordon made unwanted advances...."

His litany told the extent of conjecture rampant in conversations other than those in which Carolyne had personally participated. "How do you know Gordon made advances toward Jane Leider?"

"The walls have ears. Servants have ears. Servants have mouths. Mouths chatter. Other people's ears hear. Other people's mouths talk. Ad infinitum. Ad nauseam. Come on, Carolyne, of the can I see you for a few minutes in private, do you think you're the only lodestone who attracts information? Hell, any of us would have to live in a vacuum not to get bombarded by the constant gossip, innuendo, back-biting, and whispers, about you, the spurned woman who doesn't want the expedition to succeed and give Cornelius Ditherson more glory; about Charles, the jealous brother who equally begrudges Cornelius additional limelight; about Felix.... I'm still working on Felix, convinced it has something to do with the mystery woman, Margaret Ditherson. You wouldn't enlighten me on that point, would you?"

"Margaret isn't any longer suspected to be in anyway directly connected to Gordon's murder." Of that, Carolyne was convinced. Indirectly was another matter.

"Okay, be that way." His sensuously sexy, full lips did a very effective pout. "But don't think everyone else will be as discreet...about Felix; or about Teddy who figured Gordon was out to snatch moneybags Melanie...or about Melanie who teased Gordon without realizing the consequences. The list goes on. Even common servants, here at the ranch, are past samplers of Gordon's promiscuity which knew no social or economic bounds."

Galin's good looks and winning smile had worked overtime. "Now, if I were one of those gets as gives people, I'd insist you come clean about Felix, but I don't play the game nearly as seriously as I suspect you do. So, I'll give you another free tidbit, although stop me if you've heard it."

His pause was so extended that she thought he'd changed his mind. His smile, attractive and infuriating, invited her to beg—just a little.

"So?" That was the extent of her intended supplication.

"So, all of this crap about Alexandra wanting Gordon's baby is just that—crap. I hear she was on the abortionist's table when her obviously more Catholic brother broke down the door. Seems the little lady discovered Gordon was a philandering son of a bitch, and she didn't want any long-living mementos. Another repercussion: at least one unsuccessful attempt to throw herself down the stairs. When she fainted, upon hearing the bastard was dead, it was from pure joy. When she raves how she wants free of her brother, it's because he's determined to make her suffer the consequences."

He pushed the accelerator to the floorboard and headed the Jeep up the Tlesselan Grade. Where Richard had gone off the road seemed already reclaimed by jungle. Given respite from the ravages of man, Mother Nature could have the whole area reclaimed in a few million years.

"Where's Alexandra now?" Carolyne wondered.

"At her place, about six miles to the south. Under house arrest; guards and a nurse on twenty-four hour duty; a helicopter on the ready to fetch Dr. Seln at any sign of delivery or difficulty."

"Anything else you'd like to tell me?" He was a prime information source, and she was greedy for more.

"How can I know, if I don't know what you know, in order to

glean the difference?"

"Did *you* have reason to kill Gordon? Remember that the least likely is usually the guiltiest."

"How about my having committed the murder just as a mental and physical exercise? The Leopold-Loeb Syndrome, murder for the pure sake of murder, might fascinate me."

Carolyne chilled. "I expected something about revenge for Gordon screwing up the shoot on your *Amaz'n Galin* videos."

"Of course you did, but I figure a Yale psych major should provide something more imaginative."

"You majored in psychology—at Yale?"

"Surprised?" He'd played her; the handsome bastard.

"You tell me."

"Okay. You're surprised. I'm not surprised you're surprised. Rock stars aren't supposed to have grade points enough for Yale, and who'd chuck that for rock-and-roll stardom? Right? I did, not all that fond of being stuck in an educational display case, pinned on corkboard, and nailed with a this is it white-bread label."

He'd caught her in her own prejudices, and she didn't like the inflexibility of thought he'd spotted but she'd not recognized.

He interrupted the ensuing silence. "I wouldn't rely upon my immersion in behavioral sciences for any insights into the character of the killer, though. To say, 'I majored in psychology', is a misnomer in that I opted for a singing career before I was subjected to any in-depth probing of the criminal mind. Besides which, I'm not nearly as interested in a solution as I suspect you are. That's because someone who murdered once can murder again, and why should I aggravate him or her to murder me? I still have a lifetime ahead of me."

His insinuation: Carolyne, my dear, you're over the hill and headed down the other side of the mountain, most of your life behind you. What real loss to you, or to anyone, if you drop dead, or are dropped dead, tomorrow? Your advanced age earns you the right to meddle and the right to suffer the consequences.

"I care about Felix's motives," he said, "and about the mysterious Margaret, whom you and Charles somehow linked to Felix, to his ultimate chagrin, only insofar as no one sees that as curiosity too rampant for my own good. Exploration, as you very well know, can be a very dangerous vocation; which is why I'm who I am, and why you are who you are."

She took his warning as not necessarily based upon precognition. He'd said nothing, insinuated nothing, which established him as anything other than an innocent conduit of information. If he saw that she meddled at a higher level and that she prepared to scale even more precarious heights, she saw that, too, and just as easily knew she could be letting herself in for trouble.

By comparison to her ride to police headquarters, her identification of a teary Susan Delaney was anticlimactic. Susan neither denied who she was, nor her meeting with Richard. She did deny, and continued to do so, that she'd drained the brake fluid from Richard's car. She insisted she had never seen his car. She greeted Galin as someone sympathetic amid terrain, until then, viewed as completely alien, and she asked him how she could have known where Richard's car was, let alone what it looked like. And, what, after all, did she know about car-things, like brake fluid?

In fact, the police had mapped Susan's whereabouts since her arrival in Manaus. At five foot eleven, long legs, fantastic figure and a striking mane of auburn hair, she wasn't hard to miss. Had a career in music depended entirely upon looks, she would have been a runaway success.

"We've verified that she called Richard from Mexico City, late last night," Rodrigo Barco briefed Carolyne; Galin had been left to fraternize with the prisoner. "A maid at the ranch verified that Richard got the call. The cameramen verified that Richard left them at the burn site with instructions that they were to remain there until his return. A cab driver verified the time he picked Susan up at the airport and dropped her at her hotel. A hotel desk clerk verified when she checked in. A bellboy was with her all of the way to her room. After she tipped him, she returned to the lobby in the same elevator he did. She went out the front door at approximately the same time you followed Richard out the side door. Where they met wasn't far enough away for her to have detoured to his car, let alone found it, drained it of brake fluid, then made the meeting when you said she did. What's more, she made it back to the hotel, ten minutes later—her meeting with Richard short-lived and not too satisfactory. To soothe her nerves, she went to the beauty parlor."

"That provided three more hours of supervision." Carolyne spoke from recent experience.

"An hour and a half, to be exact."

Carolyne had forgotten that Susan hadn't quite the state of disrepair Carolyne had managed after weeks in the jungle. Susan at her worst probably wouldn't have needed three hours of maintenance.

"After the beauty parlor, she went to dinner at the hotel restaurant. Witnesses a-plenty, once again. By the time she finished eating, Richard's car had been drained of its brake fluid and had plowed into that banana tree."

Galin appeared at the doorway on the far side of the outer office and weaved through the assortment of desks and policemen. Rodrigo watched his progress and motioned him to join them.

Galin took the chair next to Carolyne. "Susan insists she's here to get Richard back. She realizes she loves him. More likely, she realizes he has the clout to stymie any kind of career for her in the music business, and she's out to make amends. She admits that jobs, even sexual liaisons, have been slim pickings on the rock circuit, since she's gotten on Richard's bad side."

"That's pretty much her story," Rodrigo confirmed. "Unless we can find someway to see where she squeezed a few more minutes out of a schedule witnessed all along the way, I don't see how we're going to prove any differently."

The phone rang.

Rodrigo answered, listened, and pushed a hold button. Line five for you, Mrs. Santire. The next office is available if you'd like to take it there."

Curious, Carolyne made the trip next door and pulled the door shut behind her. Through the partition of window that divided her from them, she could see Rodrigo and Galin in conference. She pushed the fifth button, all aglow, on the telephone base. "This is Carolyne Santire."

"This is Kyle Georni."

"Kyle? Anything wrong?"

"Just passing on a bit of information I thought you might like to act on. A spy tells me Felix is at the floating bar of the *Tropical*. Drinking ice tea. If he stays sober, it might be an opportunity to mend a few fences. Or, are you interested?"

"Of course, I'm interested."

"I thought you might be. How are things there?"

He'd get a report directly from Rodrigo, but Carolyne obliged with a preview. "Seems Susan Delaney has an alibi that accounts for way too much of her time for her to have meddled with Richard's car."

"Could she have hired someone to do it for her?"

"As far as we know, an accomplice remains a viable option, but, at the moment not to be proven. There's been no obvious contact with anyone who may be in on it with her." Carolyne figured it required someone in Manaus before Susan arrived, ideally someone who knew the terrain. It was unlikely Susan would have been able to drum up any such person on short notice, without prior knowledge of his credentials and trustworthiness. The shooting of the *Amaz'n Galin* videos had occurred far east of Manaus, so it seemed unlikely she'd been in contact with any of the city's underworld characters on that time through Brazil, unless she'd been introduced to them when she'd headed off for fun and games with Gordon.

"Well, if she's guilty of anything, count on Rodrigo to get to the bottom of it," Kyle offered by way of reassurance.

"Talk to you later, and thanks for the location report on Felix."

"Ciao!"

She hung up and returned to the adjoining office, followed by a police detective who announced he had something he thought

Rodrigo should take a look at.

Rodrigo looked, swore: "Damn!" and slammed the object of his exasperation onto his desk top so Carolyne and Galin had a good look. It was a Rio de Janeiro newspaper, turned to an inside page, where one article, with accompanying photo and headline, had been outlined in red by some diligent bureaucrat with for the eyes of Rodrigo Barco primarily in mind. The picture was of a very dead and much mauled Gordon Wentlock. The headline queried:

MAN OR MANEATER KILLS GUIDE?

CHAPTER NINE

"Do you mind...?" Carolyne asked Galin who'd given her a ride.

"Let me guess." The Rio Negro's blackish, nutrient-rich water flowed by the *Tropical Hotel* toward a meeting with the umber water of the upper Amazon; the two rivers, each two miles wide, would visibly flow side by side for the fifty miles it would take to complete a final and murky meld. "You want to speak to Felix privately." He nodded toward Felix at a table in the hotel's floating bar; Felix was engrossed, in the way of a heavy drinker, with the glass on the table before him. "You know, Carolyne, if you always insist upon these exploratory, but private, tête-à-têtes, no one is likely to have a clue if anything happens to you? 'How should I know?' each and every one of us will say. 'She didn't share what she rooted out, did she?'"

"Nevertheless...." She requested Galin's cooperation.

He fished between his muscled, bare skin and his partially buttoned bush jacket for a folded newspaper. "I'll read about Gordon's murder."

"You lifted that from the police station!" Carolyne was as appalled as she was impressed.

"There were extra copies on that desk in the outer office, weren't there?" His naughty-boy innocence was another example of conscious sex appeal. "I didn't think I should have to wait until official distribution put the paper on the Manaus newsstands tomorrow."

"Let me borrow it." She went farther: "Please."

"Take. Take. Take. Did no one ever tell you, Carolyne, that a giver benefits more, psychologically?"

"I promise to keep that in mind."

"I could order a *batida*, but I wouldn't want to be left to drink more than one. I've no desire to collide with a banana tree."

"I'll make sure you only have to drink the one."

He slapped the purloined paper against her palm with the precision of a nurse delivering a scalpel to an operating surgeon.

"Thank you, Galin."

"My pleasure, Carolyne." He bowed gallantly. His crisp about-face did any West Pointer proud, as did his march out of earshot.

Carolyne wasted no time in approaching her target. "Felix, why didn't you tell me your sister died of AIDS?" Even if the bar had been full, her modulated voice would have kept her question contained within their shared allotted space.

His looks wouldn't win many admirers in a singles' bar. His eyes were bloodshot. The grow-back of singed hair was stubby and uneven on his face and head. "Go away!" No hint of alcoholic slur. "What do we have to talk about, anyway?" He turned his glass and left fingerprints in its condensed moisture.

A waiter appeared with the swiftness for which the hotel staff was renowned. Carolyne ordered ice tea to compare it with what Felix had.

"I knew that bastard Rodrigo wouldn't keep his mouth shut. All this bullshit about a cousin with ADIS was a play to milk information from an already falling-down drunk with diarrhea of the mouth."

"Rodrigo Barco didn't tell me. Melanie did."

"Melanie?"

"Margaret and Cornelius' daughter, remember her? Little children have big ears."

"If that's true, remind me to apologize to Rodrigo."

Carolyne's tea arrived. No mistaking it for anything but what Felix had, right down to its slice of lemon and sprig of mint.

"Some of us wonder if you blamed Cornelius and Margaret

when RZ11-2 didn't prove the miracle cure it was made out to be."

"You're joking!" His hazel eyes sparked.

"You admit, the drug was flawed."

"I begged Margaret for the dosage. Didn't eavesdropping Melanie catch that part? Margaret didn't come to me looking for guinea pigs."

"The death of a loved one sometimes distorts logic."

"Margaret Ditherson was a saint. Cornelius Ditherson was a saint; he didn't miss a delivery after Margaret died. Not that I would have blamed him, because Margaret would have lived if she hadn't played Good Samaritan." He dared Carolyne to deny it. "They risked a helluva lot to give my sister and Burt a try at some quality time. I'm angry that anyone, Melanie included, should think me so small minded an ingrate to misconstrue their good intentions to such an extent that I'm plotting murder all of these years later." He drank his tea.

"Objectivity is difficult for some of us in the absence of facts."

"My sister's death is none of your business. It's none of Melanie's business. It's none of Rodrigo Barco's business, and I'll forever regret I was too drunk not to stand up to his brow-beating."

"You'd rather have it whispered that you and Margaret were meeting at *Seaman's Roost*, every Tuesday, for a roll in the sheets? That's hardly any reward for the woman who risked so much."

"It was either risk her reputation with the truth, or risk it with a lie."

"You didn't figure I'd be sympathetic?"

"You left when Cornelius married Margaret. How can I ever be sure of anything involving you and the memory of those two?"

"Cornelius gave you the impression that I was vindictive because he jilted me for another woman?"

"Cornelius never bad-mouthed anybody to me, including

you. The facts: you and he were a team envied by everyone in our business; he married another woman; you deserted him and Crystin Companies for the competition."

"I see." Actually, she didn't. She'd handled a traumatic time in her life in an exemplary manner. That others saw it differently was hurtful, insulting, and uncomplimentary.

Felix sat back and crossed his arms; it was a defensive posture any reliable psychiatrist would identify. "Then again, maybe I'm wrong. I've been the target for my share of unfounded rumor. Have you heard the one about poor Felix, chained behind a desk when he so desperately wanted to be in the field? That one is more than a little ragged from overuse, and it's true—to the deceptive extent all good rumor is based upon a trace of fact. 'The field' sounds so exotic: Amazon Basin, African Rift, Gobi Desert. I wanted it, like someone wants a gallon of ice cream at one sitting, knowing it isn't necessarily the best thing for one's health. I idolized Cornelius Ditherson, and for him I would have sat on my ass, at my desk, for the rest of my life. If this trip proved anything it's that Cornelius was right to keep me home, and I was right to know he was right to keep me there. I've hated this from the beginning: the heat, the humidity, the bugs, the claustrophobic vegetation, the people. As for Gordon's death, the jaguar, the cannibals, the whoever it was who kidnapped Charles and Teddy, the downed bridge, the river crossing: all of those were overkill. I knew the minute I stepped off the plane, the heat a hammer blow, that Cornelius and I had been right all along. Had I had any sense, I would have begged off, then and there. The only thing that kept me hanging in was the hope that I might actually make a contribution to Cornelius' memory. I had visions of being the one to stoop over in some jungle clearing and proclaim, *'Lygodium cornelius!'* Yet, all you saw was an out of shape old man, jealous of Cornelius' accomplishments, jealous of Cornelius' success in bed, tottering around this hell with the sole purpose of gumming up the works. Am I alone in seeing that as ironic?"

"If I was wrong, I apologize." She thought that was big of

her, and she didn't understand or appreciate the mocking curl of his upper lip.

"If? You see how you're not convinced, even now? No more than I'm convinced you're not a vindictive old biddy who blames two failed marriages on Cornelius dumping you for Margaret." His laugh wasn't pleasant.

She was about to show him how objective she could be if given sufficient input; her 'if' had been out of habit, not the Freudian slip he imagined.

However, Felix retained control of the conversation. "When Margaret succumbed to my pleas for RZ11-2, Cornelius in agreement, they had my loyalty for life, because they helped me help the most important person in my life. I never knew my father; my mother was a die-hard alcoholic whose liver finally gave out; but my sister, a typical, street-wise 'broad' who even embarrassed me, when at her sluttiest, was someone whose unselfish sacrifices catapulted me out of the slums and gave me everything decent I ever had. Every trick she ever turned, every illegal act she performed, including every drunk she ever rolled, contributed to my 'Felix's School Fund'. She danced nights as a stripper and worked days in a greasy spoon, as a waitress, just to see me in school with spending money. She made herself old before her time, not to mention vulnerable to the AIDS virus."

The waiter appeared to ask if they wanted another round. Carolyne said, "Yes." She wanted the conversation to continue.

"Give me a double Scotch." He amended so fast it seemed part of the same sentence, "Make it another tea."

He drained the last of what he had so the waiter could take the glass. He drew geometric designs in the puddle that remained on the table.

"'Too good to be true!' That's what Denise told me when she found Burt, after a lifetime spent getting me through school, neither extra time nor extra money having ever been available for her to form any kind of permanent personal relationships. Burt was equally tired of the rat race, equally disillusioned, equally sure his life was over, because he was too old and too used to succeed in bars, in the back alleys, or on the streets. They met. They clicked. They were happy—for a time. Burt managed *Seaman's Roost*, and Denise helped him make it uniquely theirs. They swore they could 'make the motel one of a kind' if they could ever manage the funds to entice the low life owner to sell. I was going to give them the title on their third anniversary, except Denise collapsed on the street two months before the party."

The waiter brought their tea; neither drank any.

"They got the bad news and then got on with their lives. No accusations. No blame. No, 'It was you!' 'No, you!' It could have been either. It could have been both."

"I'm sorry."

"Not nearly as sorry as I am, especially when Margaret's death caught us all unaware. We knew Denise and Burt were dying. I knew, no matter how they insisted RZ11-2 was helping that it wasn't helping enough—if at all—to save them. But Margaret? Healthy, vibrant Margaret?" He wiped his eyes. "If she'd wrecked her car before delivery of the drug, that day, instead of after, the RZ11-2 would have been found in her car; the implications for her, for Cornelius, for Crystin Companies, could have been disastrous. RZ11-2 was an experimental drug, not for human consumption." He visibly shuddered. "Three people in my life; Margaret died, and there were two. When Denise died...." To have completed the already known rundown would have been superfluous. "Yet, there are people, to this day, who think I would do something to keep a dead Cornelius out of the spotlight. Bullshit!"

Yes, Carolyne admitted that was once the case, but not anymore, as far as she was concerned, especially if, "You're responsible for this, aren't you?" She produced the folded newspaper that, until then, had been scrunched down in the seat beside her.

He didn't have to see it to know what it was. "You think so?"

"You knew someone was after the film, and you didn't trust Melanie to hold it. You stole her film chip of the corpse the very night she accused you of doing just that on your watch."

"Fears that proved right, didn't they? Firstly, when I thought she'd lost my unused substitute chip in the river. More so, when she turned it over to Rodrigo Barco with her aren't I clever attitude. Clever? She doesn't have half the smarts of her mother or father. Do you have any inkling why what she did was so stupid?"

"Because Rodrigo Barco can't be considered objective. He's too closely aligned with Kyle Georni who may have his own agenda that doesn't include jungle for *Lygodium cornelius*. Were Kyle involved, the photos would have been lost the minute Rodrigo got hold of them."

"*Were* Kyle Georni involved," he echoed. "You don't think it odd that this investigation plods along, Rodrigo and the government's Jean-Michael Teruel in conference with Kyle at every turn?"

"Story and picture here, however," she stabbed the paper, "possibly turn more objective eyes in this direction from the outside."

"I was in Rio a couple of years back. A newsman I met complained the conference he attended was deadly dull. We kept in touch."

"I'm delighted."

"At least you sound sincere."

"Believe!" She gathered up her paper and stood. In the meantime, be prepared for an angry Rodrigo. For the moment, he thinks Melanie pulled a fast one, but he won't be fooled forever."

Felix's exhausted smile didn't portray the I'm ready for anything enthusiasm Carolyne would have preferred. Still, her estimation of him had shot up by light-years.

Galin waited, not with liquor but with a map on the coffee table in front of him. "Ah, Carolyne. Was your latest private session eventful?"

"Actually, it was. What are you up to?"

"I thought a bit of sight-seeing to finish off the morning; I promise you lunch if you don't put up too much of a fuss."

On the way to the car, she told him Felix was responsible for the article and picture in the Rio paper.

"Doesn't sound like someone trying to cover up his part in a conspiracy," Galin decided.

"I don't think he had anything to do with Gordon's death." She waited for his, "And?" but he didn't do anything so predictable. "Just what are we sight-seeing, Galin?"

"Indulge me." He eased the car into traffic and headed it northwest toward Ayrao. "I promise a site picked with you in mind."

Carolyne lifted her old Australian bush hat off the backseat and squashed it down on her head; she tucked in the last of her recalcitrant curls. "Tell me more about Galin Balstrom, why don't you?" She'd make the best of her voluntary captivity.

His hair was windblown and looked good that way. His smile was broad enough to splatter incoming bugs.

She coaxed: "I'm considering doing an in-depth piece for *Rolling Rock Magazine*."

His laugh was a throaty rumble. "*Stone*, my dear, Carolyne. *Rolling Stone* magazine."

"Whatever," she confessed her stab in the dark.

"The magazine, by the way, already did a piece on me earlier this year."

"I missed it, and I continue to be curious as to what takes anyone from Yale to rock and roll."

"The sheer adventure of it. Something different from boarding school, prep school, ivy-league university, cotillion, white bread and mayonnaise. Which even you have to agree can be boring."

"Your parents?"

"Junior League, DAR, SAR, stocks and bonds; charity balls, business luncheons; cocktail parties, dinner dances; country club, boardroom. Boredom!"

"Never once kept their rebellious son in check?"

"Ever know parents, worth their salt, who didn't make the effort?"

She regretted a biological clock rundown before children she could make toe the line. Randolph, Jr., hadn't counted, in more ways than one. "Do you know I'm old enough to be your mother?" It was one of those statements meant only for herself but inadvertently broadcast to the world.

"Not my 'grandmother'?"

Her don't tempt your luck look was diffused by his only kidding grin.

"I've always been attracted to older women." It was BS, he knew it; she knew it; they enjoyed the saying and the hearing, anyway.

"So, what exactly did your mother and father say when you donned leather and spangles, not Brooks Brother and Cartier?"

"Besides, "my God!'?"

"'My God!' was assumed."

"'Please don't bring home one of those spike haired, safety pin in nose bimbos,' said my mother. 'Remember, I'm here when it comes time to invest all of those rock and roll millions,' said my father."

They'd left the city behind. A glance back: vegetation, pasture, roadway. Ahead: more of the same.

"Galin, where *are* you taking me?"

"Not much farther."

Carolyne took off her hat, ran her fingers through her hair, and returned the hat to her head. "Your parents finally accepted your career decision?"

"Did I mention they met in India, on a mountaintop, at the feet of the guru Marsheshi Boyour?"

"I'm sure I would have remembered."

"It gave me a whip to keep them in line. Whenever they bemoaned leather and platform shoes, I'd retort, 'At least, it's not persimmon robes, sandals, and begging bowls.' In the end, I guess they figured I'd end up where they are, where they want me, my road as diverse as theirs to get there."

"Will you, do you think?"

"With costly castle in River Oaks; clothes by Burberry,

Chupp, Stadler & Stadler, and J. Press; membership in The Eagle Lake 'barn'; pew at the local Episcopal church; a son at St. Paul's; a daughter at The Masters? Well, Carolyne, even I know the *Rolling Stones*—the group, not the magazine—look dumb as hell prancing the stage at their age. An eventual slide into a board of directorship slot at my father's company even now sounds better than my strutting in Spandex, mascara, eyeliner, and lipstick, when I'm fifty-five."

"You have a sister at The Masters?"

"Alas, you see before you an only child. My reference was purely rhetorical."

"I've a goddaughter there in second term."

"Can it be? Two blue bloods find each other, sans civilization?"

"I'm middle-class, through and through." She didn't boast or apologize. "I met Marilyn's grandmother at U.C.L.A. She married well; her daughter married even better; we keep in touch."

"No static from your parents when you wanted to gird your loins and trek the hellholes of the world?"

"Both my parents were teachers at a progressive coed school in Northern California. Plant hunting in hellholes sounded a fine option to them. It seemed even more so when I started making quite a success of it." Was she bragging to impress him?

Galin stopped the Jeep. His right arm automatically extended sideways to stop her forward motion, even though she'd not forgotten to buckle in. "Do you see anything that looks like a road on our right?"

"You're looking for one?"

He pulled a map from between his bare chest and jacket; it was where he'd returned the folded newspaper. "It says here: *road.*" The line was broken and squiggly.

"It's a quarter mile back." She'd spent a lifetime isolating all kinds of things from all kinds of landscapes. It's dirt, between two trees."

He U-turned; the centrifugal force took Carolyne's balance

away. "Slow a bit." The exit was now easier to spot. They bounced along it for ten minutes.

His, "Not far" was another ten minutes to a house that had seen better times. Putting it in historical context was difficult because it had so many additions.

"Galin, what is this?"

He looked amused, not sinister. "The Wentlock Estate."

"The what?"

"Cross my heart and hope to die." He did the former and omitted the latter. "From here, granddad and dad Wentlock headed out to convert the noble savage, while grandmother and mother probably waited. From here, Gordon marched off on his career of guide, part-time prospector, and full-time Casanova."

Carolyne hadn't imagined Gordon lived anywhere this close. When the expedition had officially launched from the Georni Ranch, Gordon had been in residence within the room Roy and she had so recently shared over conversation and Scotch.

"How do you know this is the Wentlock place?"

"Money and a Galin Balstrom autograph will buy me all sorts of information."

She spotted the Brazilian equivalent of POLICE LINE/ DON'T CROSS. The ribbon hadn't fared well in the heat and humidity. Once strung between two trees, one tree to either side of the roadway, it had broken off-center and fluttered each side, like a fraternity prankster's colored toilet paper on sorority shrubs. "Maybe we should check on the jail sentence imposed for trespassing in these parts?"

"Carolyne, where is your sense of adventure?" He was beyond the downed ribbon. Peeping in the window invited him more than a try of the door.

A young woman appeared suddenly from around one side of the house. She spoke rapid-fire Portuguese, and Galin's resulting, "What?" indicated he was at a complete loss.

"She wants to know who we are," Carolyne translated.

"Americans," Galin identified, but it required Carolyne to put the English into Portuguese.

The result: "She wants to know just what it is we Americans want."

The woman's black hair was long and pulled back; it dangled unruly strands that stuck to the perspiration on her forehead. Her once white blouse was soiled; her black shirt was dusty. Her feet were dirty within decidedly filthy rubber thongs.

Carolyne couldn't imagine where any of this was headed.

The woman spouted more Portuguese.

"She says," and Carolyne couldn't believe the woman thought that they didn't know Gordon dead, what with police DO NOT PASS ribbons still fluttering from the trees, "that if we leave a message, she'll see that Gordon gets it."

"Perhaps you can explain this, Miss," Galin said and stepped in closer to the woman, removed the newspaper secured within his shirt, and pointed to the grisly photograph of Gordon's corpse which had been folded into prominence.

Everything about the woman's reactions said that the revelation, supplied her by Galin's index finger banging at the newspaper photo, was the result of genuine surprise. Her eyes went wide. She bit her lower lip so hard that it actually started to bleed. Her punctuating faint had none of the artistic, theatrical grace of the one performed by Alexandra Mata Jornella Georni, upon the latter's learning Gordon was definitely dead. This faint simply pitched the woman forward, face first; she hit the ground with a resounding thud.

"Galin, for heaven's sake!" Carolyne was furious by his lack of tact, not to mention his inability (more likely his non-attempt) to have broken the woman's fall.

Galin remained unfazed. "Who do you suppose she is, and what do you suppose she's doing here?" Rather than provide better late than never succor, he headed around the house in the direction from which the woman had come.

Carolyne couldn't do much without smelling salts and/or cold water, except to turn the woman over so she wouldn't suffocate. Carolyne slapped her gently, with no success. "Galin, do give me a hand!"

"Maybe, you'd better give *me* a hand?" he offered in alternative, as he appeared with a dirt-encrusted metal box. "Seems we interrupted our little squirrel, here, digging up, or digging down."

"Put that back before she wakes up!" Carolyne didn't mean it; she knew she didn't; he knew she didn't.

"I think not." His grin was mischievous. "Retrieved from a hole dug at the side of the Wentlock house. Hers, do you suppose? Gordon's?"

Carolyne couldn't decide whether she wanted the woman awake, to protect against the rifling of private property, or unconscious, to allow Carolyne and Galin carte blanche in satisfying their curiosity.

Carolyne thought Galin had a change of mind when he put down the box and came on over without it. No doubt about her disappointment. "What are you doing?" she asked.

"Taking off my belt. I'll need yours, too."

"Why are we taking off our belts?"

"Nothing more ominous than obtaining ties for the lady's hands and feet, Carolyne. What did you think?"

Carolyne hadn't known what to think. This was new to her; she had no term of reference.

"Well, are you going to give me yours, or not?" He was down and had gathered the woman's wrists. "Mine won't suffice for her feet as well."

"Why tie her?" It was something for Carolyne to say as she peeled her belt from its loops and handed it over. She knew, as well as he did; he told her anyway.

"We wouldn't want her to wake up from her faint, see us rifling the box, and think we were up to anything we shouldn't be. She'd get upset, and somebody might get hurt."

"Maybe we should take her and the box to Rodrigo Barco."

"Maybe." It wasn't confirmation. "And, maybe, that would assure we'd never be privy to what this box contains. Do you think Felix would pass it on, before he knew what was inside, were he in our shoes?"

Felix's level of confidence in Rodrigo had been emphasized by putting the film chip in the hands of a newspaperman in Rio. Still, there was something about what they were doing, well rationalized or not, that wasn't particularly on the up and up. "Where are you going?" she asked, as he headed for the Jeep, not for the box that looked far more inviting.

"To find something to pry open the lid. The odds aren't in favor of us divining the right combination. My expertise as a locksmith, or safecracker, isn't the best. If yours is better, be my guest."

By the time he produced the lug wrench, Carolyne had the box unlocked: no skill involved beyond the memory of a combination lock on a briefcase given her by her first husband—back when they were civil enough with each other to still exchange gifts. She never had followed the instructions to change the combination from its original 0000. Apparently, whoever owned this box—Gordon? the woman? someone still out of the picture?—had been just as lazy.

"You're marvelous!" He threw the wrench back into the Jeep with a "Clunk!" and walked to where Carolyne, considerate accomplice that she was, waited with the lid opened only far enough to tell its latches were released. He squatted, both of his feet flat on the ground, his ass almost brushing the ground; it was a position Carolyne had never mastered: her feet had a disconcerting tendency to lift up on her toes and throw her off balance. "Carolyne, do us the honors, if you would, please."

She'd gone too far to stop. Divine permission had been granted when she'd so easily cracked the combination code. She lifted the lid and let it hang open on its hinges.

"Nothing immediately exciting to catch the eye," was Galin's initial, disappointed judgment.

Carolyne's heartbeat agreed and shifted into a lower gear. She picked up the weather-beaten notebook and identified it immediately as another example of something she'd seen more than once before. "A field book of record. Finds. Purchases. Sales. Trades." At first, she thought it was Roy's; Jane Leider's collection had been larger and hardbound. It wasn't Roy's, but Carolyne, who had seen only one emerald in the rough, recognized at least two of the drawn reproductions as duplicates of diagrams in Jane Leider's possession. One of those had, also, been included in Roy's record book. "The 'J' emerald." She left the page open so Galin could see the diagram and the notes indicating the peculiarities of the gem's inclusions.

"The one Melanie picked up, you mean?" He pointed to the gibberish written directly above or below notations of carat, color, inclusions, and crystal structure. "What's that?"

"Code, I expect." She flipped the pages and found what she wanted up front: a standard alphabet down one side of the page, offset by a haphazard jumble of the other letters in a parallel line directly across. "Code!" she confirmed. "And, conveniently, its key. When a gem is found, or a transaction occurs, the specifics are recorded here. If the information is, then, transferred, other than directly, the code is used to confuse anyone who intercepts but shouldn't. Who can ever know who's listening?"

"Well, you have been busy soaking up pertinent local arcana." Galin reached for the box's other content, a crumpled ball of cheesecloth.

Carolyne hadn't told him her most important deduction: she figured the notebook belonged not to the woman, not to Gordon Wentlock, but to the missing John Leider. The "J" emerald entries recorded its purchase date from Roy Lendum, but no sale or trade. The other diagram she'd recognized from this field notebook, and from the hardbound version at the villa, had a discovery date and location, again no record of sale or trade.

"Well, what do we have here?" If Galin's tone wasn't enough, the sudden flash of sunlight off green gemstone rolled from the cheesecloth caught Carolyne's attention and made her gasp.

It was definitely a large piece of emerald: part of a larger, albeit missing, piece of hexagonal crystal. The distinctive fracture of one edge zeroed Carolyne immediately to its diagram in the notebook. "It and a companion piece were discovered at a place called Aquaval." She'd bet money the same diagram, with the same coordinates, and the same accompanying information coded and deciphered, was in a book at the Leider villa.

"Aquaval?" he queried; she could tell the name rang a bell. "That's where Gordon took us for the *Amaz'n Galin* shoot, and John Leider did all the shooting—with a gun—at us." He more closely examined the cheesecloth for the gem's companion stone. When he didn't find it, he checked the box for anomalies to indicate a hidden compartment.

The unexpected scream of rage scared them. The revived woman's look of pure hatred would have scared them even more if Galin's precautions hadn't assured she could do little more than make her horrendous noise.

"Yours?" Galin had understood that much of her tirade. "I suppose you haven't heard, 'Finders keepers, losers weepers'?"

Carolyne had her own line of interrogation. "If it's yours, you know where it was originally mined, don't you?" She tapped the notebook. There was always the chance the woman had overheard or previously read the pertinent entry. Then, again....

The woman's screamed answer was translated by Carolyne to the effect that Gordon had mined and given the woman the emerald. The woman didn't have a clue where it had been mined.

"The late-dead Gordon Wentlock," Galin said, dubious in the extreme, "gave it to her because she was—his lover? his sister? his friend? his wife?"

"Seems she and he were to be married," Carolyne was soon able to supply. "When Gordon got back, this last time, he was going to take her to Paris and to Rome."

Unfortunately for this hysterical woman, Carolyne had heard the same story before, albeit from the supposedly distraught Alexandra Mata Jornella Georni.

"I'm afraid, my dear," Carolyne was now able to console, "that you're not the first woman to have heard such promises of marriage, of Paris, and of Rome—from the lips of the now-dead Gordon Wentlock."

The woman's reply, according to Carolyne, was that: the other women were playthings, toys. Gordon needed them, but only as a thirsty man needs water. Temporarily cured of such mundane thirst, he could and did throw them aside.

Galin marveled at the ego of some women. "This one special?" His voice was thick with sarcasm.

Undoubtedly recognizing a put-down when she heard one, although she didn't entirely understand its wording, the woman launched into another barrage of Portuguese at which Carolyne could only guess, in the end, came out something about: Did they think Gordon left an emerald for any of his other women?

"How do we know how many emeralds he's squirreled away, around Brazil, for how many of his bimbo ladies, lady?" Galin answered, and Carolyne relayed.

"She says he left emeralds for none of the others," Carolyne provided the woman's answer in English.

"Well, this little booklet suggests otherwise," Galin said as he reached for the record which Carolyne handed to him. "See!" He flipped the pages for the woman to see, and he immediately pinpointed three diagramed stones with no sales records.

"She says that Gordon had those with him."

Galin shrugged would you believe? "She does figure herself special," he said and made it sound as if she were delusional.

"What's your name?" Carolyne moved interrogation to a more personal level.

The woman's lips pursed tightly, without any sound.

Galin wanted more blunt persuasion: "Ask if she thinks the people around here aren't going to identify her when it's the police doing the asking."

"She wants to know if we're the police," Carolyne came back. Then, she added on her own for Galin's benefit: "The police *will* have to be notified."

More rapid-burst Portuguese from the woman that left Galin unable to catch the gist, and left Carolyne, once again, to make any sense of it.

"She insists that Gordon promised the emerald in the box would be hers."

"Tell her the police will turn it over to her, after they confirm her story."

Hearing that idea, though, the woman made protest.

"She says," said Carolyne, "that the police will keep it."

"Because they're crooked, or because they'll discover it's not really hers?" Galin wondered aloud.

"She says the emerald is her nest egg, in case anything happened to Gordon."

"And something did happen to Gordon," Galin confirmed, "except she wasn't convinced until I showed her the newspaper photo. So, why do you suppose we caught her prematurely digging?"

When asked, the woman was ready with an answer.

"Seems Gordon has always come back to her before, hasn't he? She should believe the police when they tell her he's dead but have no body to show her? No! The police are all liars. Gordon didn't trust them. She doesn't trust them, either. She still finds it hard to trust what's printed on your newspaper. She must think long and hard. As for her emerald—and it is hers, if Gordon is dead—she digs it up regularly just to see and fondle it...to touch its greenness...to taste its coolness against her tongue. Have we never had an emerald?"

"Can't say as I have," Galin admitted.

"Same here," Carolyne echoed. "So, she says we can't know the way properly to treat one. Gordon taught her to spread out whatever such gems, everyday, and to arrange them to catch the available light. 'Emeralds are miracles to be enjoyed, things so long buried they savor the light and thrive on it.' That's what Gordon told her. That's what she does—when she's not inter-rupted by American thieves—because that's what Gordon always did."

Galin rolled his eyes. "She digs up her pet rock to feed and pet it."

"She says her name is Talina, and that she is definitely Gordon's number one woman."

"Well, Talina, Gordon's number one woman, among god only knows how many other number one women...." Galin's words dripped sarcasm. "...we have to turn you and your emerald over the authorities."

Talina watched warily as Galin returned the emerald to the cheesecloth, and, then, deposited it, along with the notebook, back into the dirt-encrusted lock-box.

.

CHAPTER TEN

It was more frequent as Carolyne got older: this waking in the morning to the disgruntled realization that not nearly enough sleep had been crowded into the night before. Her daily nap never seemed long enough, either, to provide the freshness a shorter nap had once provided. In either case, the depression lasted only until Carolyne showered and donned fresh clothes.

By the time she opened the door to head down for breakfast, she was glad to be alive and knew she wasn't on her last legs by a long shot.

Galin exited his room at the same time. He was "in costume", but not the costume Carolyne expected. He smiled; she liked the way he always managed to come across as delighted to see her, whether that was the case or not.

"Crossover: is that what it's called when an artist makes the transition from one style to another?" she wondered aloud. "This look is 'country'?"

He looked good in vest, boots, and faded jeans; shirt open at the collar to show a tied black kerchief and an enticing peek of muscle scalloped cleavage; a gaucho hat hung on his back by a string anchored around the front of his throat.

He launched into a short rendition of *Home, Home, on the Range* that made the vision complete. It was the first time Carolyne had heard his singing voice, which was low and mellow, with a distinctive, gravelly purr that raised gooseflesh on an old lady who'd heard many a bona-fide western singer extol the delights of deer and antelope at play.

"I'm off to rustle up this evening's grub." He struck a pose that put all of his weight on one leg, his other leg slightly bent to give his pelvis a suggestively sexy tilt. He hooked his thumbs in his front pants pockets in a way that would have had his fingers downwardly parenthesizing his crotch if not for what was in his right hand. "There's to be a barbecue of one whole cow—or is it, one whole cattle? steer? bull? little doggie? A couple of the hands asked if I'd like to help muster up the chow."

To Carolyne, his apparent slide from one social stratum to another seemed impressively effortless; he could charm uneducated, macho, Brazilian cowpokes with the same ease he charmed his peers in the country club back home, charmed his groupies, and charmed Carolyne whenever he had a mind to. She envied him the variety of his chameleon life-style; she'd never been nearly that at ease and had an edge that rubbed some people the wrong way. "My only suggestion would be to wear those, and she nodded to the silver spurs in his hand, "on the heels of your boots, not on your fingers."

"You think they're serious about these?" He dangled the spurs. "I mean, do you believe these? How do they keep from disemboweling a horse?"

She took one and spun its serrated rowel. Satisfied, she upturned it and ran the wheel along the underside of her arm. "Sufficiently dull to be horseback effective but not cause fatal personal injury if you fall over your own two feet."

"Only if you say so." He dropped into one of the chairs that lined the hallway and fastened the spur in his possession to one boot. When finished, he duplicated the maneuver with the spur Carolyne handed over.

He stood, stamped his feet against the hall runner and produced chimes from silver against silver. "Why don't you postpone whatever you're up to and join me on roundup?"

"I think not." She'd ridden more than her share of horses; in younger days, she would have been as game as Galin. However, any horseback riding she wanted now would need be leisurely and not with good natured cowpokes out for good natured fun.

They headed for the stairs amid the pleasant jingle of his every accompanying footstep.

"Have you been downstairs yet this morning?" Carolyne recognized his youth as less susceptible to the demands for sleep, and she suspected his present clothes might well be his second for the day.

"I was stealing a piece of bacon from Melanie's plate, and checking for signs of jealousy in the watching Teddy, when this...." His gesture indicated his getup. "...arrived."

"You shouldn't provoke Teddy." Carolyne blamed Melanie for more game-playing. If the young woman cared for one man, why flirt openly with so many others?

"He didn't seem all that interested."

She stopped at the head of the stairs and stopped him with her. First things first. "It's my experience that whether Teddy looks jealous or not, he can be counted upon to be so."

"You think he sees me as competition?"

"Don't fish for compliments in these Dead-Sea waters."

He looked all "Gee Whiz!" What's more, it still worked, although it wouldn't in a couple of years when his youthful edges were completely eroded by masculinity. Not that he'd be less effective when that happened; he'd just have to exploit some equally appealing but more macho posturing.

"Any news while I slept away the morning?" That's what she really wanted to know.

He leaned against the balustrade and folded his arms in a way that invited closeness, rather than the expected opposite. "Well, Jane Leider and a handwriting expert agree that the notebook in a box is John Leider's. Jane says the 'cheesecloth emerald', like the 'J' emerald, was in her husband's possession at the time he disappeared. It seems Miss Talina, Gordon's number one woman, is still reluctant, but less so in the face of the preponderance of evidence, to believe her main squeeze has gone to the Great Beyond. That's about it."

"Developments on Felix's leak to the press?"

"Well, Felix stayed in town last night and has not showed up this morning. As far as his interrogation, I've heard no word. I can tell you that Miss Melanie is in a snit, not only because she was accused of bypassing Rodrigo Barco with those photos, but because more than one person commented upon how clever Felix was—which rather insinuated Melanie had missed the boat on cleverness, somewhere along the line."

"Who thought Felix clever?"

"Well, there's Charles, who said, 'I can't stand the bastard, but this was a stroke of genius!' Said Roy: 'I guess he proved'—to everyone but Miss Talina—'that we didn't imagine the body we found.' Said Teddy: 'Who would have ever mistaken Felix for clever?' Said Kyle: 'The important thing is having the photos, not the runabout way we had to get them.' Said Rodrigo, and this comes secondhand from Melanie, in that the inspector, like Felix, hasn't checked in with me this morning: 'I'll have you sorry for withholding key information in a murder investigation!' At the time, the 'you' referred to Melanie, who Rodrigo thought had slipped the photos to the press, but, I assume, the same now applies to Felix, the real culprit. Have I left out anyone? Ah, yes! Richard: 'What's all of this—expletive deleted—bother over a few photographs of a bloody corpse?' How's that for dialogic summations?"

"Pretty good, except the 'expletive deleted' came across a bit highfalutin from someone who looks as if he can walk in cow shit."

He rewarded her with the low rumble laugh she'd hoped for. "I wouldn't have on my boots what you just had in your mouth."

"Think you'll be able to boast as much when you're back from your roundup?"

Melanie made an appearance around the curve of the stairs. "Ah, there you are!" She elucidated, "And, don't you look mighty fine in western chic."

"Howdy, ma'am!" His drawl was pure Texan. "Didn't hear you coming."

"A few of your pardners request your immediate presence in the corral. A shoot out with the local sheriff?"

"Evening barbecue," Carolyne clarified.

"Too bad, since the local sheriff is Rodrigo Barco," reminded Melanie.

Galin had listened to her bellyaching all morning. "If you pretty ladies will excuse me?"

Melanie called after him: "Don't trip on those spurs and make mincemeat of those studly legs!" Her facial expression was way too covetous for someone already engaged to Teddy; not that any of that was Carolyne's business.

It wasn't about Galin, though, that Melanie asked when the two women drifted downstairs together. "Do you think I was an idiot to turn over to Rodrigo what I thought were the real photos?"

"It's one of those decisions better judged in retrospect, and there hasn't been nearly enough time to tell," Carolyne was gracious. "If Kyle had anything to do with Gordon's murder, and if Rodrigo is Kyle's pawn, then, yes, harm could have been done. If Kyle is innocent, and if Rodrigo is just trying to do his job, then how can he be expected to make headway when he's not been given all the available information? Ask any policeman, anywhere, how difficult it is without the *corpus delicti* and/or a murder weapon. So what that we saw both? We're rank amateurs who had Roy's geology expertise to provide us a bit more insight than the common man on the street. The more important forensics team needs the same material we had to work with, in order to give Rodrigo the facts upon which to make sense of the case. If Rodrigo makes something of the photos now, that he could have made earlier if he'd had the data to work with, then Felix was a certified jerk to bypass him. Of course, there's always the chance it was Felix exposing the film to the more objective eye of the press that got Rodrigo off his duff." She didn't continue, except to add: "It's six of one, half a dozen of the other. Not black. Not white. Grey in all its myriad shades and variables."

Melanie had already had breakfast, but Carolyne held her another minute. "Have you heard anything more about us getting back, any time soon, to search for *Lygodium cornelius?*"

"From what I can determine, we have about as much chance of that happening as a snowball has of surviving in hell. Kyle made a phone call this morning to some bigwig in Brasilia, and to another bigwig in Rio. Neither wants to risk Americans turned loose in an area even the newspapers now extrapolate has killer jaguars, natives with spears, rock throwers, and god only knows how many other potential maniacs."

"You feel Kyle is doing his best, though?"

"It sounds that way when I'm around, but who does he call, and what does he say, when I'm not around to listen?"

"I figure: give everyone the benefit of the doubt until proven differently." It was pontification she'd not lived up to, but it remained Carolyne's ideal.

She dished up ham, eggs, and hash browns. Orange juice and coffee were served at her table by one of the many servants so seldom seen or heard, at least by her.

She had a croissant for dessert and buttered a second when Charles bustled in, spotted her, and came running.

"You needn't hurry, Charles. The food won't be cleared away for hours."

"I've eaten." He sat down and, without visibly taking a breath, asked: "What's with the guards on Richard Callahan?"

The buttered croissant stopped halfway to her mouth. "What guards?"

"A couple of the ranch hands at the front door of the infirmary, another two at the back, everyone with instructions that Richard is out of bounds."

"You were making a social call?"

"I was after a tranquilizer. I haven't been sleeping all that well. One of the guards misconstrued my intentions and told me, without my asking, that Richard wasn't available. Dr. Seln pleads ignorance, or loss of memory; it was hard to tell which."

"Kyle would be more apt to have an answer than I would. They're his ranch hands," Carolyne reminded.

"Kyle went into town early this morning, but Teddy says Kyle called in the instructions to isolate Richard."

"Did Teddy know why?"

"If he did, he didn't tell me." Sure Carolyne was a dry source of information, Charles didn't stick around.

Carolyne ended up at the swimming pool after a conscious effort located Roy who was on a chaise longue, his face to the sun, his eyes shut, his shirt off. He had an exceptionally well-muscled torso, and each scar—there were three to be seen beneath a thick matting of black chest hair—undoubtedly had its own tale to tell. That he wore his pants and boots told Carolyne his presence was spontaneous, not a conscious I think I'll go to the pool.

She wasn't too old to identify his partial nakedness as a prime example of male of the species attractiveness, no more than she was too far over the hill to recognize her—if I were only forty years younger—appreciation of Galin's good looks. However, animal magnetism wasn't what put her there. Curiosity did. The object of that curiosity was a visible bulge in the right hand pocket of the bush jacket Roy had stripped from his now sweaty body and had draped over the glass tabletop between his chair and hers.

Had she pickpocket dexterity, she might have unbuttoned the pocket, lifted its contents, examined the field notebook, and returned it, Roy none the wiser. Even bumbling, she might succeed if Roy were really sleeping. However, why take the dangerous route when sight-seeing might be accomplished via a far safer route?

She fished her pockets for her notebook and pen. She flipped to a blank page and dated the paper. She wrote, "Dear Marilyn," although personal correspondence was the farthest thing from her mind. "Roy? Roy?"

"Mmmmm?" His head turned in her direction, and he squinted to see her. "Carolyne?" He shielded his eyes with one hand.

"I'm sorry to disturb you, Roy, but I wondered if I might borrow your field notebook for a moment." An approach didn't get any more direct than that.

"My field notebook?"

She knew a man caught off guard when she saw one. "I'm writing a letter to my goddaughter, and I want to tell her about Melanie's emerald. I thought I could copy down the specifics."

"Sure." He twisted for his jacket, which put his chest muscles and washboard abdominals into an attractive torque. Sweat pooled his "innie" belly button and overflowed it. He dug out the battered notebook and handed it over. He rolled back toward the sun with a helpful, "It's one of the dog-eared pages."

And so it was. She made quick notations and, then, with a glance to make sure he wasn't suspicious, she located what she really wanted, or, at least part of it, helped by a convenient date notated at the top of one page.

She flipped the pages a final time to confirm there were no handy conversion alphabets, like the key in the notebook that accompanied the cheesecloth emerald; Roy's willingness to surrender his notebook had already warned her not to expect any easily accessed key to his code.

"Thank-you so much, Roy."

He repeated the torque movement in retrieval, and Carolyne stayed on to write a letter she could probably later salvage as a real thing. She accepted an offer of ice lemonade from a servant who regularly patrolled the area for thirsty owner or guests.

Roy left, and Carolyne was gathering up her possessions when Galin's appearance in only a swimsuit, and not much of that, told her how long she'd performed her poolside masquerade.

The blond rock star entered the water on the opposite side of the pool and did so in a sharp as a knife dive that insinuated his body was as inwardly well coordinated as it outwardly appeared. With the grace of a gilded dolphin, he remained underwater the width of the pool and breached on her side with a lift to his waistline before he sunk back to his neck. The splash washed as far as Carolyne's feet. The water he shook from his hair reached her as he propped his arms on the flagstone and grinned his hello.

Carolyne contemplated whether a comment on the skimpiness of his bikini would make her sound like a dirty old lady on the make, but he took control of the conversation.

"Guess what juicy tidbit I came across while rounding up your evening beef steak?" he asked.

"The reason behind Richard's sudden incarceration?"

"Would telling you what I know only duplicate what you've already heard?"

"My other source isn't nearly as reliable as you've always been."

"Seems a drunk in a Manaus bar bragged that Richard paid him five-thousand U.S. dollars to bump off Gordon Wentlock. Seems the very same drunk came complete with enough U.S. cash on hand for him to raise certain suspicions that he just might be telling the truth."

He leaned back and pushed off. On his back, he coasted to mid-pool and rolled over as he veered sharply to the right. He began an Australian crawl, the first of several swim strokes which took him the length of the sculptured container of water.

Carolyne was so taken by his grace, not to mention by her thoughts of Richard's house arrest, she didn't know she'd been joined until, "Do you find him as attractive as Melanie does?"

"Teddy!" She tried to parry his question with, "I didn't know you were there."

He hadn't expected a direct answer. "Melanie," he said, "thinks him more handsome than Gordon Wentlock. Do you know Galin's parents are rolling in inherited dough? He'd be wealthy from trusts funds without once having had to get on a stage to bray and prance like a jackass."

Carolyne sought to diffuse a possible bomb. "Melanie has flirted before, hasn't she?"

"Confided that to you, did she?" His eyes were on Galin who performed a swimmer's turn on the deep end of the pool. "More likely, just obvious!"

"Some women are natural flirts." Carolyne did her best. "It's just the way they are. It doesn't mean anything. Melanie is still with you, isn't she? That says more than her frequently batted eyelashes at others."

"It says she thinks I want her enough to put up with a whole lot more than should be expected from someone she's supposed to love."

Carolyne would give him no argument on that score.

"It says, she thinks she has me under her thumb and that she's going to keep me there. I say, it may be time for her to think again."

"Don't do anything foolish, Teddy, will you?"

"Do you think it foolish for me to tell her that I've had enough, that her name, her money, and her social connections cost too much by way of my pride and dignity?"

There was no denying that Carolyne saw poetic justice in his pulling up stakes on a mouth opened in surprise Melanie.

"What do you know about my family background, Carolyne?"

"Not much, Teddy." She had the few specifics gleaned from Melanie, but she didn't feel it to anyone's benefit to pass them along to him, now, let alone mention where she'd heard them.

"Funny, but it's been my understanding—misunderstanding?—that you'd made it a point to know just about everything about everybody." It wasn't a compliment; Carolyne was still trying to come up with an answer when he turned and left her.

She spent the next half an hour verifying certain facts that had come her way. For one, there were ranch hands on guard at the infirmary. For two, they did volunteer that Richard wasn't allowed visitors.

"I've come to see Dr. Seln about a rash." She rolled up a sleeve and showed them the pink swath, aggravated, as she knew it would be, by her prolonged stay by the pool."

Dr. Seln had a name for it; the same name that her doctor in the States had for it; Carolyne couldn't remember it more than two minutes, no matter how many times she heard it. Again, something she already knew: "It's nothing serious." The doctor gave her some salve; she already had some.

She wanted the doctor to tell or give her something more.

"Why can't Richard have visitors?"

"All I can tell you is that Kyle called in those instructions earlier this morning. You'll have to ask him."

The opportunity for her to do so occurred when Kyle drove in as Carolyne left the infirmary.

"Some drunk shot off his mouth in a Manaus bar," Kyle confirmed. "Something about how Richard gave him money to kill Gordon. Rodrigo wants to make sure Richard doesn't go any place until the guy's story is checked." He changed the subject and asked if she'd notice any activity for the barbecue he should have been supervising hours ago.

She assured him that things, in that regard, seemed to be progressing nicely, in that Galin's wrangled beef was already basting over a pit whose wood had burned down to hot coals. When the wind blew just right, the roasting meat, complete with its honey-based barbecue sauce, could be smelled where she stood.

She went to her room and took a cool shower. She put on some of the salve from Dr. Seln, rather than dig out the tube she'd brought to Brazil with her.

She sat at the desk and opened her notebook to the information gleaned from Roy's field notes: not the data on the "J" emerald but the coded message he'd read into the expedition's radio when, that very first time, he'd appeared out of the jungle to request use of their radio. That had been before Carolyne realized a jungle prospector was likely to broadcast in code; she'd expected words, and he'd delivered a long sequence of numbers. That the leading "7,2....," were the day and month of her birth was purely coincidence. Just what they really meant needed a key to unlock, like the one provided in the transposed alphabets of the notebook found in the box at Gordon's house. Roy's key, though, wasn't as simple, obviously something kept separate so his private notations could be kept private. The chance of Carolyne inadvertently stumbling across the key was nigh on impossible. This wasn't a combination lock left at 0000; Roy hadn't been too lazy to take extra precautions.

Staring did no good. The numbers remained unchanged, without any clue to their hidden meaning. She finally gave up, not even sure why intuition told her it might be important when everything could so easily be resolved by a drunk's admission he'd been hired by Richard to murder Gordon.

She spent the rest of the day in a sociable drift among swelling and waning speculation as to Richard's guilt or innocence in his purchase of an assassin.

The barbecue was in full swing when Kyle was called to the telephone. The relative silence and inquisitive stares that greeted his return persuaded him to share what Rodrigo had told him.

"The drunk's story is still being checked. As for the photographs taken by Melanie, the original chip has finally arrived, forwarded by the newspaperman in Rio; Rodrigo has brought in several experts to give the photos a thorough going over, including a zoologist who knows jaguars. It's still too early to have any in-depth feedback, except from the zoologist who tentatively seems to find it of some interest that his cursory examination shows no apparent evidence of teeth marks on the victim and a unique pattern to the claw striations."

"God!" Melanie shivered. None of this, in conjunction with the memories it conjured, was appetizing; Kyle knew that, but it was better to give them what they wanted, rather than let their imaginations have free reign.

"There won't be anything else this evening; even policemen, forensics experts, and zoologists, need to eat and sleep. I assure you that we'll be kept abreast of all progress, or lack thereof," Kyle concluded.

"What's it mean? 'Unique pattern to the claw striations'?" Teddy was puzzled.

"All I know is what the gentleman said. 'Specifics to follow'."

Carolyne decided on a drink of hard liquor. Since her Curacao with Kyle, and Scotch with Roy, she'd gone a temperance routine of fruit juices, bottled water, tea, and coffee. In retrospect, either extreme was foolish. She ordered a *caipirinha* and watched a dark complexioned young man, behind the patio bar, expertly mix the concoction of homemade whiskey, sugar, and lime. She sipped the sweet and sour results.

"Guess where Melanie is?"

Carolyne didn't have to turn to know who asked the question. Her answer was an immediate check of the area; not for Melanie but for Galin.

"Now, ask me if I care?" Teddy supplemented.

This time, Carolyne obliged. "Do you care?"

"Not a whit." Words were cheap, and he knew it. "Trust me. I've commenced the cure."

He wandered off, and Carolyne let him.

She finished her *caipirinha* and said a dutiful good-night to her host.

She headed for the stairs and for her room and bed at the top. She was distracted from that objective by the lights suddenly going off in the den. After which, she paused and waited for sounds to confirm her suspicions; even with the door open, she couldn't hear anything until she moved in closer and finally detected Melanie's all too recognizable giggle. Good sense argued that this was none of Carolyne's business. If Teddy were resolved to the situation, who was she not to be?

What disturbed her was an ignored call for discretion and diplomacy. Even Teddy deserved better, although he'd not likely thank Carolyne for reminding Melanie and Galin of that.

She took the two steps remaining to stand her in the open door they should have had the common sense to shut and lock for the privacy they had to know that would have provided. Just the shutting would have saved them from her. The stupidity of passions so detrimental to common logic! "Hello, anyone there?"

What the resulting light provided was less compromising that Carolyne expected.

"Carolyne, join us!" Galin operated a light switch across the room. "I'd appreciate some additional feedback."

Melanie stood apart, near the center of the room. All Carolyne got from her was another silly giggle; she'd hoped for more.

"What do you think?" Galin clicked the lights off again. "Does standing here in the dark, those stuffed and mounted animals casting shadows within shadows, portray any of the mood of a night in the jungle with a man eating jaguar and head hunting cannibals?"

There was no way Carolyne could have guessed, from Melanie's schoolgirl titter, that the young woman was respected in not one but two fields of science.

"I told him faking it would never be the same as being there," Melanie barely managed.

"Galin, be serious!" Carolyne didn't enjoy her role of chaperone. People this age shouldn't need one; they weren't kids, no matter how childish they acted.

The lights came on. "You don't recognize the vaguest similarity?" he asked.

For once, Carolyne refused to be won over by his boyish charm. It might have succeeded, but only sans Melanie. "No comparison whatsoever."

"Well, of course, you two were there," he conceded. I've only the hold-over thrill of once having been hopelessly lost in the San Diego Zoo."

"Whatever turns you on." They could take that however they wanted.

Melanie infuriated Carolyne with another inane giggle; Galin chose to ignore Carolyne's fuddy-duddies—in having caught the kids at play—attitude.

Carolyne had enough. "If you'll excuse me, I'm headed for bed."

"So are we." No doubt, he meant it just as suggestively as it sounded.

Afraid of yet another nerve grating giggle from Melanie, Carolyne performed an about-face and headed for the stairs. The lights clicked off and on at least twice more before she rounded the upward curve of the stairs that cut off her view.

"Children!" She included every man, woman, and teen whose runaway hormonal glands induced runaway imbecility.

She'd never been a slave to such inconvenience, and she refused to believe she'd missed anything.

She went to bed: no surprise. Big surprise: she went to sleep. Big deception: she thought she slept far longer than the two a.m. registered on the clock by her bed when she woke up. She had the aftertaste of an unremembered dream she felt somehow important. She tried to recall any fantasies of Melanie and Galin making love in some jungle clearing, wild animals and wild natives all around, while Carolyne chided with a shaking finger. No! Nothing to do with Galin. With Melanie?

She settled back, closed her eyes, and pretended she spun with arms outstretched: a technique taught to reclaim a dream interrupted; little used by Carolyne because she seldom preferred make-believe to reality. It didn't work, probably because she'd woke up, sat up, turned on the light, checked the time, then made the attempt to reconnect.

She went to the bathroom. While there, no arms out, no spinning, she remembered the standout feature of her dream—of Gordon's makeshift funeral.

As a result, she scrounged her robe and slippers. She told herself she mustn't get too excited, because what she now planned would likely provide nothing more for her than inspirational reading for an old lady who was guilty of not doing nearly as much of that as she probably should do to prepare herself for the hereafter.

She didn't need a flashlight. First- and second-floor corridors had lights left on dim throughout the night. In case of a generator failure, conveniently located closets and/or storage spaces provided stockpiles of battery operated emergency lighting. Each darkened room had a convenient light switch just inside its door, one of which Carolyne activated once she was in the downstairs library.

She pulled the door shut and surveyed the shelves. She hoped what she wanted would leap out at her, via destiny, rather than require her mundane match of a card-catalog Dewy decimal classification with gold-leafed numbers on a book spine.

The books, though, were too uniform in their custom bindings of oxblood-dyed Moroccan leather to allow easy sorting without prior knowledge of the arrangement system. The book she chose, compliments of the card catalog, was five by seven and in such pristine condition she had to check the copyright, 1979, to make sure it wasn't a rare volume. It's aroma of tooled leather, unaired paper, and undisturbed printer's ink, was downright pleasant.

She opened the door and switched off the light. Then, reflexively, she stepped back, not likely to be spotted against the backdrop of darkened room.

Melanie, with a quilt folded in her arms, and Galin, with a champagne bottle and two glasses, weren't nearly as well blended into the woodwork, in their creep around the bend of the stairs, as was Carolyne, where she stood.

Juveniles! Carolyne watched the two in their beeline for the basement door under the stairway. She was of half a mind to jump out, yell, "Surprise!" and ask them where in the hell they were headed, just to savor the results, but she had better things to do. Anyway, too clever for his own good Galin would likely have some spontaneous rationale logical enough to stand up in any court of law.

She waited, none too patiently; quiet as a mouse. They selected two flashlights from a storage compartment to the right of the basement door, in lieu or activating the main basement lights which weren't left on after nightfall.

How much of a turn-on, Carolyne wondered: This Theseus lost in some dark, basement labyrinth with a giggling, no help Ariadne?

The basement door opened and shut, having swallowed the two explorers. Carolyne waited overly long to make sure they didn't have second thoughts.

She started up the stairs and got quite a surprise when Teddy suddenly appeared around the bend.

CHAPTER ELEVEN

Teddy's reaction: "Carolyne! Whatever are you doing up?"

Her reaction: a subconscious which had, all along been expecting him to appear. There were shenanigans afoot, but she had nothing about which to be ashamed or guilty. She had a logical explanation for being where she was; Teddy might find it less easy to explain *his* innocence in being there. "Couldn't sleep," she said and tapped the book in hand—thank God for the book! She would have hated the excuse of hot milk with an inability to produce it.

She viewed his, "Me, too," as plagiarism, then had second thoughts. He looked surprised, and, yes, even guilty, but didn't come off as a jealous, green-eyed monster in hot pursuit of a two timing fiancée and her latest paramour. He would have materialized far more quickly had he intended to keep Melanie and Galin in view.

No accompanying demand of, "Where are they?"

On his way by Carolyne, he cocked his head to read the title on the spine of her book. "That will certainly put you to sleep. I'm no longer afraid you've made off with the only good reading in the house."

She thought he'd continue down. They weren't exactly a mutual-admiration society, and his comment on her reading material wasn't exactly the beginning of pleasant small-talk.

Therefore, he surprised her with, "Why don't you join me for a small nightcap in the library? You weren't exactly falling off bar stools at the barbecue and can risk it."

He wasn't her ideal by way of someone with whom to share anything. A good time wasn't to be had in exchanging sarcastic repartee with Melanie's maybe, maybe-not, significant other. "I don't think a drink would be a good idea."

His shrug wasn't exactly sorry to hear that; it was more thank god I'm saved. It made her more desirous to leave him where he stood. In fact, they were both on their separate ways, the breach widening between them, when she reconsidered. As much as she viewed separation from the potential mess in the making, she might be a mediating influence should Melanie and Galin suddenly re-appear.

Maybe, too, a few minutes with her would catapult Teddy back upstairs and out of the way. Despite his recent assurances that he contemplated a dignified withdrawal, Carolyne wasn't anxious for Melanie and Galin to put him to the test. "Maybe I will have that drink."

He didn't turn back, and Carolyne figured he didn't hear, or, hearing, didn't like what he'd heard. Though, by the time she decided to walk the distance to join him, he had her drink poured. His smile might have passed for friendly but only in a pinch. "Curiosity get the best of you?" he baited and handed her a sherry.

She'd have to watch out for this one. "Curiosity?" She was too old and too world weary to come across convincingly innocent.

"Yes, curiosity." He took his drink and sat in one of the chairs that faced her. "As to whether I really propose to toss off Melanie and all she offers, just because she's flirted once too often with one too many other men."

"I never thought you the type who'd consider me your mother-confessor."

"I want to tell one person, so the world can know without my having personally to tell everyone."

"How obnoxious!" She'd kept a lot of confidences in her time, including the twosome at the bottom of the basement stairs.

"It could be that I resent that you're Melanie's friend." He seemed neither apologetic nor sincere. "She's not my favorite person at the moment."

"That doesn't make your insinuation that I'm the local gossip any the less rude."

"I've decided to give up trying so hard to please other people."

"Congratulations, in that you're succeeding." She gulped her drink.

"Can I get you another?"

Fat chance! Melanie and Galin would have to fend for themselves.

"Stay," he coaxed, "and I'll tell you why I come across as less than your ideal scientist and gentleman?"

She poured her own drink, thank-you, still not sure she'd stay. She didn't offer him seconds, although another swallow would drain his glass. "I once knew a bastard, literally, not figuratively," she said. She wanted this different kind of bastard to know he couldn't count on her to be sympathetic. "As a baby, he was left on a convent stoop with a note: 'I don't know his daddy, but his daddy wouldn't want him or me.' What's more, his bad luck didn't stop there. He caught scarlet fever, almost died, and had a lifetime recurring heart murmur as a result. He married and had a daughter; wife and daughter were killed in a car crash. He married again; his second wife suffered a debilitating stroke and was bedridden four years before she died. I never knew him to say an unkind word to anybody about anybody."

Teddy wasn't impressed. "You only get one living saint in your life, and that's yours. The rest of us aren't nearly as able to cope."

Many times, Carolyne had told many people: "That man is a one of a kind, living, breathing, saint."

"We're not talking a victim of love deprivation, mind you." Teddy drained his glass. "My mother loved me until her aneurysm left all the loving to my father. When my father died, my stepparents loved me enough to mortgage their home, not once, but twice, to help me through school. But, it was so much just the bare necessities, and sometimes not even those, which made me wonder if I'd ever accumulate enough material possessions to erase my insecurities. I know I'm mercenary in looking at Melanie and seeing money, homes, business, social connections, and all the other things that spell 'security blanket', but I wake up nights drenched in sweat from dreams of some catastrophe sucking dry my life savings and those of everyone I love."

He got up, poured himself a drink and carried it with him in his slow walk along one bookcase. Now and again, he tilted a book from its lineup. "I know you're fond of Melanie, Carolyne. Look upon her as the daughter you never had?" He glanced over his shoulder. "Maybe not. The half-Cornelius in her might be okay, but you could never accept the half-Margaret in her, could you?"

"What would you know?" Carolyne was amazed by how many people accessed aspects of her private life.

"I know a good deal, because you played an important part in Cornelius Ditherson's life, and I had plans to make his daughter my wife. I've since amended those plans."

"Have you, Teddy?" Could Galin and Melanie come up those stairs now, and could Teddy dismiss them with, "What the heck?"

"You take a minute, Carolyne, and think about who's more honest in my relationship with Melanie. Is it the poor kid, afraid of poverty, who makes no secret that money and background can be the pot of gold awaiting at the end of the rainbow? Is it the little rich girl who exploits by dangling the chances of all dreams come true, then pulls them back periodically for quick indiscretions? I'm frankly tired of being Melanie's have-not of the week. I'm tired of her assumption that I should look the other way while she tries out whoever is the new man or boy on the block. I deserve better than Melanie Ditherson, and I have the education for which my stepparents paid, and my reputation in the field, to keep me from starving. If I don't get super rich, or even rich enough to make me feel secure against the world, that won't make me a failure. Nor is insecurity something to which I, alone, am susceptible. How secure do you view any young woman who has this desperate need to flirt with anything in pants?"

Maybe he *could* confront Galin and Melanie with, *"C'est la vie!"*

He pulled a book from the shelf, he'd made his selection. He finished his drink and brought his empty glass back to its tray. "Be sure to turn out the lights when you leave, won't you, Carolyne?"

She finished her drink and followed him up the stairs.

In her room, she laid out the book from the library, her notebook, and a pen. In the bathroom, she splashed her face with cold water. "This fast living getting you down, is it?" Her reflection didn't answer, except by showing her a few more wrinkles and worry lines.

She went back to the desk, sat down, and opened her notebook to the number sequence she'd copied from Roy's field notebook.

There was an obvious, logical explanation for Roy to carry around his weathered, miniature edition of the *Old Testament* which he'd loaned Carolyne, momentarily, for her reading of the Twenty-third Psalm at Gordon's funeral: If there were no atheists in foxholes, the same likely applied to prospectors in the deep jungle. Someone as desirous of traveling light, as was Roy, in order to cover the most area in the shortest period of time, might conceivably see the weight advantage of a two-in-one *Bible* and codebook.

* * * * * * *

It took Carolyne seemingly forever to come up with anything, by way of decipherment, that was even vaguely intelligible. Even then....

Assigning Roy's code numbers, on a first come basis, with an Old Testament book, chapter, verse, then word (albeit, sometimes just a letter in a word) what resulted was:

"I have found rich and great abundance of—n-i-o-b-i-u-m—and as agreed I will proceed to seal off land on my way out to answer all thy questions."

A viable translation? Maybe. Except, of course, for n-i-o-b-i-u-m. Niobium? What in the hell was that? Or, had Carolyne gotten everything wrong?

The nearest encyclopedia was in the library, but Carolyne in route was blocked by an hysterical Melanie who bewailed: "It was horrible! Galin and Teddy. I thought for sure he'd killed him."

"Good God, where?" Carolyne shook the young woman until Melanie's teeth chattered like castanets; the woman making such a scene desired just such a good shake.

"Downstairs; basement." Melanie's wave of her hand could have directed anywhere. "Dr. Seln is there now."

Carolyne headed for the basement. Somebody—take her pick—had turned on the lights. Carolyne still wasn't sure where to go once she reached the bottom of the stairway: Left? Right? Straight ahead? "Dr. Seln?"

She continued her hails for direction as she headed, on pure impulse, to the right. However, she'd turned right yet again, then made a left, before she finally got any kind of response.

"Carolyne?" Not that it was Dr. Seln suddenly appearing through the open doorway only a few feet away. Nor was it Teddy.

"Galin?" He didn't look nearly dead to her. When Carolyne got her hands on Melanie, she'd wring the woman's neck for overacting. "Melanie had me written in as your pallbearer."

Galin looked as surprised as she'd been to see him. "Actually, it's Teddy down and out."

"Teddy?" Once more for incredulous emphasis: "Teddy?"

She looked beyond Galin into a storage room which hadn't changed much since the last time Melanie, Teddy, and she had seen it on their introductory tour of the house. Kyle had been disgruntled that the servant assigned as their guide had showed them: "It reeks of conspicuous consumption in its accumulation of 'stuff' from generations who confronted game populations truly assumed inexhaustible at the time," Kyle had apologized in reference to the stored collection of trophies and stuffed animals, all rejects from upstairs, all stacked, floor to ceiling, like pieces of cord wood. Except for a covering of dust, the room contents, mainly examples of artful taxidermy skills, were in good condition, except for at least one obvious exception—make that two, what with Teddy laid out on the floor between a horn-damaged toppled water buffalo and a slightly askew capybara.

Dr. Seln, knelt beside this patient, diagnosed without coaxing: "A broken nose. The assumed death rattle is only air trying unsuccessfully to find its way around crushed cartilage."

"What happened?" Carolyne's obviously flawed chain of events still had her wondering how it was that Teddy ended up a victim.

Dr. Seln opted for patient-doctor confidentiality. Galin, as usual, proved more candid. "I'd call it a case of *flagrante delicto interruptus*." He tried again: "...*interrupto*? I never was good at Latin."

Carolyne didn't smile: "Do get on with it, Galin. Save your witticisms for a more appreciative audience." She meant: "Save it for Melanie."

"It was dark, for atmosphere, you know? Melanie had predicted I'd find this room a turn-on, and she was right. She was turned on, too, since I guess Teddy isn't really as experimental at these things as Melanie would like him to be. Any wonder she sometimes goes shopping?"

Carolyne wanted to know how Teddy ended up on the floor.

"He came in, and I reacted—spontaneously," Galin put words to it.

"Spontaneously, you caved in his nose?" All of this time, her concern had been that Galin would be the one creamed.

"A guy picks up a bit of self-defense when he hangs around as many professional bodyguards and stalkers as I have on my concert tours."

Carolyne didn't need this asinine distraction. She had an

appointment with an encyclopedia.

"Could you both give me a hand? He's coming around," Dr. Seln requested.

"Doctor, I don't see that much room in which to maneuver," Carolyne complained of things as she saw them.

"Here." Galin leaned against the horn-damaged water buffalo and shifted it two feet; two capybaras and a three-pawed jaguar were pushed two feet higher up the wall; a stuffed monkey toppled from the pile with a thump. "Plenty of room."

"Let's get it over with!" Not very Florence Nightingale, but it fit Carolyne's mood. As far as she was concerned, Teddy could move himself. What happened to all his fine talk about letting Melanie go?"

Teddy groaned his equivalent of, "What the hell happened?"

"You don't want to know," Dr. Seln beat Carolyne to the punch. He stopped Teddy's exploratory hand en route to the bandaged nose. "You don't want to go there, either. Can you get up?"

Somehow, they managed, although Teddy remained wobbly and disoriented. They had more room once in the hall. Galin and Dr. Seln did most of the manhandling to the top of the basement stairs where Kyle, awake to the latest unscheduled event, had a couple of ranch hands take over. There was an exodus from the main house to the infirmary, from which Carolyne disengaged.

She went to the library card catalog: even encyclopedias melded into the uniform blood colored background. The volume she wanted told her what she wanted to know, and she Xeroxed a copy for the pocket of her robe. She closed the book and put it back. She sat down.

She had all of the pieces, now; in fact, she had one too many. What did she do with the drunk hired for murder? Accept him with the assumption that all the other culprits already shared enough guilt without murder added?

Carolyne didn't know how long she sat there until Galin performed the magic that removed the murder from the drunk's ball court; it was long enough for him to have reached the infirmary and returned. "Hear the bad news, good news, bad news about Richard? Seems he did hire a certain someone to kill Gordon, but the contract was invalidated by a downed bridge the killer decided was too difficult to go around, especially as he had down payment enough to keep him awash in booze for a very long time. Rodrigo called to tell Kyle that time sequences don't any more jive to put the guy at the scene of this crime than those others jived to put Susan with the brake fluid of Richard's car. The consensus is that the guy sabotaged Richard's car to protect money already paid for services never to be rendered. Not that any of that takes Richard off the hook. There's apparently no denying the exchange of dollars—Richard's—for a murder—Gordon's—even if the murder, by that planned means, never happened. I'm afraid Richard is in so much trouble that I'm here, this minute, to make the call to summon Dillon Crane to salvage film footage already in the can, not to mention a concept too good to blow at this stage. What's extra bucks to assure a completed and quality music video package?"

"You'd like to use the phone?"

"The house is full of phones; I don't particularly need this one."

"Be my guest." What she had to do couldn't be done in the library, patting herself on the back while bemoaning the greed and avarice of certain people. "I was on my way out."

She went to her room and got dressed, without a shower. She put *Bible*, notebook, and Xeroxed reference in a tote bag. She went downstairs and successfully ran the gauntlet of possible encounters. The only exception: the man at the motor pool who had her sign out the Jeep.

Out on the road, she felt safer but no more content. An unpleasant picture was made more so by the people painted as villains. She'd truly, more than once, almost swallowed some of their lines of bunk. The duplicity of their corruption made her ache. The world was something far less likable because of them. She was bolstered by a need for justice, or she would have wished she'd been less clever: ignorance is bliss.

She didn't go to police headquarters. Nor did she plan to look up the government representative, Jean-Michael Teruel. No confrontation with any fox in its own lair. She drove to the *Tropical Hotel Manaus* and asked the desk clerk to ring Felix who'd checked in permanently once he'd grown tired and disgusted with the company at the ranch. Smart man!

"I'm sorry, Mr. Tenner checked out earlier this morning. I believe he's returned to the United States."

Was that one bit of information passed on that morning to Kyle, lost in the relay to Carolyne through Galin? No way could Felix have left without Rodrigo's okay.

"Could you check to see if his plane has left the airport?" She didn't need him personally for the name of the newspaperman in Rio. She could call Felix at the airport and get it. Would he answer a page?

"I'm afraid it left fifteen minutes ago," the hotel desk clerk informed.

She thanked him and asked if he'd book her on the next flight to Rio. She didn't really need Felix at all; it wouldn't be difficult tracking down the reporter who'd written the piece on, and printed the photo of, the dead Gordon. Mainly, she wanted to clear her conscience and let Felix know she knew him guiltless. His departure from Brazil had merely saved her penance for another day; that was all.

She told the desk clerk she'd changed her mind. She hadn't, but it struck her unwise to add her name to any airport computer readout that could be accessed from police headquarters. She'd come too far, gleaned too much, to be careless now. One man had been killed; one dead woman, more or less, wasn't too much additional ante for the pot of this one particular poker game.

She cashed traveler's checks in three different banks, none for a sum large enough to cause any interest. In combination, she had enough cash to clear out of town.

She drove to the airport and called the ticket counter from outside. Was the next flight for Rio full? No; would she like to make a reservation? No; she'd be a last-minute passenger, squeezed in just under the wire. If a fully booked plane meant she'd miss out, she'd fly a last-minute to Belem, or to some other spot, on from there to Rio. No international flights, because she didn't want to show her passport.

All wrong, Carolyne! Everyone would notice a last-minute. The help would be ticked at needing to rush her thorough. People for other flights would be reluctant to let her crowd in, no matter how loud, her, "I have to catch a plane!" and they'd remember her nerve.

She went inside, said she was Maria Lanis, a name picked out of a hat, and bought a ticket to Rio.

She located a nondescript corner and tried to blend into it. She had an hour until flight time.

She wasn't thinking clearly. She should have waited nearer to departure before buying her ticket; she was vulnerable to anyone flashing her picture.

"Why would they flash your picture?" Her mumble was undecipherable but loud enough to garner a couple of curious glances. So much for fading into the woodwork.

No one knew she was here. No one knew she knew what she knew. How could they? She hadn't known until that morning. She had her worksheets and reference material with her.

She wasn't up to cloak and dagger. She was a scientist, better suited to benign plants not malign people.

She couldn't relax. She went over the facts, and the implication of the facts; she didn't want Felix's friend in Rio thinking she was a lunatic. She had to be lucid, intelligent, and well-meaning. There was a story here for him if she only got it across in a way that didn't have holes or wasn't shaded by emotion.

She considered too trivial for consideration the mess Melanie and Teddy had made of their lives, with the help of Galin. So, why did all of that intrude into her every thought and mix its banality with the really serious issues?

There were fifteen minutes to flight time, her plane actually scheduled to leave on time, when she surrendered to the nagging, but persistent inconsistencies in the Melanie, Teddy, and Galin ménage-a-trois. It would only take a few minutes to clear them up; then, maybe, she could devote full concentration on things really important.

She dialed the ranch and asked for Melanie or Galin.

She got Galin. "All I needed was the library phone for a few minutes, Carolyne. I didn't mean to drive you out of the whole house."

"It's the first time I've been up early in ages." True. "I decided to take advantage and squeeze in a bit of nonsense shopping." False; there was nothing nonsense about buying her ticket to Rio.

"Don't bother to stop by to say hello to Felix while you're in town. The word going around is that he's outbound for the States."

Carolyne at her most innocent: "Oh?"

"Seems his story checked, whatever that story might be. Think you'll ever tell me about Felix and the mysterious Margaret? Rodrigo let him slip the noose. Felix was spending way too much time at the hotel bar, getting sloshed; hotel guests were complaining. We all know how fast the law acts when tourist groups, with their dollars, start to complain."

Carolyne wished she could be headed home, too.

"What's up, Carolyne" Galin fed the pause.

"Did I hear you right: you'd never been in that storage room before? Not alone, not with Melanie, before last night?"

"You called for the latest scoop on my love life?"

"Be a pal, Galin. Indulge me. I know you enjoy the subject."

"Do you want to preface this with heavy breathing? Mine? Yours?"

"Give it a rest, Galin!"

"I don't know whether to be flattered or hurt that you chose a phone call instead of the kind of private tête-à-tête you granted everyone else."

"Galin!"

"Okay. When have you known me not to play your game?"

They announced Carolyne's flight as ready for boarding.

"Carolyne, you there?" Galin sounded doubtful.

This wasn't important. It was the voyeuristic curiosity Galin said it was. Which made her what: a dirty old lady, with a raincoat, whose next stop was a theater balcony showing sex flicks?

"First time, Carolyne," Galin intruded. "Last night, I mean. Although, I would have been there sooner had I known about it."

Hang up, Carolyne. "What time did you head down to the basement?"

"I had other things in mind besides the time, Carolyne." Nevertheless, he followed with an estimate that matched hers for him.

"Did you or Melanie come up for air, once you were down there?"

"It was a basement storage room, Carolyne, not the deep, blue sea. You have Melanie and me confused with seals, dolphins, or whales. Walrus?"

"Did either of you leave once you were in place?" The last of the boarding passengers disappeared through the gate. "Did you go for more champagne?"

"Saw the empty bottle, did you?"

She'd seen the full one, hadn't she? "Did you go for another blanket? Did you want a snack and go get one?"

"We were settled in for what we thought was the duration, Carolyne. Blanket spread; lights out; door shut but unfortunately not locked—definite oversight, but who expected visitors? Shadowy and easily imagined menacing wild animals stacked to the rafters; glasses filled with champagne to be imbibed by flashlight: a fantasy to compete with any x-rated novel. Then, Teddy spoiled the party. Just opened the door and appeared, no by your leave, or here I come."

She could have caught the plane, but she didn't. She spent the next hour summarizing on paper all of her facts and suspicions. After which, she called the newspaper in Rio and got the name, Manuel Marlin, of the reporter who'd submitted the published article on Gordon. Carolyne mailed Manuel all the information she had, plus all her extrapolation on it, and she headed back to the ranch.

Intuition told her she was missing something, right in front of her eyes, that could be lost forever if she ran away without personally tracking it down while she had an investigative "edge." Her sixth sense had done right by her too many times for her to ignore it now.

There was especially something off-kilter about this latest business with Melanie, Galin, and Teddy. If her thought process was operating true to form, her subconscious might already have identified the inconsistency and have the solution; it merely needed coaxing to slip into conscious mode.

She pulled in at the infirmary and passed by the guards at the door with, "I'm here to see the guy with the broken nose." In pantomime, she pinched the bridge of her nose and shifted it left, then right.

Teddy occupied the bed that Richard had had before the latter's involvement in a scheme to buy a murder had secured him a room all his own. Teddy's voice was strange without benefit of amplification through nasal passages now stuffed with cotton. "I know, I know, Carolyne, you want to hear how I could, one minute, tell you I'm tossing off Melanie and, the very next minute, proceed to make a jealous fool of myself."

"You can certainly try."

"I just wasn't in as much control of my emotions as I figured I was. The idea of her and Galin together just...well, need I go into green-eyed monster detail?"

"You followed them into the basement?"

"I had my methods of tracking them down. You're not the only one able to utilize a bit of detective skills. If they had found it such an ideal spot for what they had in mind, they couldn't have chosen a better place for me to take on Mr. Rock Star and Miss Rich Bitch without disturbing anybody else's sensibilities with something that was best settled in private."

She wished him speedy recovery and headed for the house. She didn't slow down to talk to Kyle and Rodrigo Barco who turned up in the infirmary as she left it.

She found Melanie by the pool.

Melanie saw her coming. "Oh, Carolyne, give me a break and don't start with the third-degree. Pleeeease." She pulled her wide-brimmed straw hat to cover her face.

Carolyne sat on the adjoining chaise longue. She paid no attention to Melanie's put upon posturing. "When I left you and Galin in the den, you were soon to be headed upstairs." No need to reveal how she'd spotted them, later, coming back down. "How did you end up in the basement?"

"I remembered the storage room. That's all. I knew if Galin thought the den kinky, with lights out, he'd love the other." Her voice was muffled through her hat.

"You went to his room to tell him your great idea?"

"I didn't have to go to his room, did I, Carolyne?" She pulled her hat abruptly away and stared—I wish you'd mind your own business. "As I suspect you very well know. I was already in his room at the time."

"Game-playing to make Teddy jealous?"

"Maybe." She was uncertain. "Maybe not. This time was somehow different from the others, even insofar as I actually thought Teddy didn't...." She left it.

"Didn't what, Melanie?"

"It's a point made moot by his actions that proved he obviously did care."

"Do you know he went out of his way to convince me he didn't care? He said he was tired of you walking all over him, and he planned to drop you like a hot potato and get on with his life."

"He told you that?" She was incredulous. "Why on earth would he tell *you*?"

Good question. Carolyne knew what he'd said was the reason: "He thought I would get the word around."

"Oh."

Carolyne would have appreciated an argument against the suggested tell a phone, tell a graph, tell Carolyne mentality.

"Why don't you tell me exactly what happened?"

"Why on earth should I?"

"Because I'm a woman, a sympathetic ear, and talking about it will help clear the air, maybe let you get things in perspective, maybe let you sort out if you like Galin, and why; whether you like Teddy, and/or just maneuvered him into a position wherein he could prove, once again, how much he desperately wants and needs you."

The argument sounded good, but Melanie had to insist, "There's really not that much to tell. I was with Galin, and I thought of the storage room downstairs. I said, 'If you thought the den was a turn-on with its lights out...*et cetera, et cetera.*' He said, 'Let's grab a blanket, some champagne, get flashlights, and do some exploring of the possibilities.' We did. Teddy showed up. End of story."

"With the exception of a fairly different twist on the antici-pated end."

"I thought I was in a ninja movie. I never saw anyone act so fast as Galin when Teddy barged in and turned on the lights. He jumped up and automatically executed some kind of twirling that landed his foot in Teddy's face. Teddy went down and made all sorts of horrible snorting sounds. I ran for Dr. Seln."

"You're sure this was the first time you'd mentioned the storage room to Galin?"

"Until I did, I'd completely forgotten that Teddy, you, and I had even seen the room on our grand tour."

"You had no sense of Teddy following directly in your foot-steps down the basement stairs?"

"If he were anywhere so close on our heels, how come he left us in the room for so long before he barged in?"

"Letting the incriminating evidence accumulate?"

"All the other times, the whole purpose was his not letting it go that far. Besides we would have seen or heard him if he'd been directly behind us. The basement was pitch dark. He would have needed a flashlight, unless he could see in the dark, like a bat. If he'd flipped on the hall lights, we would have seen that, too, at least while we were loose in the corridors."

"You didn't ever suggest to Teddy that you and he, instead of you and Galin, might take in the storage room for fun and games?"

"Suggest that to Teddy?" Melanie laughed so hard she dropped her hat. "Let me tell you about Teddy, if you want some serious girl-girl talk. I'd put his sexual repertoire on par with that of a missionary. You ever hear of the term 'missionary position'? I think Teddy invented it. His background, middle-class mores, sees sex as something a little dirty and unseemly even as a means of procreation. I didn't suggest to him that we might go down into the basement for fun and games. One, he would have bridled at the mere suggestion that I needed any extra stimulant when he was doing his best. Two, I already told you, I hadn't thought of the room until Galin in the den obviously sparked the dormant memory."

Carolyne's next stop was the basement, and that one particular storage room in question.

Slowly, she surveyed what was there, including the empty champagne bottle; two champagne glasses, one broken: so much for a hundred bucks worth of bubbly and another hundred worth of Baccarat crystal; the wrinkled blanket, and the evidence that Galin and Melanie were into safe sex: give them credit for that.

Her once-over completed, she began again, this time slower, more analytical. She was a scientist, used to isolating the forest from the trees, or vice versa, and there was something here to be isolated. Some vague memory told her she'd spotted it before. Her chief disadvantage was in not knowing for what she looked; her chief advantage was her inherent knowledge that she'd know "it" when she saw it.

Macaw. Capybara. Monkey. Sloth. Tapir. Peccary, puma, possum. Jaguar, jararaca. Rattlesnake, sloth, turtle. In duplicate. In triplicate. In quadruplicate. Evidence of species that had known better times and better accommodations.

She didn't know "it" when she saw it, after all. She knew it when she didn't see it.

Galin greeted her at the top of the basement stairs. "If our phone-con got you so hot and bothered that you rushed back, you should hear the dirty talk of which I'm really capable."

"Later, Galin." That promise should put the fear of God into him. "For the moment, could you spread the word that I'd like to see Kyle and Rodrigo Barco in the library? You'll find them at the infirmary. Also, I'd like to see Roy at the same time, if you can find him somewhere."

"Damn, Carolyne, another of your now-famous private sessions?"

"Jean-Michael Teruel wouldn't be around, would he?"

"The government man? Come on, Carolyne: not even you can expect to bat a hundred."

No major loss. Jean-Michael, she suspected, would have the specifics within minutes of her saying them.

"For being so good about it, Galin, I'll let you sit in on this one, if you've a mind to do so." There were advantages to having a witness.

"Well, that's more like it. Don't you dare start without me."

She didn't. He was there when she faced the other three men in the room.

Be still, beating heart! "Gentlemen, it's about time you and I had a little discussion about coded messages, greedy sonsof-bitches, the intended rape of an ecological system, rampaging natives, a downed bridge, and niobium." That got their undivided attention. "When we're through with that, and I've registered my complete disgust and disappointment, I'll tell you about a man-eating jaguar, emeralds, and how we might just entrap Gordon Wentlock's killer."

CHAPTER TWELVE

The zoologist and forensics people were noncommittal. After all, photographs weren't the same as a body. They could only admit to the *possibility* of what Carolyne suggested. After more examination, and/or more proof, they *might* well agree with her completely. For the moment, they preferred to make no definite statement, pro or con.

To catch the killer, the decision was taken to pretend less indecision: The photos would be insinuated definitely to show certain anomalies, and the lab boys would be insinuated as hoping to have a firm explanation in only a couple more days.

Rodrigo moved Richard out of the infirmary to police headquarters in Manaus. The ranch hands on guard duty returned to their normal work assignments.

Rodrigo returned to the ranch just after nightfall. His car concealed, he accessed the main house through a backdoor. Later that night, he was joined in the basement by Carolyne, Kyle, and Roy; an attempt was made to dissuade Galin, but he showed up, too.

At one a.m. the following morning, Teddy Rhingold, his nose bandaged and his face black-and-blue, carried a three-paw, stuffed jaguar from a basement storage room and was arrested, and charged with the murder of Gordon Wentlock. The ensuing search of this room turned up a cache of priceless emeralds.

"Well, Carolyne, you did us proud," Galin said. Melanie, Charles, Carolyne, and he were in the library. Kyle, Roy, and Rodrigo preferred a lower profile until the expedition left on a flight scheduled out of Manaus later that afternoon. Galin would stay on to complete his video; Dillon Crane would fly into Manaus in two days to take over where Richard had been forced to leave off shooting the video because of continuing legal difficulties.

"I just couldn't make Teddy's confrontation with Melanie and you in the storage room fit its lead-in," Carolyne downplayed. "He'd gone out of his way to let me know he was breaking with Melanie and could care less what she was up to with you."

"Without saying it in so many words, Teddy insinuated the same to me," said Melanie who'd had trouble with that at the time.

"A fortune in twice-stolen emeralds no longer made Melanie the only pot at the end of the rainbow," Charles concluded. "He didn't want us wondering why Melanie was suddenly no longer the prize she once was."

"His explanation of 'inability to control' his passions, could have been valid," Carolyne admitted. "We all act in ways our brains tell us not to. It was his elaboration to include how the 'privacy of the spot' made it so ideal to 'spare our sensibilities'; Melanie had already told me at the river crossing that Teddy preferred public confrontations where there was no mistaking his she's-mine mentality. If he really wanted privacy, why not Galin's room where Melanie and Galin were holed up until they headed for the storage room? I wouldn't question Teddy barging in there, but how logical was the basement, through a maze of dark corridors?"

"He could have spotted them en route." Charles saw that possibility.

"We would have spotted him, in turn." Melanie reiterated the reasons why, given Carolyne the day before.

"I was in the doorway of the library and spotted their entrance to the basement," Carolyne admitted. "No sign of any servants to pass Teddy the word. Granted, Teddy appeared shortly thereafter, but he wasn't hot on their trail. He came around the bend in the stairway, so there's no way he saw them. The acoustics are so poor he couldn't have heard them; Roy and I hardly heard the fisticuffs between Charles and Felix—you all remember that ruckus—until we made a visual around the bend of the stairs."

"We were quiet," Melanie assured; Galin nodded.

"Even if he had seen, or heard, he would have had to pinpoint that one room, among so many; no easy task, especially since the spot is so well insulated against outgoing and incoming sounds; I couldn't hear Galin and Dr. Seln, and they didn't hear my calls until I was only a few feet away, the door wide open at the time. Nor was it a case that Melanie ever gave Teddy any indication the room had any special appeal to her or to Galin. She'd pretty much forgotten the storage room until Galin became so infatuated with the possibilities of the den with its animal trophies. Galin and she suddenly in the storage room had been too spontaneous for Teddy to have had foreknowledge."

"So, he was there for some other reason." Charles wondered if he'd have reached the same conclusion.

"I'd seen the room with Teddy and Melanie on our grand tour," Carolyne reminded. "My second time there, Teddy unconscious on the floor, was too eventful for me to register the three-paw jaguar, except in my subconscious; despite the haphazard storage arrangement, the other trophies, except for the water buffalo with its horn obviously damaged during the fight, weren't missing paws, or eyes, or stuffing; nor had the jaguar been so obviously missing its forepaw my first trip through."

Only in retrospect did Galin follow how, "Teddy decided to kill Gordon and remembered the potential of the stuffed jaguars in the basement room. He took a forepaw, complete with its claws, and used it and them to make it look as if Gordon was the victim of a wild animal attack. The comments of the zoologist about no teeth marks and unique claw striations worried him that someone might figure out it wasn't a real jaguar after all; the storeroom might occur to someone as a logical source for whatever was needed to make a mauling look cosmetically correct to an untrained eye."

Charles saw as plain as day that, "He hadn't bothered to dispose of the full trophy, when he cut off its forepaw, because he'd figured no one would make the connection, Gordon dead and buried; the storage room wasn't an often visited place, in that Kyle considered it something of an embarrassment."

"Teddy planned to kill Gordon for emeralds as far back as when we first came through." Melanie made it a statement. "It was a way for him to end his quest for financial independence without marrying me, or marrying anyone else, to get it."

"Teddy was on the balcony, outside Gordon's room, and spotted Gordon and the emeralds through a breach in the curtains," Carolyne confirmed. "Gordon had a habit of taking the gems out regularly and fondling them for the pure pleasure of it. He continued doing the same in the field, often slipping away just for that purpose, and Teddy saw that as his chance. Hit from behind, Gordon dropped the gems; Teddy missed the 'J' emerald in his haste to pick up the others."

"Emeralds that had already been stolen once by Gordon who murdered John Leider." Melanie thought she had that pat.

Carolyne: "Everyone knew of John's fantastic success in the field, and Gordon knew something big was up at Aquaval when John drove away him and the *Amaz'n Galin* film crew at gunpoint. When Richard stormed off, Gordon ran off with Susan Delaney but only long enough to drop her and head back to Aquaval, kill John, and steal the emeralds John had collected for sale to Prince Mahoud Najheez."

Galin imagined Susan who left the fat goose Richard for true love Gordon, only to have her one and only wave good-bye before the honeymoon.

Charles asked, "Why didn't Gordon take the emeralds and run? He didn't need the money we paid him, as guide, with that fortune in stockpile."

"Several things kept him in check," Carolyne explained. "His fetish for emeralds made them hard to part with. Also, he didn't want to pull up stakes too soon after John was reported missing, because people knew there was bad blood between them; not only the shooting incident that involved the *Amaz'n Galin* crew, but because Gordon tried, but failed, to put the make on John's wife. It was best to have things appear business as usual. Finally, those emeralds were very important gemstones, inventoried carefully in the field, and, again, at the villa; that duplication of records was made perfectly clear by the entries, coded and uncoded, in John's notebook that Gordon stole with the gems. Gordon couldn't unload such stones locally, or Jane would have gotten wind of it. Even selling them abroad may have gotten back to her. His best bet was to sit on them until John's disappearance became really old news, then slip away, break the emeralds into smaller, less identifiable, stones, and live happily ever after, no questions asked."

"Live happily ever after with Talina?" Galin only half-kidded.

"Someone once said, 'Love isn't something one plans; it just happens, between the strangest people, at the strangest of times.'" Carolyne admitted. "Those two certainly weren't a match I would have thought made in heaven, but why couldn't even a promiscuous sonofabitch like Gordon have one special woman to come home to? It had to mean something that he planned for her well-being by parting with one of his precious stones; a very impressive gem it was, too."

"Why didn't he break the gems into smaller stones right away, so Jane wouldn't trace them?" Charles asked.

"Gordon was hardly known for his prospecting skills," Carolyne pointed out, "and would only have raised eyebrows if he suddenly had some story about lucking out on some major emerald discovery, or even a smaller one, so close on the heels of John's disappearance. Why focus any kind of limelight on himself when it wasn't necessary? Also, he held out hopes that he'd eventually locate someone able to buy the large stones, without word getting out to Jane; there was a considerably larger amount of profit to be had from leaving the stones in their larger form than in breaking them down into smaller, albeit more easily disposal, units; much the same kind of problem that Teddy would have had to deal with eventually, but for which he figured he had plenty of time to come up with lucrative solutions."

"I'm amazed how you put it all together as the result of one stuffed animal without its forepaw." Galin raised his glass in toast to Carolyne. The others followed suit.

Carolyne was modest. "Remember, Teddy was the only one to see the 'killer' jaguar: 'Big as a house.' 'Heard it growl.' 'Fired at it; may even have hit it.' Once I got over the major obstacle of realizing there might not have been a real jaguar, I naturally had to examine Teddy's credibility."

"Why the jaguar at all?" Charles thought there was an easier way. "Why not kill Gordon, get the emeralds, and hide the body?"

Galin answered. "He didn't want a missing person. Death by jaguar allowed no mystery, plus a body, so no one would be out looking, and, no matter how high the odds against, stumble on the body wherever Teddy had stashed it, and start asking questions. This way, it was merely an unfortunate accident until Roy threw in the monkey wrench about the river rock. Teddy planned for the body to be safely buried, because he'd made sure, by taking out your radio, that no one could be called in, and the body couldn't be hauled out. By the time anybody came back to find otherwise, if they even bothered, the environment would have made sure there were no answers except for those Teddy had already given."

"Teddy hit Felix on the head, wrecked our radio, and stole our satellite relay device to make sure the body would have plenty of time to decompose," Charles said, "but what were we supposed to make of the damage and theft of our equipment?"

"He didn't care what we made of it, as long as we didn't connect it to Gordon's death." Melanie thought herself damned clever to see that. "Only in books are all the strings neatly tied, and the resulting package complete with no tears or tattered corners. Teddy figured—and why shouldn't he?—that it didn't matter if we all asked, years later, 'Who knocked Felix, smashed the radio, stole the satellite gizmo; and why?'"

"It started to fall apart when Roy asked, 'What's that river rock, there, doing here when it shouldn't be?'" Carolyne said and accepted Galin's offer for a refill of Scotch. "That question tied the destruction of the radio to a conscious effort by a murderer to delay any expert examination of the body. When Melanie photographed the corpse, and I came up with a means of possibly preserving the body until experts could get to it, Teddy knew he was in trouble."

"Not to mention how the 'J' emerald suggested a motive for murder," Melanie said and held out her glass; Galin did the honors.

Charles: "Why did Teddy risk playing jealous lover the night before he murdered Gordon?" He had one answer: "Because he didn't figure anyone would doubt the jaguar did the deed?"

Carolyne saw other alternatives. "Teddy couldn't risk going against character. He'd made a habit of publicly displaying his macho whenever someone moved in on Melanie. Remember, at the time he'd not yet begun to paint himself out of the relationship; if his bid for the emeralds was unsuccessful, he'd still need her. So, he played his usual role and knew any investigation would prove none of the other men he'd fought for her affections had ever ended up dead. Besides, who would have thought him careless enough to give himself even a tentative motive for murder before committing one?"

"You know what brings me up short," Charles confessed, "is how Teddy disposed of the body and the 'killer rock' after we put them in the cave and headed for the ranch. Wasn't everyone's time accounted for, except for Roy's when he headed off on his own to look for Teddy and me when we were kidnapped?"

"Which was why when I decoded Roy's message and read where he'd discovered a large deposit of niobium and would 'proceed to seal off the land,' on his way out to answer questions, I originally figured Roy, Kyle, and their puppets Rodrigo and Jean-Michael, were guilty of Gordon's murder as part of that 'sealing process'," Carolyne conceded. "What better way for them to get us to move out fast than our guide dead, a man-eating jaguar, or a two-legged murderer, to blame? Soon to be supplemented by the possibilities of cannibals on the rampage. That was the way I put it in my summation to Manuel Marlin. Only afterwards did I think 'sealing off' might include cannibals never seen or heard, and a bridge suddenly down. If Roy had merely intended to look for Charles and Teddy, instead, heading off to plant skulls on a stake, and whittle green shafts for arrows, and chop the bridge down, he didn't have enough time to backtrack to the body. He could have figured Kyle's men would be sent back to the cave to dispose of that evidence and just say it was gone, but we know that didn't happen from Charles who accompanied the rescue team; no corpse was there when they got there. As Charles boarded the copter at the last-minute, Kyle or Roy couldn't have planned for that eventuality to send out another copter before it. As no one protested when Charles went along, that indicated clean consciences, especially as Charles came back alive."

"Where did Roy come up with skulls on a stake and arrow-heads, on such short notice?" Galin asked, poured more of the booze, and settled into a comfortable armchair.

"It wasn't short notice," Carolyne begged to differ. "He'd planned for just such a major strike for years, and he knew the necessity for a strategy to discourage anyone from nosing around, when the time arrived, until all the preliminary paper-work was in and a work team in place. He had the skulls and arrowheads waiting: souvenirs collected over the years. It was only a case of putting them where they were most effective."

"You never figured Roy had an accomplice to kidnap Teddy and me, then dispose of Gordon's body while Roy took care of skulls, arrows, and chopped down the bridge?" Charles didn't find an accomplice theory a fantastic one. "What about the English guy who called Teddy, 'Yank', tied us up, and cut Teddy's face with a ring?"

"Several things led me to believe Roy had no accomplice," Carolyne explained. "There was no mention, when we headed out, of anyone but Roy in the area. Why wouldn't someone have mentioned it at the time; it was prior to Roy's broadcast of the discovery? Then, there was the coded message. Not once, but twice, 'I': 'I have found....' 'I will proceed....' Also: '...on my way out....'" Not 'we,' not 'our'. On the receiving end, Kyle would have known Roy had a partner, so why hide it, especially in a message that went out in code?"

"So, when did Teddy dispose of the body?" Charles persisted.

"When he was supposedly kidnapped," Carolyne was ready with the answer.

"Supposedly?" Charles protested. "Carolyne, I was there!"

"I didn't say *you* weren't kidnapped, Charles. You were. By Teddy."

Melanie saw it. "You never saw or heard your assailant, did you, Charles? He came at you from behind, knocked you out, tied you up, blindfolded you, gagged you. Teddy did all the seeing and hearing. You didn't even know Teddy was around until he untied your hands and said, 'Here we are, survivors!', then showed you his scratch and rope burns."

"A scratch and rope burns that could be easily self-inflicted," Carolyne verified. "The scratch Roy got from a branch on our run through the fire looked as easily made by some brute's ring."

Charles was incredulous.

"Teddy knew there was no jaguar to eat you and no dangerous animals sighted in the area; as for the natives, Roy was only then planting the signs of them," Carolyne continued. "Everything told Teddy you'd survive until he got back to collect you as his alibi. Even if any of us came looking, you couldn't move or scream to make you anything more than a very small needle in a very big haystack."

"The bastards!" Charles decided and for not the first time.

"Your case of no faking it dysentery cleared you of any suspicions as the kidnapper of Teddy, out to dispose of evidence," Carolyne gave his bowl problem her blessing.

"What exactly did Teddy do with the body?" Galin asked Carolyne, decidedly appreciative of her very fine mind. "Finally do with it, I mean."

"What he probably should have done with it from the start: dropped it in the river. Likewise, the murder weapon to become just another river rock. And the jaguar's paw eventually to decompose and disappear, after having first used it to press pug marks into some of the loose dirt around the cave to make it look as if the cat had absconded with the corpse."

"Teddy cut the ropes of the raft and sliced off the flaps of my backpack." Melanie saw that, too.

"He couldn't trust the water to oblige, so he swiped the film chip, Melanie's bogus replacement to Felix's bogus replacement, before he was last to leave the far shore, then jettisoned the chip while on the guide line," Carolyne verified. "He cut the raft ropes to make sure all evidence of his hasty rifling of Melanie's pack was deep-sixed. Even if everything was lost, we were close enough to the ranch to make it back, especially with Roy's knowledge of the area."

"Didn't Roy worry about a killer on the loose who could stumble upon his secret as easily as any of us?" Charles wondered.

"Roy denies knowing from the start that one of us killed Gordon, but he must have suspected," Carolyne decided. "There was no one but him and us in the area, and he was familiar enough with the region to know that. When Teddy and Charles disappeared, then reappeared with claims of kidnappers, Roy must have seen Teddy behind it. When the raft came undone, that must have cinched it. He probably even had the emeralds figured out as Teddy's motive. However, he had bigger fish to fry, and everything Teddy did that hurried us out and offered a warning to others to stay away, played into Roy's hands."

"What exactly is niobium?" It didn't any more ring bells with Charles than it had with Carolyne when she'd broken Roy's code.

"These days, Carolyne was more informed: "A platinum-grey metallic element that alloys with nickel and steel to withstand exceptionally high temperatures. In nuclear reactors, it allows neutrons to penetrate easily; I don't know what that means, but it's a definite plus. Best yet, at low temperatures, it's a super-conductor, and the attempt to find a complete disappearance of electrical resistance in metals above absolute zero has become the new darling of research."

"Money to be made, ecological systems to be destroyed." Charles got the none too pretty picture. "No way is any country in debt going to pass up the potential for exploiting such mineral wealth for hard cash."

"Not even Kyle, with his original ecological good intentions to stop slash burnings and allow us in for plant research, was able to pass on the temptation of that much money in profits," Carolyne said, saddened by that fact. "No one ever has too much money, especially when the money to be had can make the difference between rich and super rich. I somehow believe Kyle still feels he has something to prove to Jane Leider for past rejections, and there's no denying that Jane can be impressed by cold cash."

"If Roy knew Teddy was guilty, but kept it a secret because it played into his hands, insofar as a killer, a man-eating jaguar, and cannibals weren't an open invitation for anyone to inter-fere until Kyle and Roy had their own well-protected work team in place, weren't you taking a chance, Carolyne, when you confronted Kyle and him to enlist their help in catching Teddy? Neither Kyle nor Roy, by your own admission, had much to gain by Teddy behind bars."

Galin was delighted to toot Carolyne's horn for her: "She had me along as a witness to the confrontation. More to the point, the news out about the niobium discovery, via the letter Carolyne had mailed to the newsman in Rio, suddenly had Kyle and Roy needing to devote all of their efforts toward keeping a firm hand on a situation that would suck in undesirables like bees to honey. They didn't want to have to waste time dealing with rumors they'd murdered Gordon to protect their invest-ment. Suddenly, it behooved them to pluck at least one bother-some fly from the ointment."

Galin did have one final question: "If Roy and Kyle used

Gordon's murder as a bonus, why was Rodrigo, their puppet, so upset when he got hold of the Rio newspaper? Publicity like that was bound to keep more people away than it invited in."

Carolyne had the answer, albeit male-chauvinistic: "Rodrigo was simply angry because someone had put something over on him. It didn't help that, at the time, not knowing it was Felix, he had it figured as Melanie—a woman."

Not that much later, airborne over Brazil, Charles was still free with compliments: "You are a number-one amateur sleuth, Carolyne. No doubt about it."

"And a big zero as a plant-hunter and environmentalist, this time around. There's no way we access that area again until it's mined clean and probably stripped bare of *Lygodium cornelius*, and all other flora and fauna, in the process." She turned to the window and looked out. Although miles from the Georni ranch, there was no seeing the jungle below because of all the smoke from all the burning trees set afire by all those men seduced into exploitation of the environment by dreams of livelihood and profit.

ABOUT THE AUTHOR

WILLIAM MALTESE, an international best-selling author of non-fiction and fiction articles, short stories, and novels, including his popular Wildside Mystery Double, *Incident at Aberlene* and *Incident at Brimzinsky* (Spies & Lies #1-#2), has published (under various pseudonyms) over 200 books in genres ranging from straight mainstream, to straight and gay erotica, as well as mystery, romance, western, adventure, espionage, cooking, wine, young adults and children, plus twenty-four science fiction/fantasy/horror novels, beginning with *Five Roads to Tlen* in 1969 (as "William J. Lambert III") through *Bond-Shattering* (2007). He's anything but a newcomer by way of writing fictionalized autobiographies and biographies, including his *Diary of a Hustler* (with "Joey"), *Slovakian Boy* (with "Pavel"), *Amen's Boy* (his exposé on sexual abuse in the Catholic Church, with Jacob Campbell), and his shocking Lambda-Award-nominated *ARDENNIAN BOY* (written with eminent gay scholar Professor Drewey Wayne Gunn) that raised more than a few eyebrows, while gleaning rave reviews, in its graphic portrayal of the scandalous literary and sexual relationship between the French poets Paul Verlaine and Arthur Rimbaud. For a comprehensive list of his literary output, see *Draqualian Silk: A Collector's and Bibliographical Guide to the Books of William Maltese, 1969-2010* (Borgo Press, 2010). Maltese enlisted in the U.S. Army, where he achieved and was honorably discharged with the rank of Sergeant (E-5).

You can email him at: williammaltese@yahoo.com

You can locate him on the internet at:

http://www.williammaltese.com
http://www.facebook.com/williammaltese
http://www.theglutenfreewaymyway.com/
http://www.facebook.com/backoftheboatgourmetcooking
http://www.facebook.com/winetastersdiary
https://www.facebook.com/DinnerWithCecileAndWilliamACo
okbook?fref=ts
http://www.facebook.com/evengourmandshavetodiet
http://www.facebook.com/flickerwarriors
http://www.facebook.com/draqual
http://www.myspace.com/williammaltese
http://www.myspace.com/draqual
http://www.myspace.com/flickerwarriors

William's Xocai® chocolate site:

http://www.mxi.myvoffice.com/williammaltese/